MONEY SHOT

Scott Hildreth

DEDICATION

No matter how old I get or how many children I have of my own, I will always be a little boy.

My mother's little boy.

Mom, this one is for you.

PROLOGUE

June 6th, 2013

I believe there comes a time in every man's life when he questions the loyalty of his wife or girlfriend. Right or wrong, it eventually happens. A pattern of strange disagreements, her taste in music changing drastically, and a constant need to stay late at the office had raised my eyebrows, but it was when she cut her hair that I actually *knew*.

Her long blonde hair had been her trademark since we met, and as many times as I asked her to change it, the answer was always the same. After ten years, I stopped asking. Roughly five years since I had last asked, she came home with her hair cut well above her shoulders and colored bright red.

I remember standing there admiring her as she walked in, wondering what had changed. As she walked past me and turned toward the bedroom with a bag of new clothes swinging from her elbow, it hit me like a ton of bricks.

She hadn't done it for me.

She had done it for him.

Now, standing in his driveway glaring at him through the window of his truck as he fumbled to find what I was sure to be his gun, I felt incompetent, incapable, useless, and half sick at my stomach.

I lowered my chin slightly and shook my head. "If I were you, I wouldn't."

"Look, I uhhm," he said as he shifted his eyes toward me.

"I told you once, get out of the truck, Motherfucker. Just get out, and don't reach for that console again. I ain't planning on killing you, but I sure as fuck will if I have to," I said flatly.

I could have brought a few of the fellas, or the entire MC for that matter, but as far as I was concerned, my soon to be ex-wife's lover wasn't club business, it was personal. As much as I loved my club brothers, and as much as I trusted them to watch my back, I also knew the importance of keeping my personal life just that, personal.

He glanced down at my clenched fists and did his best to reason with me. "Look I don't want to…"

I had never been a patient man. Even as a kid, I would peel the wrapping paper away from the Christmas presents and see if I could get a peek at what was underneath long before the day arrived to unwrap them. Often, while sitting on my motorcycle at a stoplight, I lose my ability to sit and wait, and simply ride through the red light.

My mother always said I lacked tolerance.

I couldn't agree more.

I pulled his truck door open with one hand and grabbed a fistful of his hair with the other. Although I had a reasonable amount of practice pulling men from their vehicles by their hair, attempting to pull him out by his provided an entirely new experience altogether.

As his head followed the force of my hand pulling him toward the open door, his eyes widened and he began to scream. A short second later, and I had his entire head of hair in my hand, and he sat free of my grasp in the seat of his truck.

And he was as bald as billiard ball.

Quite confused at what had happened, I gazed at my hair-filled hand and tried to make sense of it all. The amount of time it took my mind to understand I was holding his hair hat and he had become a free man was just enough for him to do what I had clearly told him not to.

I tossed his toupee toward my bike, leaned inside his truck, and reached for his right arm. As I squeezed his wrist with my left hand, preventing him from reaching for the open console, I began to punch him in the face repeatedly with my right hand, all the while continuing to pull him from the truck and explain why I was doing what I was doing.

I felt fifteen years of my life had been wasted, and that I had been devoted – and loyal – to a lie. With every ounce of frustration packed into each swing of my fist, I continued to pummel him until he was a bloody mess.

When I finally released him from my grasp he fell to the ground. Covered in blood and with both eyes swollen almost shut, he was still conscious. I stared down at him, wiped my knuckles on my jeans, and drew a long, slow breath.

Looking back on the events of my past, there seemed to always be things that I had done in fits of rage or in a moment of desperation that I later regretted. I'd always referred to them as brain farts, and I had plenty of 'em in my days. Several of the fellas would later claim that this night produced a brain fart, but I didn't agree with them.

I believed my actions were justified, considering I was married to the woman for fifteen years. If nothing else, I felt it would cause her to remember me for who I believed I was.

A very loyal man with an extremely short temper.

As I gazed down at him, I reached for my pocket, pulled out my knife, and flicked the blade open. As he continued to moan and attempted to roll on his side, I pressed my boot down onto his shoulder and held him in place.

"Hold on, Motherfucker, I'm not done with you. Just a little reminder of who was here," I growled.

After glancing over each shoulder, I knelt down, pulled up his bloody tee shirt, and carved a very distinct "V" down from each of his nipples to his belly button.

With his screams of pain echoing into the night, I wiped the blade of my knife against the thigh of my jeans, folded it, and clipped it in place in my pocket. I needed a fucking cigarette, but I'd almost given up on the habit of smoking. *Almost.* After leaning into the truck and taking his gun from the console, I shoved it into the waist of my jeans and walked to my bike as if what had just happened was a common occurrence.

But it wasn't.

Natalie and I had been together since we were in high school. Although I never would have guessed we would have grown apart, it happened, and now I was forced to deal with the thought of her being with someone else.

I coughed a light laugh as I tossed my leg over the seat of my bike. Brain fart or not, I liked the end result of my actions.

Her new man had my initial carved in his chest.

She had always liked seeing me with my shirt off, but my guess was that she was going to have the new guy leave his on in the future.

I released the clutch lever and twisted the throttle back. A thirty minute ride and I'd be back at the clubhouse; one day wiser, and with one less woman in my life.

With the street lights rushing past me, and the warm summer air pressing my cut against my chest, I thought of what my life had become; and what I felt I had thrown away with Natalie.

Fifteen fucking years.

The only relationship I had ever been in.

I knew one thing, and I knew it for sure.

The next woman, if there ever was another, would have one hell of a time proving herself to me.

SIENNA

June 8th, 2014

With my heart beating out of my chest and my mind racing in ten different directions, I brushed my hand across the face of the screen anxiously. The page didn't move. I carefully pressed my finger against the screen and flipped the page in the other direction. After a quick study, and confirming it was the page I had previously read, I swept my finger across the screen again and stared at the end of what appeared to be the last page.

There was no doubt.

I had reached the end of the book.

"Are you fucking serious? A cliffie? You bitch!" I screamed as I tossed my Kindle across the room and into the wall.

My favorite author had just become a worthless heap of steaming shit. After falling deeply in love despite all of their differences, being torn apart and then reunited, the hero proposed marriage; and I was prepared for a wedding. Instead, in the last chapter, out of the fucking blue, the hero was arrested for murder. Who in the fuck would end a story in such a place, leaving the reader to wait anxiously with knots in her stomach for the next book?

A fucking idiot, that's who.

Although I generally tried to give myself twelve hours to digest a book before writing a review, I rolled off the edge of my bed, grabbed my glass of wine, and commenced to downing it as I walked over to my desk. As I waited for the computer to go through its startup procedure, I walked to the kitchen with my empty glass and grabbed the remaining bottle of Madeira.

After roughly two seconds of considering how much wine I should pour into the glass, I uncorked the bottle, raised it to my lips, and took a much needed drink. I tossed the cork on the counter beside my empty glass and stomped toward my bedroom with the bottle dangling from my loosely clenched fist.

I walked into the room, sat down, slammed the bottle against the desk, and began to type.

Kindle throwing alert

I'll be taking donations from anyone wishing to fund a new Kindle purchase, because after reading this book, my Kindle is in a thousand pieces.

Can you imagine the story Cinderella ending with the prince finding Cinderella's glass slipper, but not searching for – or finding – her?

Or maybe in The Notebook, the story ending with Allie receiving Noah's letters from her mother, but not acting on her feelings?

You can't, can you?

Neither can I.

The reason I can't imagine it, and I'm sure you'll agree, is because most authors follow a proven pattern in the crafting of their stories for romance novels. They have a hero and heroine meet, fall in love, and eventually some type of conflict tears them apart. We frantically flip through the pages, saddened by their separation, and jump with joy

8

when they eventually reunite. At some point the book ends, alluding to them living happily ever after.

I reached for the wine, drank a quarter of what remained, and wiped my mouth with the back of my hand. I slid the bottle beside my monitor, inhaled a shallow breath, and turned on Bruce Springsteen's "*Santa Claus Is Comin' to Town*." After a few minutes of bobbing my head to the music, I commenced typing.

That, my friends and followers, is not the case in this book.

Not at all.

The author seems to have misplaced the memo explaining the necessity on not only writing a novel, but completing it.

When I reached the point where the book stopped (I refuse to call it an ending)...

I stopped typing, searched through my files, and inserted a .gif of a wide-eyed woman's head exploding. After laughing to myself for a few long seconds, I took another drink of wine and continued.

I realized the author must have run out of time. Maybe she needed to meet a deadline, and decided finishing the book would push her past her date or time. Who knows? But what I do know is this...

She sure as fuck didn't finish writing it.

Now, for the beginning of the book, and what transpired between that point and when the book simply stopped?

I loved it.

As I read through this book, I was relieved that it had it all. A hero I could sink my teeth into. A heroine I wanted to sit down and have a glass of wine with. Scorching hot love scenes, more scorching hot love scenes, and conflict I saw coming, but hoped never came to fruition. After a hundred or so well-written angst-filled pages, the H and h were reunited, and then…

   Something ridiculous happened and the book just fucking ended.

   Up until the last chapter, this was a five star read for me. After reading all the way to the point she ran out of desire to finish it, I'll have to give it one and a half stars.

   And I'm only doing that because I'm half-drunk and a hell of a lot happier than I was when I started this review.

   I inserted a .gif of an obviously drunken woman sitting on the edge of her bed in her underwear with a bottle of wine between her legs.

   As I read the review, I finished the bottle of wine. After rereading it, I wished I had another bottle, but knew I had no business driving to get one. Hoping a search of my kitchen would produce a bottle, but knowing damned good and well I had drank my last one, I published the review, excited at the thought of all of the comments I was sure to have when I woke up. I glanced up and stared blankly at the small hole in the wall, and slowly filled with drunken regret for throwing my Kindle. After a few insanely long alcohol induced seconds of lusting over my newest book boyfriend while Bruce Springsteen's "*Merry Christmas Baby*" played, my doorbell rang.

   The sound startled me, causing me to jump from my seat and almost pee in the process. As my mind filled with thoughts of some mass murderer going door to door in search of his next victim, I tossed my glasses on my desk and ran to the window to get a peek at the scum. I carefully pulled the blinds away from the window frame and peered outside.

   Dear God.

   A big, rough, muscular, tattooed biker stood on my porch in his leather vest, jeans, and biker boots.

It was like Christmas in June.

I rubbed my drunken eyes with the tips of my index fingers, blinked a few times, and continued to admire him from the privacy of my bedroom.

He got more handsome with each passing second.

He pushed his hands into his pockets, shifted his weight from one foot to the other, and slowly turned around. His bare arms were covered in tattoos and muscles. Even his muscles had muscles. After a few seconds of watching him walk toward the street, my curiosity – and the fact I was sexually deprived – got the best of me.

I released the blinds and made it to the bathroom in three quick strides. I glanced in my mirror, attempted to fix my hair, and ran toward the front door. Dressed in a reasonably clean pair of Victoria's Secret's best sweats, I looked pretty presentable – at least for a late Sunday night. After clearing my throat and second guessing my thoughts for a few seconds, I yanked the door open and did my best to look sleep deprived. In my half-drunken state, it wasn't much of a stretch.

"Hello," I said in what I hoped to be a sensual whisper. The words escaped my lips as a raspy drunken cough.

Half way to his motorcycle, but fully illuminated by the security light in my driveway, he paused and turned around.

Holy fucking shit.

He looked like no other biker I had ever actually seen, but exactly like the ones I had developed in my head from the MC Romance novels I had spent so much time reading. If it wasn't for the warm and extremely humid summer air blowing in my face and making me half nauseous, I would have thought I was dreaming.

As he walked in my direction and spoke, my heart began to beat rapidly and my palms began to sweat. As the low rumble of his voice explained the situation he was in, my mouth fell open and I stared at him as if he was being offered to me by the God of sorrow.

"Listen, this is going to sound like complete bullshit, but I ran out of gas and this is where I ended up," he said as he waved his hand toward the motorcycle parked by the curb.

I glanced at the vintage Harley, shifted my eyes to where he was standing, and stared. Common sense, which was something I often seemed to lack, should have caused me to turn toward the house, go inside, and lock the door. Instead, I stepped from the house onto the porch and asked for more details.

After clearing my throat of the sweet wine that still heavily coated it, I widened my eyes at the sight of him. In an effort to look cute, but more to lure him a little closer, I tossed my hair over my shoulder. The move threw me off-balance, causing my drunken ass to almost fall flat on my face.

"So, you need a ride?" I asked in a fractionally more sultry tone.

He took a few steps toward me, crossed his arms in front of his chest, and sighed heavily. "Well, not exactly," he said. "I don't want to leave the bike here."

I turned my palms up and shook my head from side to side. "I don't have any gas. The maintenance men cut the grass and stuff, so I don't have any need for it. But…"

I paused and studied him as I considered what else to say. He rocked back and forth nervously on the balls of his feet as he seemed to consider leaving his motorcycle in the street. He looked rough, but not in a homeless unkempt way. He seemed to be, at least by his appearance, stature, and stance to be a guy no one would ever want to cross, and I suspected very few had successfully done so. His hair was dark, short, and as close as I could tell in the dark, well-cut. His face was covered in a day or two of beard growth, and it complimented him quite well. His bare arms were nothing but muscle, and were covered with various tattoos.

All things considered, he was perfect.

I'm sure most women would have offered very little, if anything, to help him. A biker running out of gas in an upscale residential neighborhood on a Sunday night in the summer wasn't a common occurrence, and by most people's standards, wouldn't warrant much assistance. After what seemed to be an eternity of admiring him and thinking, I blurted out what must have been a subconscious thought.

"What? You don't have a phone?" I asked.

"Like I said when I walked up, I knew it would sound like bullshit, but it's the truth. I was riding down Central, and I ran out of gas. I wanted to coast off the main street and get under a street light. So, I kicked it into neutral and coasted as far as I could. That got me to *there*," he said as he turned and pointed at his motorcycle.

"And no, I don't have a phone. Long story," he said as he turned to face me.

I nodded my head and grinned as if I understood. Half-drunk from my wine induced book review, and half-horny from the shitty romance novel without an ending, I gazed at the sexy biker and gave him my best resolution to his problem.

"Tell you what. Push your bike into my garage and we can lock it up all safe and happy and then we'll go get gas in my car. Will that work?" I asked.

"Safe and happy," he said with a laugh.

"Just wait until I get the car out before you try and shove your bike in," I said.

Still facing me, he nodded his head in apparent appreciation.

Proud of my pearly whites, I smiled a tooth-revealing smile and nodded my head in return. The expression on his face reminded me that my teeth probably weren't white, but wine soaked. The half-bottle of Madeira I had guzzled while reviewing the book undoubtedly had my teeth looking like I'd just finished eating a raw steak.

"I appreciate it," he said as he turned away. "I'll owe you one."

I turned toward the house and did my best to wipe my teeth clean with my index finger as he walked away. After carefully backing my car out into the driveway, I got out in enough time to watch him push the Harley into the garage. He situated it perfectly against the inside wall of the garage, studied it for a moment, and turned to face the car. As he walked toward me, I made note of the fact he wasn't wearing a wedding ring, but I doubted many of his type did, even if they were married.

"*This* is your car?" he asked as he walked around it with his hand on his chin and his eyes glued to the flawless black paint.

"Only one I got, yep," I said proudly.

"1966 or '67?" he asked.

I shook my head. "It's a 1965. Year my dad was born. He left it to me when he died."

"Well, it's a damned fine looking Continental, that's for sure. And I'm sorry about your pop," he said as he opened the door.

He carefully got into the car, fastened the seat belt, and looked around the interior as I got inside and situated myself. His expressed appreciation of the car and his careful manner of opening the door and getting inside led me to believe he wasn't only a big tough biker. At least

14

a small part of him was kind and considerate, and it was apparent.

"I'm Sienna," I said as I turned the key and started the car.

He coughed a laugh and grinned as he turned his head in my direction. "Call me Vince. And I'm guessing this fucker ain't stock?"

The rumble from the exhaust made sneaking around in the car almost impossible. My father had built it as a show car, and planned on using it as a trophy of sorts, only driving it on special occasions. He had a 521 cubic inch 600 horsepower motor built by a local professional shop, and I helped him install it right before he died.

His instructions to me upon his passing were clear.

Drive the car, Sienna. Drive it and enjoy it. And if you ever decide to sell it, don't sell it because you want something different; sell it because you don't love it anymore. And only sell it to someone who does.

He had the car as long as I was alive, and actually had purchased it a few years before I was born. His entire life had been spent making the car perfect, and perfect was how I intended to keep it.

"521 cubic inches of earth shaking Big Block Ford, six hundred horsepower to be exact," I bragged as I backed out of the driveway.

"No shit?" he said with a grin. "You know your cars, huh?"

"I'm an only child, and a daddy's girl. The only time I spent with him was in the garage," I said. "So, I know a little about cars, and a lot about *this* car."

He nodded his head as he glanced around the interior of the car admiringly.

"So where were you going?" I asked as I shifted the car into drive. "You know, when you ran out of gas."

"Nowhere, just riding. I go out on Sunday nights and just ride, it clears my mind before starting a new week. Had a poker run yesterday, and as that fucker started spittin' and sputterin', I remembered I forgot to fill it up after. I can get two hundred miles on a full tank, and not a mile more. Runnin' out is the price I pay for not keeping track of my miles, I guess," he said.

"Well, the station up on Douglas will loan us a gas can. Just remember, two hundred miles," I said with a grin.

He stared at me for a moment, narrowed his upper lip, and revealed his teeth. As I gazed back at him rather confused, he narrowed his eyes and pointed to his teeth with his index finger.

"You've got a big piece of meat or something in your front teeth. Sorry, but it's driving me nuts," he said as he tapped the tip of his finger against his tooth.

I glanced in the rearview mirror and curled my lip upward. The side of one of my two front teeth was as red as a ruby. I had obviously wiped the other tooth clean with my finger on the front porch, but missed whatever wine-soaked matter was stuck between my other teeth.

"Shit, sorry," I said as I alternated glances between the road and the mirror.

He shook his head and grinned.

"I was eating crackers and cheese and drinking wine. Typical Sunday night at my house," I said as I turned into the gas station.

I pulled in front of the store and after a few seconds of the engine running, decided to shut it off. The sound of the motor running while parked against a brick building became rather annoying very quickly, the low rumble from the high performance camshaft made the car sound like an old school race car.

"This fucker was shaking the windows," he said as he opened the door. "You got to love the sound of all that power."

I grinned, proud of what my father and I had built. He pushed the door open slightly and paused. Time seemed to stand still as he fixed his eyes on me and cleared his throat.

"Need anything?" he asked.

I had no idea of who this man was, but on the outside he was everything I wanted in a man. I may have licked my lips before I responded, but if I did, he didn't seem to notice or care. After a few seconds of admiring his muscles and handsome looks, I shook my head from side to side and shrugged.

"A toothbrush," I laughed.

"Be right back," he said as he stepped out of the car.

After carefully closing the door, he walked into the gas station, talked to the guy at the register, and turned toward the back of the building. In the well illuminated store, I could see every detail of what he was wearing. The back of his leather vest had a patch of a winged skull with two crossed rifles sewn on it, and had a "Kansas" rocker. I'd read enough books about bikers that I recognized the diamond shaped one percenter patch, and considering he was wearing a cut with the patch and rockers, there was no doubt he was a fully patched member of the club.

Selected Sinners.

I'd seen a few of the members of the club from time to time over the years, riding down the road or in a bar in Old Town. For a one percent club, they sure seemed to have their shit together, and never made the news for doing anything stupid, at least not that I'd seen. As I sat in the car and watched him walk toward the gas pumps, I recalled seeing on the news that one of their members had donated gold coins to the Salvation Army during Christmas time.

I glanced in the rearview mirror and admired his reflection. He was far too handsome to be standing there alone. I opened the door of the car and shuffled toward the gas pump. With each well thought out step, I realized although I was far from sober, I was not as drunk as I needed to be to offer myself to him.

I was single, lonely, and really needed to be fucked, but I was far from a slut. The thought of being ravished by a biker was always something lingering in the back of my mind, but actually allowing him to do it was a different thing altogether.

"So, one of your guys donated a bunch of gold on Christmas a while back. Right after he got back from the war. He was some special forces guy or something," I said as I walked up to the gas pump.

"Sure did," he responded.

I shrugged my shoulders as he placed the nozzle back into the pump. "Not the kind of thing most people think of bikers doing."

"Probably not," he responded.

Wow.

Don't feel like talking?

I stared down at my flip-flops and realized my toes were in desperate need of polish. Half embarrassed, I turned toward the car as he began to step past me. As I glanced up from my toes, I noticed a man standing beside my car with his hand on the front fender. Before I had a chance to say anything, Vince barked out a demand in a tone of voice that caused the hair on the back of my neck to stand up.

"Step away from the car, Motherfucker," he growled as the pace of his steps quickened.

The man, obviously drunk, turned his head toward Vince and all but fell into the fender of my car. After taking a few more steps, Vince

18

SCOTT HILDRETH

placed the gas can beside the car, walked up to the man, and gently pushed him to the side by pressing his left forearm against the man's chest. As the man stumbled backward, Vince stepped between him and my car.

"Expensive paint job, Brother. Just want you to be careful," he said.

"Get your fucking hands off me," the man howled.

In a split-second, the man produced a knife and began swinging it toward Vince. Immediately, it was apparent Vince was no stranger to fighting, protecting himself, or disarming a knife wielding drunk.

Kick his fucking ass, Vince.

As the man grunted and lurched forward with the knife, Vince raised his left arm high in the air, wrapped it around the man's right arm, and quickly turned around. With his back against the man's chest and the man's arm pinned in Vince's armpit, he reached for the man's wrist and turned it to the side.

As the drunk wailed in pain, he dropped the knife. As soon as it hit the pavement, Vince stepped on it and pushed the man to the side.

As the man stumbled, Vince bent down, picked up the knife, and shoved it into his back pocket. I stood in awe at what I had just seen. No differently than the men in my MC Romance books, Vince was not only a biker, but a bad-ass biker. Standing and waiting to see what his next Judo move might be, I was surprised to see a police officer walk from inside the store and onto the sidewalk in front of my car.

"Kid inside told me what happened. He saw it all. You want to press charges for assault?" the officer asked.

Still standing between the man and my car, Vince crossed his arms in front of his chest and shook his head. "Simple misunderstanding, Officer."

19

"Kid inside said he pulled a knife on you," the officer said as he tilted his head toward the drunk.

"Nope. He took a swing at me and missed. Didn't see a knife," Vince said with a shrug of his shoulders.

"A swing and a miss, huh? Anyone here had too much to drink?" the officer asked as he glanced at each of us.

It had only been thirty minutes since I finished the bottle of wine, and although I wasn't shit-faced drunk, I was definitely not as drunk as I was going to get. With each passing minute, I felt a little more incapable of standing without teetering over. A sobriety test would land me in jail for sure.

"Can't speak for him," Vince said as he tossed his head toward the drunken man. "But, she's had some wine. Good thing I'm driving."

The officer cocked an eyebrow. "You're driving?"

"That's what I said," Vince responded.

The officer pointed his finger at me. "Kid inside said *she* drove up…"

He turned and pointed his finger at Vince's chest. "*You* got gas…"

He swiveled to the side and pointed at the drunk. "And *he* attacked you with a knife when you walked up to the car."

"Believe only half of what you see and nothing that you hear," Vince said.

Wow. He just quoted Edgar Allen Poe.

The officer turned to face me, pressed his hands on his hips, and sighed. "So what *really* happened?"

Raised by a father who was wrongly accused and subsequently wrongly convicted of a crime he didn't commit, I had very little respect for police officers, especially our city's finest. Based on my desire to spend more time with Vince and less time standing and talking to a cop,

I shrugged my shoulders and smiled.

"Exactly what he said happened," I responded.

The officer raised his hand and pressed his thumb against the bill of his hat, raising it slightly. "And how much wine did you drink tonight?"

"Not so much that I'm blind or stupid, but too damned much to drive," I responded.

He nodded his head in confirmation, apparently disappointed he wasn't able to make a few arrests.

"How'd *you* get here?" the officer asked as he turned toward the drunken man.

Obviously not an intelligent man, the drunk tossed his head toward a truck parked a few stalls away from where we were standing.

"Have a nice night," the officer said with a nod as he grabbed the man by his upper arm and pulled him onto the sidewalk.

After carefully placing the can of gas in the floorboard between my feet, we got into the car and turned to face each other.

"Keys?" Vince asked as he held his hand out.

I reluctantly dropped the keys into his hand. Other than my father and me, he would be the only other one to ever drive the car.

He reached into his front pocket, fumbled around for a moment, and then reached toward my lap.

"Here," he said as he dropped a small tube of toothpaste and a toothbrush in my lap.

I glanced down and smiled. As ridiculous as it seemed to actually think of the toothpaste and toothbrush as a gift, I immediately felt warmth developing in my heart as I gazed at the items. Short of my father, it was the only gift a man had ever given me.

"Any secrets to starting it?" he asked as he pushed the key into the ignition.

I turned to face him and immediately my mouth curled into a grin. He had captured my attention in a short period of time, and I had no desire to let him slip away without trying to learn more about him. Before I embarrassed myself by staring, I shifted my drunken eyes away from him and responded.

"Pump it once and turn the key," I said as I opened the glovebox and placed the items inside.

He started the car and slowly backed out of the parking stall. Relishing in the recollection of Vince's one-sided fight, I glanced out the window and toward the building. The officer was giving the man a sobriety test on the sidewalk, and it was pretty obvious he wasn't going to pass it. As I shifted my eyes once again toward Vince, I wondered just how well I would have performed the same test in my flip-flops.

"I appreciate you saying you were driving," I said.

"No problem," he responded. "I appreciate you taking me to get gas."

"No problem," I said in a mimicking tone. "But we're not even."

"Oh we're not?" he asked over his shoulder as he pulled into the street.

The muscles on his tattooed bicep flared as he turned the steering wheel. He was torturing me and he had no idea he was doing so.

I shook my head and swallowed a mouthful of desire. "Nope. I want a ride on your bike."

He turned his head in my direction as the car came to a stop at the traffic light. After cocking an eyebrow comically and fixing his eyes on mine, he responded.

"I don't give just anyone a ride on my bike," he said flatly.

"Well," I said as I raised my eyebrows slightly. "I'm not just anyone."

VINCE

June 8th, 2014

I had told myself over the course of the last year that a woman would have to prove herself to me to get me to even give her a moment's notice, but in the end, that wasn't necessarily the truth. A stupid mistake on my part had landed me in an upper middle class neighborhood, and within an hour, I had a gorgeous half-drunk brunette on the back of my bike, and was riding down a county road on my way to nowhere.

As interesting as she was, and as different as she seemed to be, she was still a woman, and without a doubt would have all of the characteristics of one - and a woman wasn't something I needed in my life no matter how cute she was, how well she filled out her filthy sweats, or how cool her car was.

In the end, she was a woman, and women were evil.

For a short ride through the county at midnight, however, having her on the back of my bike was enjoyable. It reminded me of better times, the feeling of being complete, and not necessarily living with much desire to do anything but exist.

The city quickly turned into a few randomly placed rural housing developments, and eventually the developments diminished into a few sparse farm houses. After a matter of minutes, we were ten miles from the city and riding into the path my headlight cut into the otherwise completely dark road ahead.

As I became almost hypnotized by the bouncing beam of light, her hands lightly gripping my waist reminded me of Natalie. The thought was equal parts comforting and sickening at first, and after a few minutes, comforting was the clear winner. The fast approaching rural stop sign reminded me not only had we reached the highway, but that I needed to maintain my focus on the road, and not my passenger's hand placement.

I stopped at the intersection, pulled out along the side of the highway, and rolled to a stop on the paved shoulder of the road.

"Is something wrong?" she asked as I kicked the heel of my boot against the kickstand.

I flipped the ignition switch off and reached down and turned the key, killing the lights.

"Nope, just stopping for a bit," I responded.

We both stepped off the bike at the same time, and stood staring at each other illuminated only by what little moonlight escaped through the low passing clouds. I broke her gaze, glanced toward the ditch, and nodded my head in the direction of the large concrete storm water drain passing underneath the intersecting road.

"Grab a seat," I said as I tossed my head toward the large piece of exposed concrete.

Being subtle had never been one of my strengths, and I wasn't going to try and change things now. In being honest with myself, riding with her on the back of my bike rekindled feelings I was sure had long since passed. Natalie hadn't been on the back of my bike for a year before we divorced, and she'd been gone for roughly a year.

The last two years I had ridden alone, and although I had many requests to take women on rides, I never fulfilled them. Now that I had decided to, for whatever reason, I wasn't sure I liked the result.

"I got to be honest with you," I said as I sat down on the edge of the concrete.

"Okay," she responded as she crossed her arms and gazed down at me.

"Sit," I said as I patted the concrete beside me.

"I'll stand," she responded.

"I'm thirty-three years old. Married for fifteen years, and divorced a year ago. I'm a different kind of guy than you'd probably ever meet, and a damned far cry from most bikers you'd ever run across." I paused and patted the concrete again.

She stood, staring down at me, and shook her head lightly. Standing there in the moonlight, still dressed in her sweats and flip-flops, no one could dispute her beauty. As I gazed up at her and fully realized just how beautiful she was, I reminded myself that external beauty acted as a distraction to what was on the inside.

"I was faithful. For fifteen years. I didn't spend time at strip clubs with the fellas, or any more time at the bars than I had to. When I did, I always played it cool, and never let myself do anything stupid, short of fights and stuff. You know, never messed around. Then, I found out she was in a relationship with a guy. Hell, I guess I should have known, considering the way she treated me..." I hesitated and started to stand up.

She pointed to the concrete. "Sit."

She walked to my side, sat down, and turned to face me. "Go ahead."

"Well, fuck. I don't know why I'm even telling you this. It's just. Hell, I don't know, having you on the back of my bike made me think of her or something. I mean, I'm done with her, but you grabbing my waist in your hands reminded me of her. I either liked it a lot or I hated it, I just can't decide which it was," I said.

She brushed her ponytail over her shoulder and twisted her mouth to the side. "Did you actually think of *her*, or did having my hands there make you feel something you haven't felt in a while?"

I considered what she said, turned toward her, and wrinkled my nose. "You a fucking psychologist or something?"

She shook her head and grinned. "Just read a lot."

"Yeah, me too," I said as I gazed down at my boots.

"Really?" she asked.

Still focused on my boots, I nodded my head. "Like I said, you'll never meet another like me. I sit at home every night and read. Probably five books a week. Rarely sleep. I'm either at the clubhouse, home reading, or somewhere in between."

"A soft-hearted biker who loves to read," she said.

"A soft-hearted biker with a short fuse and quick fists," I said as I kicked the toe of my boot against the concrete.

"I noticed that," she responded.

"Been an outlaw all my life. Figured joining the MC was my best bet at finding my true calling, and it seems I was right. They put my Pop in prison when I was a kid on a conspiracy to commit murder charge, and he died of pneumonia after a few years. When I turned eighteen I got his old bike running, ten years later I joined the MC, and now I finally feel at home. Don't care much for the government, can't stand cops, and most of the time I think the country would be better off if Axton Bishop was President," I said.

"I'm sorry about your father. That's crazy. My dad did five years for a burglary he didn't commit. He was at home asleep at the time, but because of an old assault charge, he was in the system. Someone picked him out of a lineup. I'll never forgive them for what they did to him. He was gone the entire time I was in high school. Motherfuckers," she said as she tossed a rock into the ditch.

"You said he passed," I said as I shifted my eyes toward her. "Can I ask?"

"Colon cancer," she said with a nod.

"Sorry," I said.

"Yeah, me too. And who is Axton Bishop?" she asked.

"Huh? Oh. He's the president of the MC," I said with a laugh.

"I'll write him in next November," she said.

"You won't be the only one," I said.

"How about when we leave, I'll wrap my hands around your chest or maybe your neck? Maybe that'll make you feel more comfortable," she said.

"Wrap my hands around *your* fucking neck if you ain't careful," I said.

"Don't make promises you aren't willing to keep," she said as she stood up.

Just saying it caused my cock to begin to twitch. Realizing it had done so made me begin to worry about it, and my worrying kept the thought in the forefront of my mind. Within a few seconds, I had a full-blown hard on, and although I wasn't necessarily embarrassed, I wasn't proud either.

But, as I had said many times in the past, subtlety wasn't a strength I possessed.

"You ready?" I asked as I stood.

She turned to face me, and her eyes quickly fell to my crotch. After a short pause, they worked their way up to meet mine.

I grinned and nodded my head toward the bike.

"Guess so," she said.

As I walked toward the bike, she continued.

"So what'd we decide? You going to wrap those hands around my neck?" she nonchalantly asked.

As I threw my leg over the seat of the bike and acted as if I didn't hear her, I knew if I ever chose to see her again, I'd damned sure have my hands full.

And I wasn't totally convinced that would be a bad thing.

Not totally.

SIENNA

June 29th, 2014

I sat in my living room flipping through Netflix's available shows. After thirty minutes of searching for something new, I decided Netflix never had anything new and chose to watch another episode of *Orange is the New Black*.

For some reason, the thought of being tossed into a women's prison was a constant fear of mine, and watching the show was a good reminder of how much I did *not* want to be in prison. For me, and I was sure for many women, the show had proven to be the best deterrent of crime that was ever invented. As much as I hated the thought of prison, I couldn't stop watching the show.

Three episodes later, I was bored, even more afraid of being fucked by a woman who looked like a dude, and as always, lonely. It really didn't seem to matter who I had chosen for a boyfriend in the past, every one of them seemed to want the same thing in the end, access to my late father's wealth. I wasn't a rich woman by any stretch of the imagination, but I could easily live the rest of my life without working, as long as I was careful about what I spent my money on.

My father sued after his wrongful conviction, and after many years and two attorneys, won the case, leaving him, and upon his death, me, with the proceeds. Nothing, however, would even be enough to pay for what they took from him.

I lived in his home, had only utilities to pay, and had no car payment. Most would consider me wealthy. I, on the other hand, considered myself fatherless, and no amount of wealth would ever replace the void his death left inside of me or in my life.

My father's absence in my life left me constantly searching for a male figure to step in and provide the comfort he supplied me for a lifetime. The problem was that I seemed to have some type of attraction to douchebags. Old ones, young ones, skinny ones, gym rats, I had dated them all. The common thread between them all was that they were douchebags. Either unwilling to commit or incapable of doing so – and always a liar – they seemed to flock to me like bees to fucking honey.

I suppose it was quite possible I was attracted to them, and somehow in a subconscious frenzy of idiocy I chose them, knowing they would eventually pull some douche move and be tossed aside like the others, but I didn't quite believe I was the one at fault. I liked to blame them, because in the end, they were the douchebags.

I sat and blankly stared at the little squares of Netflix choices frozen in time on the screen of my television, angry that I hadn't received my Advance Review Copy of a new Erotic Romance novel I was supposed to review. After a few moments, I began to think of Vince, how out of nowhere he appeared in my life, and how much it ended up we had in common.

My father described fate as *the unexpected result of the natural development of life*. I guessed Vince's appearance was nothing short of that, and as I continued to sit and stare at the television, it angered me that he didn't have a phone. He explained how he decided he didn't want a phone after his divorce, and that he had lived for the last year without a television, and relied solely on music for at-home entertainment. At first I didn't want to believe him, but after talking for a while about it, I realized he was being truthful, and more than likely imposing some weird type of punishment on himself for something he didn't even do, or deserve to be punished for.

Sitting on the couch gripping the remote control like I was trying to squeeze the last unavailable ounce of toothpaste from an empty tube, I became mad at his ex-wife for treating him the way she did. No one deserved to be heartbroken, and even bad-ass bikers were included.

I seriously doubted I could ever be in an actual relationship with someone like Vince, and I further doubted that I would ever see him again, but the thought of it was pretty satisfying for the time being.

I relaxed onto the couch and daydreamed about riding on the back of his motorcycle in cut-off jean shorts, sneakers, and a ripped up tee shirt. With one hand wrapped around his waist and the other resting in between his thighs, we'd ride across the country without a worry, fucking at every place we stopped.

His ex-wife would call him back, and after a few angst-filled weeks of separation, we'd end up back together and his ex would get run over by a train. Together, we'd go to the funeral, only to meet the newest ex-husband, who would be with a girl twelve years his junior.

A true romance novel in the flesh.

The sound of a motorcycle woke me from my not-so-deep sleep. I sat up on the couch, confused as to whether the sound was something from my dream or reality. The silence provided all of the proof I needed that the motorcycle was in my dream. Frustrated and in need of a drink of some sort, I tossed my legs over the edge of the couch and wiped my eyes.

A thud against my front door startled me, and the sound of the doorbell that followed did more of the same. Slightly confused and maybe a little overanxious, I ran to the window and pulled the blinds.

Vince's bike sat in the driveway. I ran to the door and yanked it open.

Vince was leaning against the frame of the door, and his shoulder pressing against the wooden frame seemed to be the only thing holding him up. His head hanging down, and his face out of view, I suspected he was drunk and was attempting to make a bootie call.

A mild version of flattery filled me, and I reached for his arm to guide him in. As my hand touched his wrist, he glanced upward.

"Holy shit!" I gasped.

Someone had beaten him into an unrecognizable mess. Both eyes were swollen, and his face was covered in blood. As he fell into my arms, I noticed both of his lips were mangled. Far too much for me to hold up on my own, and with his entire weight pressing against me, he eventually fell from my arms and onto the floor.

As he tried to stand, he turned his mangled face toward me and did his best to smile. His once white teeth were covered in blood.

"You should…"

"Shhh, let me call an ambulance," I said.

"No!" he grunted as he tried to push himself up from the floor. "No ambulance, no cops."

I nodded my head in acknowledgement as he raised himself onto his elbows.

"You look half-dead," I said under my breath as I reached for his arm.

"You should…see…the other guy," he murmured.

And he collapsed onto the floor.

VINCE

July 1st, 2014

I did my best to open my eyes and tried to focus on my surroundings. The unfamiliar room was dark, illuminated only by the streetlights shining in through the cracks between the blinds. After a few long minutes of my eyes adjusting, I tossed my legs off the side of the bed and attempted to stand.

With each breath I took, it felt as if a knife was being inserted into my chest. I sat on the edge of the bed and searched my mind for memories of what had happened. After a few more minutes of confusion, I recalled the events of the Sunday night that got me to where I was.

A disagreement about a parking spot turned into a fight, and the fight was over almost before it started. The mouthy – and very disrespectful – driver of the truck was put in his place with half a dozen quick punches and a short choke hold. The other three passengers in the truck were a totally different story. While holding the driver in a choke hold and doing my best to explain the benefits of being respectful – all the while attempting not to actually choke him – one of his three friends blindsided me with a punch. Before I knew it, I was on the ground being kicked and stomped by three cowboys.

As they laughed and turned to walk away, I cut the calf of one of them. Through the leg of his jeans – and from the back of his knee to his ankle – I dug my knife as deep as I could, dropping him to the ground as he turned to walk away. As his two friends carried him away, I crawled to my bike and rode the three blocks to the closest place I knew to go.

Assuming I was still at Sienna's home, but not sure of anything, I once again tried to stand. As I moaned in agony and relaxed on the edge of the bed, the bedroom door opened.

"Don't you dare try to get up," she said as she opened the door.

Although I couldn't see her clearly, her voice was enough for me to know who she was. After a short and almost blind stare on my part, the bedroom light came on.

"Got to, I got a job I got to do tomorrow," I said as I shaded my eyes with my hand.

"Tomorrow being Monday?" she asked as she walked to the edge of the bed.

I sighed softly and nodded my head. "Yeah."

"I don't understand how in the hell you do anything without a phone, and it's Tuesday, so you're a day late," she said harshly as she stood in front of me with her hands on her hips.

"Fuck. Tuesday?" I asked as I glanced upward.

She sat down beside me and cleared her throat. "Technically, yes. It's about 1:30 am. And Monday's passed, so yeah. It's Tuesday. You've been asleep on and off for twenty-four hours."

"Swelling's gone down quite a bit, and the stitches look pretty good," she said as she closely inspected my face.

"Stitches? You stitched me?" I asked as I reached for my face.

She slapped my hand away from my face and shook her head. "Don't you dare touch it, it'll get infected. And, fuck no, I didn't stitch you. You'd look like some pieced together sock monkey if I did. I got a

36

nurse and a PA over here and they took care of you."

I gazed down at the floor, swallowed heavily, and nodded my head. At the time, I only wanted to get somewhere where I felt safe. Coming to her house was inconsiderate on my part, undoubtedly unexpected on her part, and troublesome at the least.

"Look, I don't want you thinking I'm some weirdo, 'cause I'm not. You live two blocks from the busiest intersection in this city, and although I don't live close to here, I ride by here a couple times a day…"

"Save it," she interrupted.

I shook my head. "No, just hear me out."

"Some of the fellas run in packs, and some hang out at the clubhouse and do whatever comes up. I'm a loner. I mean, I'm loyal to the MC, and I love the brotherhood, but I run alone. I just don't trust people. Not really," I paused, inhaled a shallow breath, and winced from the pain.

She shook her head and tilted it toward my mid-section. "He said you probably have cracked ribs. Based on the boot prints, anyway."

"Feels like it," I coughed.

"How many stitches?" I asked as I raised my hand toward my cheek.

Another slap of my hand and a sharp exhale reminded me of her obviously protective nature.

"Thirteen on the big cut, and I think four on the small one," she said as she leaned in front of me and inspected my wounds.

"You look a lot better than you did," she said.

I shifted my eyes toward the floor. "I'll pay for whatever it cost. You got friends in the medical field, huh?"

"Nope. I did my best to drag you in here, and gave up half way. I made a quick Craigslist ad in the personals. Got a lot of responses, too. It was the only thing I could think of that wouldn't get the cops over here," she said.

Still staring down at my bare toes, I nodded my head in shame. "Appreciate it."

"So, as I was saying. No phone, and riding alone as always, I was up at Central and Rock. At *Walt's*. Place was packed. I pulled in from the east, and there was one stall left. Some truck was just sitting there, and I sat there on my bike and waited for this prick to park, and he just sat there. So I parked and hopped off the bike. As I'm walking toward the bar, the driver gets out and calls me motherfucker for taking *his* spot. Ended up beating the shit out of his cowboy ass, but his buddies got the best of me. I'd have never made it to the hospital, and someone had already called the cops and an ambulance, so I left in a little bit of a hurry. I'm sorry," I said.

"Don't worry about it," she said. "So, you've never said. Just what is it that you do? You know, for a living?"

I stared down at the floor and thought of the best way to explain my situation. After a short pause, I glanced in her direction. My eyes were swollen, I had a throbbing headache, and I was still a little dazed from the beating, but it was pretty easy to see that she was an extremely beautiful woman.

She looked different than she did when I met her. On that night, in her filthy sweats and half-drunk with her hair in a ponytail, there was no doubt she was an attractive woman. Tonight, however, she was even more so. With her hair down over her shoulders and her concerned brown eyes studying me, it was difficult not to stare at her. After a short time of enjoying her beauty, I once again shifted my eyes to the floor.

"Resolutions manager," I said flatly.

"That didn't sound very sincere. And what does that mean anyway?"

she asked.

"I resolve things," I said as I glanced toward her.

"Be more specific," she said.

"Debt collector?" I said as I shrugged my shoulders. It came out with a hint of uncertainty, sounding more like a question than an answer.

She chuckled and turned her head in my direction. "What, you're not sure?"

I glanced upward. "I'm sure. It's just not something I have to describe very often."

"Look, I've read enough books that I know club business isn't up for discussion, so don't worry about explaining anything if you don't want to," she said.

"What books?" I asked, almost bursting into laughter while I spoke.

"Lots of books. MC Romance books," she responded.

I coughed a laugh and reached my aching ribs. "What the fuck is an MC Romance book?"

"It's a love story about a member or members of a motorcycle club. Most of them are a series of books, each one about a different member of the MC. You know, one will be the president, the next the sergeant-at-arms, maybe a prospect, or the enforcer, or whatever. It's a subgenre of books. They're pretty popular," she said.

"I'll be fucking damned," I said.

"You hungry?" she asked.

"Kind of," I responded.

In actuality, I was starving, but I didn't want to impose any more than I already had.

"Eggs, bacon and hash browns sound good?" she asked.

I did my best to smile and nodded my head.

"Be right back," she said.

She stood from the edge of the bed and studied me with smiling eyes for a moment before turning away. There was no doubt in my mind that whoever ended up securing Sienna as a wife or girlfriend would have someone very special.

I just knew that person would never be me.

SIENNA

July 3rd, 2014

I sat outside the coffee shop sipping my coffee and reading as droves of people needing a caffeine fix came and went. A couple in their mid-twenties got out of an SUV and walked toward the entrance, pushing each other playfully as they made their way across the parking lot.

I watched until I was almost disgusted by their groping, giggling, and grabbing, and finally turned away. I took a drink of my coffee and propped my legs on the chair opposite of where I was seated, and tilted my Kindle away from the sun.

The coffee shop was one of my few escapes, and provided entertainment in the form of people watching, really good coffee, and a peaceful place to read. I had read many books from start to finish at the same location over the years, and my memories of the place were quite fond.

Once while parking my car, I got into an argument with another person attempting to park beside me at the same time, and was rescued by a patron of the establishment. The gesture of kindness led to sharing a cup of coffee, which prompted a date, and the date included sex.

He swore at the time he was single, lonely, and on the tail end of recovering from a case of heartbreak, but it all ended up being a lie. Facebook, Instagram and Twitter are not your friend when you cheat on

41

your wife, and a girl who is unemployed has nothing but time on her hands to figure such things out.

Since the incident with the married man, I had chosen to sit on the other side of the coffee shop, feeling as if the side I was sitting on that particular day was now tainted.

My house had been reminding me of Vince, and I hoped a trip to the coffee shop and a good book would clear my mind and allow me to make it through a day without me obsessing over thoughts of him and the possibilities of us becoming an *us*. It seemed, however, that everything I did or saw, including reading my dark erotic novel, reminded me of Vince.

In the process of reading my new book, no relief was provided, but I did have a few pretty vivid fantasies etched in my mind, all of which included Vince and me in a basement with handcuffs, a blowtorch, a Tanto blade (whatever that was) and a box of Frosted Flakes.

I had no reason or right to be obsessing over Vince, and in my lifetime had never done so over any man. Men, generally speaking, obsessed over me, making ridding myself of them entirely an almost impossible task. I was beginning to feel a strange guilt, and almost as if I was becoming exactly what it was I detested, a stalker.

Two chapters later, and I was writhing in my seat. In my mind, Vince was the Hero and I the heroine. The problem, for me, was that the author had done a remarkable job of painting the sex scenes in a vivid manner, and had left me to suffer.

Frustrated, horny, and for some odd reason wanting a bowl of cereal, I decided to call it a morning and go for a drive. I needed to clear my mind of Vince and try to become normal again.

As I picked up my coffee and turned off my Kindle, three motorcycles pulled in the lot and parked on the sidewalk by the entrance. I did my best to act uninterested, but as I walked toward my car, I checked over my shoulder.

One, a massive man almost seven feet tall, stood beside another slightly shorter, but rather muscular man. The second man, with a huge beard, much more full and long than Vince's laughed as he walked, and the third man, considerably more handsome and with a darker skin tone than the other two, talked as they walked toward the entrance.

All three wore vests adorned with the patch of their MC.

Selected Sinners.

Here we go again…

VINCE

July 4th, 2014

Sunday nights were reserved for dinner at my mother's home, and as much as I tried over the years to change it, I wasn't able to do so. Disputing my mother's practices, procedures, or rituals was something rather simple to do, but having her agree with me was another story. Although this particular day wasn't a Sunday, it was a holiday, and one that my mother perceived as worthy of a family meal.

And arguing with her wasn't an option.

"Eat your fried chicken, Stephen," my mother said.

"I'm eating it as fast as I can, Mother," I responded.

"You're picking. I don't like it when you pick. Pick, pick, pick. It's all you've done since you got here. Did you eat with those boys before you came?" she asked.

"No. I told you, I came straight from home. The food's good, I just…"

She reached below the table and handed Bradley another chicken bone. "You just *what*? Stephen Vincent Ames, you need to forget about that woman. She's gone, and she's not coming back. You deserve better, and it's been what? Two years?"

"Don't feed him chicken bones. It'll kill him. And it's been a year," I said.

Bradley, an English bulldog, was my mother's best friend. She talked to him as if he understood every word she said, and fed him whatever he would eat. According to my mother, Bradley was my younger brother, and she even held birthday parties for him, making him wear a hat and eat birthday cake every year.

"He's a walking garbage disposal, he'll be fine. And don't think changing the subject will make me forget what we were talking about. She didn't even want kids, Stephen, it was only a matter of time. And I haven't seen her for two years, so it's hard for me to remember exactly when you were divorced, but she left you long before you were divorced, I can tell you that, " she said.

I inhaled a shallow breath and cleared my throat. "I'm not thinking about her."

I scooped up a forkful of some strange corn, bean, and vegetable salad she had prepared and carefully lifted the substance to my mouth. Fried chicken on the Fourth of July was one of her rituals, and it generally included several side dishes, many of which she now obtained off of Pinterest. Some of the new recipes were great and some were nothing short of awful. I did my best to swallow the unidentifiable spicy mixture, but it was proving to be rather difficult. As I rolled it around in my mouth and reached for my glass of water, she raised her eyebrows and sighed.

"You don't like the corn salsa?" she asked.

"It's *salsa*?" I asked as I pressed my tongue against the roof of my mouth in an effort to rid myself of the taste.

"Yes, what did you think it was?" she asked.

I shrugged my shoulders. "I don't know. Hell, you've got a gallon of it there in that bowl, I thought it was a salad or something."

"Salsa, Stephen. It's corn *salsa*. I got if off of Pinterest. Suzette likes it, and so does Randy," she said.

"Well, take it over to Suzette and Randy's house," I said.

She reached over the table and smacked the back of my knuckles with her butter knife.

"God damn it," I howled as I pulled my hand away. "Fuck."

I raised my hand and stared at the back of it, fully expecting to see blood. A three inch long red welt began to rise before my eyes.

"You hear that, Bradley? We're two dollars richer," she said as she pointed toward the top of the refrigerator with her chicken leg.

I knew better than to argue. I stood, pulled out my wallet, and walked to the refrigerator. After digging through my wallet and finding two one dollar bills, I pulled the jar from the top of the refrigerator and dropped the money inside.

"You smell like smoke. Have you been smoking?" she asked.

"No, I quit," I said, telling the truth for the most part.

"I think you were telling quite a fib to Bradley and me earlier when we were cooking the chicken. I want you to know that, Stephen. You're my little boy and I can see right through you. It's what mothers do," she said.

I continued to eat, acting as if I didn't hear her.

She paused and pointed her half-eaten chicken leg at me. "You've been riding since you were six years old. You and I both know you didn't wreck your father's motorcycle. I want to know who beat you up. What happened?"

"I dumped it in some sand," I said.

"Stephen Vincent. Both your eyes are stitched up, and you look like hell. What happened?" she asked.

I pointed at the jar with my fork.

She shook her head. "Hell isn't a curse word, it's a place. And it's a place you're going to end up living if you keep telling your mother fibs."

"I dumped the bike, Mother," I sighed.

"It doesn't have a scratch on it," she said, shaking her head from side to side as she spoke.

I cocked my head and stared in disbelief. "It's covered in scratches, how would you know?"

She raised her index finger in the air and glared at me. "I rode on that bike for years. I know where every scratch is. Fine, Stephen, just fine."

"I met a girl," I said flatly as I picked through the pile of chicken.

"Pardon me? I would have sworn you said you met a girl," she said.

"I did," I said as I continued to pick through the chicken. "Did you buy a breastless chicken?"

"Here, take mine," she said as she handed me her chicken breast. "Now, about this girl. Is she the reason you got beat up?"

"No, I met her one night when I ran out of gas. She gave me a ride to the gas station. She was really nice. It's nothing, I was just making conversation," I said as I bit into the chicken.

"Bradley's starving, give him your bones," she said as she waved her hand toward my plate.

"He shouldn't eat chicken bones, and he weighs fifty pounds anyway. And thirty of it's fat," I said.

"Take it back, he's not fat," she said.

"You can't take things back after you say 'em, and he is too," I said.

"You sure can. You say 'I take it back.' Now, who's this girl? Does she want kids?" she asked.

"How the hell would I know? I told you, she gave me a ride to the gas station," I responded.

One thing my mother always detested about Natalie was that she was outspoken regarding her lack of interest in having children, and my mother dreamed of the day she would have grandchildren. It was a subject Natalie and I discussed often and never quite agreed on.

"Is she pretty?" she asked.

I nodded my head. "Beautiful. Dark hair, like yours."

"Does she have tattoos?" she asked.

"None that I could see," I said.

My mother accepted the fact I had tattoos, but believed everyone else with tattoos was an obvious criminal or had spent time in prison. Women with tattoos, as far as she was concerned, were trouble.

"So are you seeing her?" she asked.

I dropped my chicken breast onto my plate. "Gas. She took me to get gas. That's it."

"Did you get her phone number?" she asked.

I rested my forearms on the table, glared at her, and raised both eyebrows.

"You need to get a phone, Stephen. This is ridiculous," she said. "Everyone has a phone."

"I *had* a phone and now I don't. No worries, I know where she lives," I said. "I could always stop by."

"Don't be a stalker, Stephen. It's not nice," she said as she reached for her glass of tea. "I saw on *Bluebloods* the other night what happens to stalkers."

"Jesus…" I sighed as I reached for my chicken.

"Take her some flowers, tell her thank you, and ask her to go to dinner. That's what a proper man would do. In the same situation, it's what your father would have done, and you know it," she said.

As I ate my chicken, I considered her advice. She was right. So far, I'd troubled Sienna twice with my problems, and had never really taken time to thank her properly for everything she had done for me.

"I'll take her some flowers," I said with a nod of my head.

"And dinner. Take her to dinner, Stephen," my mother said as she lowered another chicken bone below the table.

Bradley took the chicken bone from her hand, waddled toward the refrigerator, and flopped down on the floor beside his bowl of food. As he gnawed on the bone and grew another few ounces fatter, and one step closer to choking to death, I shifted my eyes toward my mother.

"Fine," I said. "And dinner."

"You're a good boy, Stephen. Now eat the rest of your salsa," she said as she pointed her butter knife at my plate.

I had no intention of eating the remaining salsa, but I did think taking Sienna flowers and going to dinner was a good idea. My mother might have been difficult to bullshit, and impossible to win an argument with, but she always gave good advice. Her only concerns were, and had always been, what she believed to be in my best interest.

As I sat and ate the remaining portion of my Fourth of July meal and mentally prepared for the fireworks display we were certain to discharge in the driveway later, I knew one thing for sure.

I would always be her little boy.

SIENNA

July 9th, 2014

I had three books to review, was out of wine, and was about half as drunk as I needed to be. One of the books was an absolute disaster, written by someone who was so full of herself she wouldn't even take my constructive criticism as advice. In my opinion, if an author of a book didn't know the difference between two, to, too, four, fore, for, or their, they're and there, they had no business publishing a book without the assistance of a professional editor.

And if the author was so pretentious she believed a book reviewer couldn't have an effect on her ability to sell said book, she was dead wrong. My offer in the form of a private message to help her with a few things was met with a response that was beyond rude and completely uncalled for. I glared at her message decided a response wasn't necessary, only an appropriate review.

Sienna,

*I appreciate your opinion, but remember, I am **THE AUTHOR**. Putting my thoughs on paper is my job, and yours is to review what I gave wrotten. If you don't like my choice of wrods, maybe you should write your own book and have me review it.*

Thanks anyway.

Not.

Diamond

She couldn't even write me an email without making mistakes. The sad thing was that the book had a reasonably interesting storyline, but the problems with syntax, grammar, and her weird prose prevented me from enjoying it, and from completing it. The opinions on not finishing a book and providing a review were all over the place, but I was of the opinion if I did my best to read a book, and because it was a disaster was incapable of finishing it, my follower should know my opinion.

I stared at the screen and tried to decide the best thing to do. After a moment, I began to type.

My Sister, My Lover, by Diamond Phelps was interesting enough for me to attempt to read it, but I was incapable of finishing it due to the constant errors and problems with her shifting from past tense to present tense and from first to third person - sometimes in the middle of sentences.

"I walked to the edge of the pier, wondering what he was going to do about our baby. Strangely, I wasn't even sure it was his. He walks up beside me and held my hand, shows me he loves me without speaking, and pats me on the back softly. I snap out of my subconscious state and turned around, and he lifts my chin and says "it'll be just fine" with his green eyes.

Words were not spoken, but they didn't have to be spoke. He says all that he needs to say because we were loving each other, and we were always going to be lovers.

You never should walking away from a man who deep down inside loved you like he loves me and I knew this, but the fight within me building with each passing moment.

The fire inside of me was intense, and it burns eternally...."

I think the above excerpt says it all.

Now, to pre-squash the question I'm sure throngs of people will ask, "Sienna, is it fair that you one-starred a book you DNF'd? You didn't actually finish it." I will offer this answer in advance.

If I started the book, decided to go on vacation to Belize, and didn't finish it for that reason, only to DNF and one star the book, yes. Yes, that would be wrong in my eyes.

Or, if I started the book, set it aside to go get a glass of wine, and tripped over the carpet in the living room where it meets the hard wood (which I am known to do on my 2nd or 3rd glass), and ended up in the hospital with a broken hip and a terrible case of 'I'm stupids', only to return and find my Kindle had been stolen? Yes, that would be bad of me to DNF and one star.

But, life is too short to read bad books or wear ugly shoes.

So, I CHOOSE to not finish this book based on the fact there are many others out there worthy taking up space in my head.

One star. DNF.

I read the review, decided using the excerpt from the book was probably best, and pressed the button to publish it. It was an extremely short review, but I believed it provided the prospective reader with enough information for them to develop their own opinion.

As I stared at my notes from the second book, the doorbell rang. Slightly startled, but becoming fractionally more used to the sound of the doorbell since I met Vince, I walked to the window and pulled the blinds to the side. I hoped it was him, but before I even glanced toward the porch I knew it wasn't, because the sound of his motorcycle didn't come first.

Much to my surprise, what appeared to be Vince's silhouette stood waiting on my porch. Dressed in my plaid pink pajamas and a wife beater, I considered changing clothes, but quickly decided not to. So far, neither my P!NK sweats nor my jeans had much of an effect on him, and I hoped my most adorable pajamas would cause him to see me a little differently.

I ran to the living room, attempted to pace my breathing, and pulled the door open slowly. Vince stood before me with a smirk on his face and a vase filled with flowers in his hand.

"Good evening," he said.

Feeling almost as if I was in shock, I stood and stared.

"I wanted to say thanks for everything," he said as he handed me the flowers.

The only thing I could think of that would come close to describing how I felt would be to compare it to how and what I felt on Christmas morning with my father as a little girl.

"Thank you," I murmured.

As my heart began to race and my palms broke out in a profuse sweat, I turned toward the inside of the house and prayed I didn't start crying.

"Come in," I said as I walked toward the kitchen.

I assumed the flowers would need water, but in looking at the vase, they didn't.

"I didn't hear your motorcycle, you surprised me," I said as I placed the vase on the counter.

"I uhhm. I drove the truck. I couldn't figure out a way to get those on the bike," he said.

He was dressed differently than normal, and wasn't wearing his cut. Dressed in a black tee shirt, jeans, and boots, it seemed that he was dressed up for the occasions.

"You're not wearing your cut," I said.

He shrugged his shoulders. "No cuts in cages. Surprised you haven't read that in your little MC books."

"Well, I haven't yet," I said as I shifted my eyes toward the flowers.

"I can't stay, I got to go do a quick job, but I uhhm. I have a question," he said.

"Okay," I said as I shifted my eyes in his direction.

"You want to get lunch next Sunday? Maybe like meet up or something?" he asked.

Holy shit.

"Sure, sounds fun," I said.

"How about let's meet at that place on 21st and Rock, the new steak house?" he asked.

I did my best to contain my excitement. "Sure, what time?"

"Noon?" he asked.

He was big, covered in tattoos, and I knew from the night we got gas he had the ability to be violent, but for that moment, he seemed rather innocent.

"Sure."

"Alright. Now remember, I don't have a phone, so don't be late," he said.

"I won't, I promise," I said.

He nodded his head, shifted his body toward the door and paused. "Alright. Well, I better get. Thanks again, for everything."

"Any time," I said, and then immediately wished I would have said something else.

He walked to the door, opened it, and glanced over his shoulder. His eyes fell to the floor and slowly worked their way back up to my face. "I like the pajamas. They're cute."

"Thanks," I said.

I waved as he turned and walked toward his truck, just like I used to at the passing floats in the parades when I was a little girl, and then felt like a complete idiot for doing so. Hell, I didn't know what a proper departure salute for a biker was, my books hadn't addressed it. Maybe I should have pounded my fist to my heart and shot him the peace sign. After he got in his truck and drove away, I shut the door and ran to the kitchen.

I closed my eyes, buried my face in the flowers, and inhaled a long slow breath through my nose. As I lifted my head I opened my eyes and gazed down at the magnificent arrangement. They were perfect.

They were…

The unexpected result of the natural development of life.

VINCE

July 16th, 2014

The meal with Sienna was far more enjoyable than I ever expected it to be. As gorgeous as she was, and as womanly as she appeared to be, being in her presence reminded me more of hanging out with the fellas than eating a meal with Natalie. She was calm, she spoke about whatever was on her mind, and she didn't seem to have reservations regarding any of the subjects I chose to discuss. I found myself intentionally trying to cause her to be uncomfortable, but nothing seemed to shake her. As our meal came to a close, I had to continually remind myself that being in a relationship was the last thing on earth I needed to do.

But I *really* enjoyed being with her.

"So, you don't work?" I asked.

"Not right now, no. I did up until last year, but I got..." She paused, raised both hands in the air, and made cute little finger quotation marks before continuing. "Let go."

I couldn't help but grin. To see her was to witness beauty, but watching her live life defined *cute*. I gazed at her for a long minute, mentally stumbled, and finally spoke.

"I see," I said.

She twisted her mouth to the side as if she were thinking and reached for her glass of tea.

"I'm kind of just hanging out right now. It's my father's old house, and I don't really have any bills, so…" she raised her glass, took a drink, and chewed on a cube of ice while she gazed at me innocently.

"And on Sundays you get drunk and review books?" I asked.

She swallowed the ice and quickly got another. As she chewed it, she responded over the loud crunching sound. "Pretty much. It's a ritual. I generally start about seven or so. It's the only day of the week I drink."

Over the years I had learned a lot about people. My job required that I have a knack for reading people or develop an ability to do so based on my experience. I suppose my successes in my work could be attributed a little to both. Naturally I was able to read people better than most other men, and over time I learned a lot about expressions, tell-tale signs, and mannerisms while working. Sienna's willingness to do something as simple as sit and chew ice cubes told me some things about her.

She was comfortable around me, and she had no hesitation to be herself in my presence. I studied her for a moment and eventually raised my index finger. As her eyes shifted up toward my hand, I grinned.

"I have a question," I said.

"Okay," she responded.

Her brown eyes were filled with innocence, but my experience with people told me she was far from an innocent woman. I knew I wasn't mentally or physically ready for a relationship, but letting her slip away completely was unthinkable.

"I told you about my ex-wife, and how I didn't trust women," I said.

She nodded her head as she raised her glass of tea. "Yep."

"Well, what if we started doing this every Sunday? As friends and nothing more, just two people enjoying each other's company. What would you say to that?" I asked.

She shuffled an ice cube around in her mouth and eventually spit it back into her glass of tea. After wiping her mouth on the back of her hand, she shifted her eyes to meet mine and smiled.

"I'd like that," she said.

And, with those three words, my life was completely changed.

SIENNA

August 10th, 2014

My life was much different than what I had become used to, and now included everything I ever wanted it to; with the exception of sex. It was easier for me to dismiss the sex than I would have thought, and I attributed it not to my being satisfied to Vince's ability to make me happy, but to my feeble mind's belief that one day the sex would come. It had been two months since the day we met, and as much as I hoped the relationship would develop into something more than us merely being friends, he had made no indication to lead me to believe it ever would.

It was pretty obvious he loved only one woman in his life, and her infidelity left him feeling alone and cheated, but more than anything, he felt as if someone he trusted had broken a promise. I truly believed of all things, her breaking her vow of marriage was what hurt him the most.

Vince was a man different than anyone else I had ever met, and was no doubt different than anyone I would ever encounter, regardless of how many men I chose to meet in my lifetime. He collected debts not for his club, but for any and everyone who hired him to do so. I had learned he was well known in the city, and everyone from drug dealers, bail bondsmen, and even local attorneys who didn't want to get their hands dirty hired him to resolve their money matters or find someone who had skipped out on a debt or a commitment.

He explained one reason he felt no shame in doing what he did was that men had a responsibility to honor their word, and no one should ever break a promise. He viewed a debt as a promise, and always made sure they understood when he arrived to collect that he was there because they had *broken a promise*.

Vince was involved in all of the club's activities, and viewed the members of the motorcycle club as his family. He had a pretty strong relationship with his mother from what he had said, but his family was the MC. His choice to be alone in life wasn't some form of self-imposed punishment in my opinion, but a protective measure to make sure he didn't expose himself to the pain and heartache associated with people not keeping their promises, commitments, or the possibility of them not meeting his expectations.

On one of our lunch dates, he did take the time to explain that if he had no expectations of anyone, he would never be in a position to be disappointed. Getting him to agree to a standing Sunday lunch was difficult, but he eventually agreed, stating if I ever decided not to show up, to call him at his home, and leave a message on his answering machine. His not having a cell phone made things with him extremely difficult, but if it did nothing else, it kept me conscious of my commitments.

After this short period of time, I respected Vince almost as much as I respected my father.

I glanced at the clock on the dash and shook my head. Sunday traffic at noon was ridiculous on the east side of the city, as almost every street had half a dozen churches on it, and church ended at the same time for every one of them.

Dealing with the indecisive minds of the slow driving idiots in front of me was about to get the best of me. Traveling the last two blocks had taken me fifteen minutes, and in five minutes, I was going to be late. And being late wasn't an option with Vince.

You don't know whether to shit or wind your watch, do you old man?

In the middle of the city wasn't a great place to pass a car, nor was it legal. Sometimes, just to keep my sanity, it was necessary. I gripped the steering wheel, peered to the left, and pressed my foot against the gas pedal.

The transmission shifted down two gears and the rear throttle blades of the massive four barrel carburetor kicked in. With no time to think, and very little time to react, I pulled the steering wheel to the left and passed the three idiots in front of me in just enough time to miss the truck in the oncoming lane.

Having in excess of six hundred horsepower in a street car sure wasn't necessary, but it was a hell of a lot of fun. After a few light applications of the brake pedal, I slowed down to eighty miles per hour, only fifty miles an hour above the posted speed limit. Traveling at that speed, I flew past every car on the road, leaving them where they belonged, behind in my wake. The traffic light ahead would be impossible to stop at, and as I continued to blow past the Sunday drivers, I checked the signal. The light changed from green to yellow, so I hammered the gas pedal again, launching the car through the intersection like a rocket. I grinned as I pulled into the restaurant with two minutes to spare.

A quick search of the parking lot produced no motorcycle, and I sighed in relief as I shut off the engine. As I sat and listened to the end of *"Christmas in Hollis,"* by Run DMC, someone approaching the car startled me.

"What the fuck are you listening to?" he asked.

"Oh shit, I didn't think you were here," I said as I opened the glove box and flipped the switch to turn off the stereo.

I opened the door to the car, admiring his growth of beard as I got out. "Sorry, I was just chillin'."

"It's the middle of summer and you're listening to Christmas music?" he asked.

"I like Christmas," I said as I locked the car.

He shook his head and laughed. "At Christmas time, maybe."

"Run DMC's "*Christmas in Hollis*" kicks ass all year round, sorry," I said.

He shrugged his shoulders. "Run DMC? Christmas rap?"

"Shit keeps me in a good mood, what can I say. You ready to eat?" I asked.

"Yeah, I'm starving. It was a late night," he said.

We walked toward the entrance side by side. The entire time, I tried not to stare, but he really looked great. His beard was a little thicker than the two or three days growth that he generally wore, and had grown rather full since I had seen him only a week prior. Instead of wearing his normal tee shirt, he had on a wife beater, and his vest was unbuttoned. As he walked his walk of confidence, periodically checking over each shoulder as we made our way to the entrance, I felt safe, secure, and almost blessed.

"Fuck, maybe I should try listening to it all year round," he said as he pulled open the door to the restaurant. "Maybe I wouldn't be so hard to get along with."

"You're not hard to get along with," I said as I walked inside.

"As long as you keep showing up for Sunday dinner, we'll get along fine," he said.

"Two," he said to the young girl at the reception desk.

64

"Summer will help you," she said as she motioned toward a girl with dreadlocks who stood beside her.

"Follow me," Summer said cheerily.

"After you," Vince said as he pointed toward the bouncing locks of filth in front of us.

Of all people, I believed I was truly a fan of individuality and expression of one's true self. I never, however, found much value in dreadlocks. As far as I was concerned, they made whoever was wearing them seem dirty, unhealthy, and just shy of screaming for attention.

After the dreadlocked girl tossed the menus on the table and walked away, we each sat down.

"You like that shit?" I asked as I picked up the menu.

He cocked an eyebrow as he took a sip from his glass of water. "What shit?"

"Dreads?" I asked as I tossed my head toward the waitress.

He shook his head. "The Rastafarian chick? Nope."

"Yeah, me neither," I said.

"Personally, I like your hair," he said as he nodded his head toward me. "Dark, clean, well-cut, and always done up a little different. Hell, it never looks the same, but it's always perfect. I like that."

My face felt flush, and I was sure that I was blushing, but the compliment was genuine and it made me feel great. Based on who I had received them from in the past, I generally categorized compliments as attempts to get in my pants. With Vince, I knew better. Whatever he said came from the heart.

Hearing him say such things made me want him more, and the want was almost a dull pain. As a matter of respect to him, I never asked for anything else, but I wanted him more with each passing week.

Each time we met, I expected him to finally reveal a portion of his personality or being that would cause me to turn away under the realization he wasn't what or who I thought he was, but it never happened. If anything, he continued to confirm he was just what I expected – and hoped – him to be. He was a man with tremendous devotion and commitment to what and who he believed in, and it just so happened he used a motorcycle as his means of transportation.

He intertwined his fingers, turned his palms to face me, and extended his arms as he cracked his knuckles and yawned. Seeing his biceps and chest flare was something I would never get used to, even if we remained nothing but friends for a lifetime. His body did a pretty good job of defining perfection, and although he wasn't a conceited or arrogant man, he often accidentally flaunted it.

And each time he did so, my heart stopped for a few beats.

"So tell me about today's reviews," he said as he leaned back in his seat.

"Uhhm. Well, I've got one stepbrother book I finished earlier in the week that was a good solid three and a half, and a werewolf shapeshifter deal that was actually pretty good. I'm back and forth between four and four and a half. We'll see how I feel after lunch," I said.

He leaned forward, pressing his forearms into the edge of the table, and cocked an eyebrow in what had become his signature gesture of concern. "But you only read romance, right?"

I took a drink of water and nodded my head. "Yep."

"Don't tell me a stepbrother book is…"

Before he had a chance to continue, I interrupted. "Sure is."

"Do they…"

"Sure do."

"The brother and sister?"

"Uh huh, but they're 'steps' so it's okay," I said as I raised my glass.

He pushed himself away from the table and shook his head. "It's wrong as fuck. And you're telling me people like that shit?"

"Sure seem to," I responded.

"And a werewolf what did you say? Shapeshifter? It is a romance, right?" he asked as he leaned onto the edge of the table again.

"Yeah. He shifts back and forth between being a werewolf and a man. He falls in love with a woman from Massachusetts, but he's originally from Canada. A long way from the pack, you know," I said with a laugh.

He scrunched his nose and shook his head again. "A chick fucking a dog?"

"Well, they only bone when he's a man, but in a sense, kind of, yeah," I said.

"I fucking swear. And people wonder why I'm a loner. The world's full of fucking weirdos. *Sense and Sensibility, Pride and Prejudice, Midsummer Night's Dream...*" he shoved himself away from the table in clear frustration, grabbed the edge of it with his fingertips and pulled himself close to the edge again.

After shaking his head in disgust, he rested his elbows on the edge of the table and leaned into the center, pressing his palms against his jawline. After a few seconds of staring blankly at me, he cleared his throat.

"Laugh as much as you choose, but you will not laugh me out of my opinion," he said. "Have you read *that* book?"

"*Pride and Prejuduce*? Yeah, several times," I said.

"Can I interest you in our buffet?" the Rastafarian girl asked.

"Come back in ten, we're in a heated discussion," Vince said with a wave of his hand without so much as shifting his eyes away from me.

"You notice there weren't any werewolves or shapeshifters or fucking stepbrothers in it?" he asked.

"Yeah, I noticed," I responded.

"Here's what I think. I think the world is so full of people that have lost hope in conventional love – all because no one is willing to give it unconditionally anymore – that they read to be shocked, thrilled, or disgusted. They no longer read to be filled with promise or hope, because they no longer believe. A modern love story has become the most unbelievable fairy tale ever. And now, people read those BDSM books like they're going out of style because it makes them wet. That sure as fuck doesn't make it a good novel. A porno movie will make them wet too, but it sure doesn't mean it's a good movie. I fucking swear," he said.

I shrugged and tried to force myself not to smile. He was right. The book world had changed drastically just in the amount of time I had been out of school. It seemed the erotica genre was not only based on sex, but most of the books lacked the base ingredients to give them even a hint of romantic element.

"You know, in a romance novel, it's the first kiss. *That*, Sienna, is the money shot," he said.

I coughed out a laugh and tried to keep from spitting my ice cube out. "I thought the money shot was when, you know. When the guy shot his load on a chick's face."

He shook his head and waved his hand in my direction. "See? That's *your* perception, based on modern day bullshit books. A money shot, by definition, is the essential element that causes a book, movie, or magazine to succeed. The selling point. In a romance novel, it should

68

be *that kiss*. Not a face full of cum. Don't get me wrong, there's a time and a place for a cum shot, but the money shot? It should be the kiss. The *first* one."

I was really, *really* starting to like this guy. Before I could give my opinion, he continued.

"People need to learn to believe in love again. They need to desire that feeling that happens deep down in their inner being that only love can give. And true love sure as fuck isn't something that causes your crotch to ache, either. That's where all the confusion lies," he said as he reached for his glass of water.

"My heart aches," he said as he raised his glass and held it in the air.

I did the same.

"Here's to the lost art of loving," he said as he clanked his glass against mine.

"Hear, hear!" I said.

My heart swelled a little as I took a drink of my glass of water. If I was reading a book about a romance novel reading biker who was a debt collecting ass kicking member of a MC, I'd probably laugh until I peed myself. But, he sat before me in the flesh, talking about *Pride and Prejudice* as if it was sacred and something he held dear to his heart.

"So, are you ready to order?" Dreadlocks asked.

Vince turned to face her and grinned, exposing his shiny white teeth. As she smiled in return, he widened his eyes, took a shallow breath, and all but came unraveled.

"Sure, I'll have a plate of devotion, a side order of commitment, and a thick slice of I promise not to break your heart. Be sure to make it untoasted and hold the butter, so I don't choke on it. Oh, and a shot of your best bourbon to wash it all down with," he said without so much as taking a breath.

"Huh?" she said as she tossed her dreadlocks over her shoulder.

"Exactly," he said as he wagged his eyebrows at me. "See?"

It was *that day*. On the Sunday at the buffet place on Webb Road. That was the day that a large part of me fell for Vince.

And fell hard.

VINCE

September 11th, 2014

September 11ᵗʰ, 2014

There were very few men I respected as much as my father. Axton Bishop was one of those men. I didn't respect him because he demanded it or because he wore the "President" patch. I respected him because his actions, his words, and where his heart was required that I do so. To not respect him for who he was would do nothing but provide support of me being incapable of seeing just what it was he offered me as a man and as a member of the club.

"Got a minute, boss?" I asked as I leaned inside the office door.

"I've always got time for you, Vince," Axton said as he closed the ledger.

"Headed to the bar with Toad," Otis said as he stood from his seat.

"Otis," I said as he began to walk toward the door.

"Vince," he said with a nod of his head as he walked past.

"So what's on your mind?" Axton asked.

"Just wondering about a few things," I said.

"Flunked mind reading in school, Brother. You're going to have to enlighten me," he said as he leaned back in his chair.

"Got a question about a woman," I said as I sat down across from him.

He snapped the rubber band he wore around his wrist a few times,

71

more than likely subconsciously, inhaled a long slow breath through his nose, and then exhaled out his mouth. The process, for Axton, had become somewhat of a ritual.

"My thoughts on women have been made pretty clear. Don't have much use for them, they can't be trusted," he said. "So what's your question?"

"You think a man can be friends with a woman, or does it always turn to shit?" I asked.

He popped his rubber band once and leaned forward in his chair. "You got a woman friend, have ya, Vince?"

"Sure do. Just don't want to hurt her, or have her expecting things of me. You know, things I'm not willing to give," I said.

"So this is some girl who's a *friend*, and you're not throwing her any of that cock, right?" he asked.

"Right," I said.

"And you're not planning on changing that?" he asked.

"Not planning on it, no. It'll just fuck things up. She's cool as a fan, Boss. Drives a '65 Continental, she's pretty as fuck, and kind of a mouthy little bitch, but not in a disrespectful way," I said.

"Sounds interesting," he said as he leaned back in his seat. "Well, you and her can be friends no doubt, and I wouldn't tell all of the fellas this, believe me. You're a weird fucker, Vince, and we both know it. I'm sure if you say you're not going to give her any dick, you sure won't. But I can tell you one thing for fucking sure…"

"What's that?" I asked.

He rubbed his jaw between his thumb and his forefinger and lowered his chin as he locked his eyes on mine.

"There'll come a day when she wants that dick. And it'll be a deal breaker. Then you'll have to decide for sure," he said.

"Always comes to that, doesn't it?" I asked blankly.

"Sure does," he responded. "Damned sure does."

"So how's business?" he asked.

"Pretty good, thanks," I responded.

"Face looks better now that it's good and healed. Scars make you look more like a one percenter and less like a book reading hermit," he said with a laugh.

"You're one to talk. You read as much as I do," I said as I stood.

"I read a lot, that's a fact. Now don't leave mad. You still need to talk?" he asked as he stood.

"Ain't mad," I said. "Just thinking."

"You wanting to start fucking this girl? Just between you and me?" he asked.

I shrugged my shoulders. "Fuck I don't know, kind of."

"So what you're really wanting to know is if you can fuck her without fucking up the friendship, right?" he asked.

"I'm not sure. It's just. Fuck, I don't know. I've never been around a woman as cool as she is. She reads books. Reviews them online and stuff. We meet every Sunday for lunch, and have been for three or four months now. We sit and talk about books, cars, bikes, people, politics..." I paused and shrugged my shoulders before I continued. "Shit, you name it, and we've discussed it. God damned woman is drop dead gorgeous, but that ain't what I like about her. I like it that she's so down to earth. No fucking drama. No bullshit. No whining, bitching, or acting like a little girl."

"Believe me, that'll all change," he said.

I turned to face him and nodded my head. "That's what I'm afraid of."

"Listen, I'll never shack up with a woman. Every motherfucker in this club knows that. They're good for one thing and one thing only, and that's shovin' 'em full of dick. That's it. Beyond that, I don't have much use for 'em. But my opinion on women shouldn't be your opinion on women. There's sure plenty of men on this earth who are happily married, in solid relationships, or shovin' the single neighbor gal next door full of cock, and doing it successfully. Does it mean this girl's for you? Only you can answer that question, Vince. Only you," he said.

"I think I'll probably keep doing what I'm doing and see what happens," I said.

"Sounds like a good move," he said.

"Devil looks after his own," I said as I clenched my fist and held it at arm's length.

He pounded his fist against mine and grinned. "He damned sure does."

As I walked out of his office and into the shop, I didn't feel any better about the situation I was in. Axton was right, the only one who knew what was best for me was me, and no one else.

What it came down to was whether or not I was ready to take the risk of being hurt again.

And I didn't know much, but I knew the answer to that question.

I wasn't.

SIENNA

October 5th, 2014

I stared blankly at the monitor. The book was a disaster, the wine was aplenty, and the night was yet another spent at home alone. I wondered if I died in my sleep some night or fell into a wine induced coma and was unplugged from life support by some nurse who hated cool bitches just who would write and read my eulogy. I considered what it might say, based on them somehow finding someone who knew me well enough to write *something*.

She drove a cool car and her hair was awesome.

She had a nice butt when she wore those jeans from The Limited.

Her nail beds were nice, but she rarely chose a good color of polish.

Her eyebrows needed work.

Thinking about it, I came close to crying. I had no one, was falling for a man that would probably never fall for me, yet I couldn't fathom ever wanting any other man. My life had become a disaster. I was twenty-six, single, and had spent a lifetime in and out of relationships with losers. My father was probably turning over in his grave at the thought of his precious daughter withering away as an unmarried woman now pushing thirty years old.

My father, not unlike me, was constantly reading something. Everything from cookbooks to old folklore could be found beside his bed on any given day. He was a sponge willing to soak up anything he could gather from reading. Me? I became a dreamer while he was away in prison, and began reading romance novels as fast as I could flip the pages. As soon as I got a Kindle and learned of the *one-click* option, my savings account began to dwindle, and my TBR list grew into the thousands.

Romance novels were my weakness, and living the life depicted in them had become my dream.

Before my father went to prison, he told me *persistence is rewarded in a manner indifference will never know.* I applied it all through high school, and my grades were a reflection of his wise words and my desire to make him proud of his little girl.

I considered the advice of my father, and decided unless I applied it to my life, I would simply fall back into a proven pattern of slipping further and further away from what it was I deserved.

I deserved to be loved as much as I was able to love.

My eyes eventually focused on the monitor, and I realized I had spent an immeasurable amount of time wallowing in my sorrows. Spiraling into a state of self-pity wasn't something I needed to do, and I knew focusing on my review should resolve the issue.

I grabbed the bottle of wine, raised it to my lips, and took a long drink. Much to my surprise, the flow of the sweet substance abruptly stopped, leaving me holding a useless glass paperweight over my bobbing head.

How in the fuck did that happen?

I blinked my eyes and stared at the bottle. It was definitely empty, even though I had opened it only a few minutes prior.

I swear, they're making these bottles smaller. Maybe the glass is thicker and they hold less...

I shook the bottle, gazed blankly at the bottom, and shoved it onto the desk beside my monitor. After teetering back and forth for a few seconds, it stopped quivering and came to rest upright and...

Empty.

The bottle's ability to hold itself upright after I tossed it across my desk was all the proof I needed that the wineries were making the glass thicker, and providing me with much less of the nerve soothing potion I required to complete my Sunday night ritual.

Fuckers.

I glared at the screen, angry about the wine situation. "Have Yourself a Merry Little Christmas" by The Pretenders calmed my nerves as I began to read my glorious review.

You're probably reading this review wondering just what book I read. Well, don't let all the five star reviews fool you. I'm drunk enough, experienced enough, and lack fear of retribution enough to give an honest opinion.

And here it is.

This book was awful.

And regardless of how many tens of thousands of followers the author has, I'm not afraid to admit it.

I refuse to fall in line with every other reader or reviewer who states this book is a "great read" or "fabulous" just because the author is a well-recognized figure in the industry.

Newsflash.

Five star reads are NOT books that have unbelievable characters doing unbelievable things.

This book read like an episode of the Jerry fucking Springer Show.

I fell in love with the guy who raped me as a teen, and used to come to my house as a babysitter and tie me up in the basement and stick broom handles in my twat. He beat me unconscious when I was twenty, and my family moved away, but I decided to stay because I truly loved him.

Then, after a few years of suggesting and me willingly complying with his requests to have threesomes with him and his brother, I woke up and decided to break it off.

After six months of sulking and smoking meth, I decided to give his other brother a try, only to fall in love with the stepfather.

Are you fucking kidding me right now?

As I read this worthless piece of shit, I held my breath in wait of the trip to Tijuana and the Shetland pony show. That's really all this book was missing.

Great read?

I think not.

Hot sex scenes?

No.

Well written?

Yes.

But I don't care to read another hot sex scene when the h is mentally challenged and incapable of standing up for herself against an H who is overbearing, has a thirteen inch cock, and can fuck for twelve hours straight without the aid of a Viagra.

"Fuck me and my brother, okay?"

"I don't want to, it's not right…"

"How can it be wrong if I want it and you love me, Aphilia?"

"I guess it can't. Okay, I'll do it, but only because I love you…"

That, ladies and gentlemen, is a direct quote from this five star read. I'm sorry, but I about barfed.

And who in the absolute fuck names their kid Aphilia, anyway?

Nobody.

Want a five star review?

Write me a book about a girl named Sienna who gets her brains fucked out by a bearded biker.

My rating? Half a star because I liked the dedication, but with great reluctance I must give it one star because Goodreads won't allow zero.

I published the review and reached for the bottle of wine. After raising it to my lips, I realized it was the same empty bottle I had so eagerly abandoned earlier.

Heavy, but empty.

Fuck.

After removing my glasses and tossing them to the side, I pushed myself away from my desk, stood, and sang backup for Madonna's "*Santa Baby*," which was the only thing that saved me from my wine deprived state of being. As the song came to a close, I smiled and fell back onto my bed with my arms outstretched.

After a moment of staring at the ceiling I rolled over and smashed my face into the closest pillow.

My lunch with Vince earlier in the day had been perfect.

Vince was perfect.

And I was sure I could be perfect for him, I just needed an opportunity.

I wrapped my arms around the pillow, squeezed it tight, and within a few seconds, began to softly cry. And on that night, in a slightly drunken state of being, I cried myself to sleep for the first time in five years.

VINCE

Our meeting ended, and a mandatory ride supporting Toys For Tots had been discussed at length. With Christmas fast approaching, the weather was less than favorable to ride, but as long as there wasn't snow on the ground, we continued, regardless of the temperature. With all of the club's heavies gathered on the side of the shop, I sauntered toward my bike as I pulled my stocking cap over my head.

"Vince," Otis said with a nod as I walked past.

I raised my right hand slightly and nodded my head. "Fellas."

"Headed to Toad's barbeque joint for a few beers and some chow if you're interested," Axton said.

"Appreciate it. I think I'll just..."

"Excuses are like fuckin' assholes," Biscuit said. "Everybody's got one."

I turned to face the group. Toad, Axton, Otis, Hollywood, and Biscuit were a club within the club, and for the most part, were a closer knit group than the club was as a whole. They really didn't let the other fellas in their little group, other than to meet for a drink or take a short unscheduled ride out of town for a show of presence.

"I need to..."

"Need to loosen up, Brother," Biscuit said. "Tell you the truth, you ought to knock you off some pussy. Been walkin' around this motherfucker for the last year like a motherfuckin' zombie. Come on, I got a story to tell that'll make your toes curl."

I glanced at my watch out of habit. Still stuck at three o'clock, it wasn't much help. Hell, I didn't have anything else to do, and I did need to eat something.

"Sounds good," I said.

"Saddle up," Axton said as he tossed his head toward his bike.

"Last one out lock up," Axton said over his shoulder as he fired up his sled.

The thought of being part of their group for a short period of time was satisfying, but doing so on a long term basis wasn't something I could ever do. It was far too easy to get caught up in patterns, routines, and eventually develop expectations of the men as friends, and eventually someone would fuck up and I knew enough about myself to know I would lose faith not only in the men, but in the club as a whole. Not exposing myself to the members as individuals protected me from being disappointed in their actions or broken promises, which, over time, were bound to happen.

The six of us rode the half mile to Toad's barbeque joint, and carefully parked our bikes in front of the building side-by-side. After confirming my bike was perfectly parked beside Otis', I turned toward the entrance and shoved my keys into my pocket.

"Hardcore motherfucker, ridin' that Shovel. You work on that pig all the time or what?" Biscuit asked as we walked toward the door.

"Quite a bit, yeah," I responded. "But it was my Pop's bike, and..."

"Yeah, I heard that. Cool as fuck you kept it and all," he said.

"Shovel's are powerless," Otis said as we walked inside.

I shook my head in disagreement. Harley replaced the Panhead motor with the Shovelhead in 1966, and in 1971 a world record was set by a man on a Shovelhead powered Harley. The bike was the first in the world to travel the quarter mile in less than nine seconds in a drag race. Propelling two wheels from zero to one hundred and sixty-eight miles an hour in less than nine seconds, and doing so in 1971, was a tremendous accomplishment.

"The first nine second bike in the quarter mile was a Shovel," I said.

"Bullshit," Otis snapped back.

"God damned truth," Axton interrupted. "Man's name was Joe Smith. Out in San Diego, I think."

"Los Angeles. West Covina to be exact," I said.

Biscuit coughed a laugh as we walked up to a table large enough to seat us. "Fuckin' bookworm."

"But the man's got his facts straight. A god damned Shovel is bulletproof," Axton said.

I nodded my head in his direction as we sat down, appreciative of his support of my bike in the presence of the other men. Each of them rode an almost brand new Harley, and with the exception of Axton's bike, they were all pretty much unaltered and had very little personality.

My bike was a hodgepodge of parts, and looked the part of an old school hard-core biker's bike. With faded black paint and very little chrome, it was loud enough to wake the dead. It had the same straight pipe exhaust my father rode it with, and the ape hanger handlebars were the only modification I made to it since obtaining it from my father. Older bikers gathered around it at every rally and poker run I attended. The younger bikers simply walked past it, most not even knowing what it was or what it was capable of.

Personally, I loved the thing.

"Cool old bike, if you ask me," Biscuit said as we sat down.

Excluding Axton, of all of the men, Biscuit was the most genuine. He was the club story teller, and a practical joker. He reminded me a little of me, as he was against technology in many respects. He didn't have a television, rarely carried his phone, and never cared to read the newspaper or hear anything about the world's current events. Toad was a war hero of sorts, and had never really mentally came back to civilization after the war. He had a quick temper, was a martial arts specialist in addition to being a Marine, and was a walking time bomb. Otis was the Sergeant-at-Arms and acted as the protector of the club, but no one short of Axton ever really knew what he was thinking. He was six foot six and muscle from head to toe, so the SAA slot was a great place for him to be. Hollywood was another loner of sorts, and lived in the middle of nowhere, keeping to himself if he wasn't with the smaller group of men. Of the group, I trusted him the least. My father always said *the eyes don't lie*, and Hollywood's eyes always were constantly filled with concern or worry. He was a club brother, and as much a *Sinner* as me, but it didn't mean I had to trust him wholly.

And I didn't.

"Everyone hungry?" Toad asked as he turned toward the kitchen.

The five of us glanced around the table and nodded our heads in confirmation.

"I'll get ribs, links, and brisket coming. Sound good?" he asked.

"Sounds good, I appreciate it," I said over the others grunting and nodding their heads.

After being gone a few minutes, Toad returned with a round steel tray filled with bottles of beer. As he reached for one of the beers, Biscuit began to tell his story.

"So, this gal was a waitress at Hooters, and built like a brick shithouse. She had tits the size of that pumpkin that was sittin' on my porch 'till Halloween and a waist about twenty-six inches at most. So, one of the El Forastero's and me was havin' a beer and this gal walks up to the table. 'Are you a real biker?' she asks. I said, 'If having a Harley and a ten-inch cock makes me a real biker, I guess so.' She stands there for a minute, tilts her head to the side, and says, 'show it to me.' 'Shit,' I said, 'the motherfucker's right outside the window, see for yourself.' She grins like a shit eatin' possum and shakes her head. 'Not the bike,' she says. 'Show me your cock.'" he paused and scanned the group for a reaction.

"Bullshit," Hollywood chimed in as he took a drink of beer.

Biscuit turned toward Hollywood, cocked an eyebrow, and rubbed his beard with his right hand. "Might be a lot of things, 'Wood, but a liar ain't one of 'em. You don't wanna hear this tale, grab you a rib to go and hop on that sled and point her west."

"Go ahead," Hollywood said with a heavy sigh.

"So I looked at Ol' Red Wing and winked. Then I turned toward the gal with the titties and pulled out my meat right there at the table. Now, this all happened in about ten seconds, so I didn't even have a chance to work me up a chubby, but I yanked the Hankster out and he was about half limp, but just half. So I get it out, and I shake it at her a little bit. And she covers her mouth like *this*," he paused and raised his hand to his mouth.

"Gal's eyes get wide as a couple dinner plates, and she says, 'It ain't even hard, is it?' Hell, I drop my cock in my lap and shake my head. 'Do you think I walk around with a stiff cock all day, Lady?' I ask her.

85

'It makes me dizzy if I do'," he said as he slapped his hand against the table.

"So what'd she do?" Otis asked.

"Well, if you'd stop fuckin' interruptin' I'd sure as fuck tell ya. Anyone else want to ask any stupid questions before I continue?" Biscuit asked as he surveyed the group of men.

Axton shook his head from side to side and twisted his index finger in a circle. On his signal, Biscuit continued.

"So she glances over each shoulder, stares down in my lap, and shakes her head. Now she don't know it cause she's checking to make sure there ain't gonna be a crowd gatherin' around the table and not payin' attention, but I been stroking this fucker for about thirty seconds at this point. So anyway, she looks down in my lap and she does *this*…"

He paused, covered his mouth with his hand, and inhaled a sharp shrill breath.

"She stares at it for a minute, and without lookin' up, she says, 'Holy shit. Does it get bigger?' I stop strokin' it, look over my shoulder, and turn toward her. 'Only if it's in a gal's twat. But she's got to have really big titties.' I tell her. And she looks at me like she won the lottery. Now I ain't shittin', fellas, not one bit. She looks at me, drops her hand away from her mouth, and this crazy bitch says, 'Oh my god, I've got *huge* titties.' Red Wing spit out about half his beer, and I just widened my eyes and said, 'Hell, I didn't even notice.' It wasn't ten minutes, and I was balls deep in that gal's twat in her SUV in the parking lot. Motherfucker had three of them kid seats in the back, which was kinda weird for a minute," he said.

"You're a fucking whore," Otis said with a laugh.

"And damned proud of it," Biscuit said. "But that'll be the last she's gonna see of me."

"Why's that?" Toad asked.

"Are you fucking kiddin' me? I ain't lookin' to raise another man's kids," Biscuit said.

I found it strangely satisfying that all of the men at the table were single, and for the most part, short of Biscuit, none of them were actively pursuing women. Biscuit's pursuit was more of a hobby or sport than a desire driven by any means of attraction, and excluding him, the men shared the same feelings regarding women.

I sat quietly, thinking of Sienna as the food showed up. As everyone reached for a plate, my mind began to wander to the *what ifs* and the *why nots* of being in a relationship with her. All things considered, I was more of an individual, and never conformed to the patterns or opinions of the masses, these five men included. If I was going to be in a relationship with her, it was going to be for all the right reasons, and although I believed sex was always an important part of a relationship, it wasn't the sole reason to be in one.

As I ate a rib and paid very little attention to the next story Biscuit began to tell, I decided the next time I saw Sienna, we were going to have a talk.

A serious talk.

SIENNA

November 9th, 2014

With perfect hair, perfect nails, perfect makeup, a great pair of jeans, a bad ass pair of 2" heels, and a sweet as fuck wool coat, I raced through traffic as I alternated glances between the road and my rearview mirror.

My eyebrows looked *reasonable*, as always.

As The Eurythmics "*Winter Wonderland*" blared out of the speakers, I weaved in and out of traffic with my typical five minutes to spare and four minutes of driving left. While stuck at a traffic light, I once again checked my eyebrows in the mirror.

I looked like I had turned a three year old loose on my face with a molten brown crayon. I seemed to never get my eyebrows to reach the point of perfection. The light flashed green just as Bryan Adam's "*Run Rudolph Run*" began to play.

Now that's more like it.

I mashed the gas, lurched through the intersection, and quickly changed lanes in front of the old man in the pickup truck who had been beside me for the entire trip. After another lead-footed display of the Continental's awesome power I was far enough ahead of him not to raise his temper, so I hit the brakes and turned right into the Bradley Fair shopping center. A quick scan of the parking lot and I found the perfect spot - on the end and in the front.

No door dings for Sienna.

I pulled in the spot, hugging the far side for safety's sake. I shut off the engine, opened the glove box, and flipped the switch to the stereo. Vince's bike was parked up front by the door on the sidewalk.

A quick glance in the mirror further confirmed I was nothing short of a spastic eyebrow plucking idiot, so I opened the door and began my shameful walk to what I was certain to be the impending death of our six month old friendship.

Death by bad eyebrows.

I pushed the door open and glanced toward the seating area.

Sitting immediately beside the door on a long leather bench, Vince tapped the face of his watch with his index finger.

"Sorry, I was early," he said. "This thing's hit and miss. I thought I had it fixed, but it quit again. I didn't want to be late, and I wasn't sure what time it was, so…"

"Well, by my clock in the Lincoln, I was one minute early," I bragged.

"Pretty typical," he said. "I have no idea how you do it with consistency."

"I wait down the block until there's one minute left, then I haul ass to where we're meeting," I said.

He nodded his head. "Wouldn't surprise me."

His beard was full, typical of what most men with beards do for winter time, I supposed. He had on a black canvas jacket over a long-sleeved khaki shirt, and a black stocking cap pulled down low on his head. The jeans he was wearing were perfectly worn, from wearing them, not because he bought them that way. I admired him as he stood, wondering how he got each and every hole in them, and just what it was that happened to cut the hole above his right knee.

He interested me so much it made me sick.

"I'm following you," he said as he pointed into the restaurant.

I walked through the restaurant toward the blazing fireplace. It wasn't quite winter yet, but it was much cooler than what we had been used to, and was just a few degrees shy of fifty.

Vince had picked a time that was well after lunch, but a few hours before dinner. Because it wasn't necessarily the holiday season just yet, the restaurant, short of us and one other couple, was empty. Being almost alone with Vince was enough of a change to fool me into thinking we were on a romantic date, and I was pretty sure after I got my book reviews done for the night, I would pleasure myself daydreaming about it.

"I like it here by the fireplace," I said as I flopped into the seat.

"Your hair looks nice," he said as he sat down.

"Oh, thank you," I said.

"So do your heels," he said. "I like heels with jeans."

"I just grabbed what was at the end of the closet, thanks," I said.

Actually, I had spent almost an hour trying on shoes and trying to pick the perfect pair. Some made me look ridiculous, some for whatever reason seemed to no longer fit, and a few of the others killed my feet. This particular pair of 2" black heels felt great, looked great, and didn't break the bank when I bought them.

Shoe sales are the best thing ever.

"I like your jeans," I said with a grin. "They're awesome."

"My jeans?" he asked in a slightly sarcastic tone. "Why's that?"

"Because they're worn out, but I know you wore them out. You didn't buy them like that. I like worn out jeans," I said.

"I've had these fuckers for years," he said. "And you're right. I wore these fuckers out for sure."

"Well, I like them," I said.

"Thanks," he responded as he waved to the waitress.

"I'm sorry, you order at the register," she said as she walked up to the table.

I shrugged my shoulders. "Never eaten here."

"Me neither, one of the fellas recommended it," he said as he pushed his seat away from the table.

We walked side by side to the register, where a six foot tall wooden menu was on display. Quite surprised I didn't see it or stumble into it on my way inside the restaurant, I chuckled and pointed toward it.

"Probably missed it because it's so small," I said with a laugh.

The menu was a good foot taller than I was. Vince laughed and nodded his head as he studied the descriptions painted on the wooden display.

"I'm going to have the pizza and salad deal," I said after looking over the menu.

"Which pizza?" he asked as he continued to stare at the options.

"The one with artichokes and roasted garlic, sounds good. And I don't have to worry about kissing anyone, so no worries," I said.

A man walked in, stepped behind us, and peered over Vince's shoulder toward the menu. After a glancing over his shoulder a few times, Vince sighed and turned around.

"Something I can help you with, Brother?" Vince asked the man.

"Just looking," the man said cheerily as he repositioned himself to see over Vince's shoulder. He stood a mere twelve inches from Vince.

"Why don't you give my girl and me some space for a minute," Vince said calmly as he took a step toward the menu.

My girl?

"Ain't got to be a dick about it," the man responded under his breath.

Oh shit.

Vince turned around completely, and swept me to his side with his hand as he did so. I watched as he spread his feet shoulder width apart and raised his right hand to half way between his waist and his chest. The dip-shit staring in our direction didn't seem to notice, but it was apparent Vince was preparing to stomp this guy's ass.

"Now the last thing I want to do is drag you out in the parking lot and kick the living shit out of you for being disrespectful. If I was alone, I can give you my solemn word you and I wouldn't be talking right now, I'd just be beating your ass. So, I'm going to need you to apologize to my girl for being a rude prick and breathing on her shoulder, and I'll let the dick comment slide," Vince said.

Vince's right hand quivered as he tightened his jaw and prepared for what was going to be his next move. As I stood and waited for the guy to either tell him to fuck off or apologize, I wished I was a guy and could tell people off from time to time, because sometimes they sure as fuck needed it.

The man stared down at his feet for a moment, glanced toward me, and cleared his throat. "I'm sorry for crowding you."

I smiled and nodded my head. "Apology accepted."

Vince lowered his hand, turned toward the menu, and inhaled a short breath.

"I'm having the calzone," he said calmly.

"Yum," I said as I turned toward the register.

As we placed our order Vince pulled out his wallet and thumbed through the money inside.

"Twenty-two forty," the man said after ringing up the total.

"Here's fifty," Vince said as he handed the man a fifty dollar bill. "That'll cover whatever the guy behind me is getting."

"Him?" the cashier asked as he tilted his head toward the guy who was still studying the menu.

"You got it," Vince said with a nod.

"And the change?" the cashier asked.

"Keep it," Vince said with a nod as he reached for his glass of tea.

As I reached for my tea, I turned toward Vince and grinned slightly. He was looking away and he didn't notice my admiring stare, but I didn't do it for that reason. He was different than any other man I had ever met, and I liked it.

I liked it a lot.

I dreaded the day he found a woman who actually interested him. The thought of ever losing him, especially to another woman, scared me to death. In his presence, nothing else mattered. There was no real concern with time, where we were, or what we were doing. I was as satisfied as I had ever been, and I wanted nothing else but for our time together to stand still. It never did, and always eventually ended, but one thing I could always count on was that he would return the next Sunday for lunch, to sit, talk, and enjoy time with me.

And for that, I respected him.

But, because of who he was and what he stood for, I was slowly falling in love with him.

"So, they bring it to us?" he asked as he sat down.

I shrugged my shoulders as I removed my coat. "I guess?"

"Tea's good," he said as he raised his glass.

I took a drink of the tea and nodded my head. It had a slight hint of

94

peach, but it wasn't overbearing. "That *is* good."

"So, what happened since we last met?" I asked.

"Other than my watch crapping out?" he asked.

I shrugged my shoulders and grinned. "I dunno, anything. I just like hearing about what you've done. I mean, the stuff you can tell me."

"Well, we went on the toy run, donated a bunch of toys. All of us rode except Tater, and he drove a truck full of shit. Fucking Axton went insane this year buying and trading for toys. Crazy fucker traded a shipment of guns for toys last July, and kept 'em in the shop for the last six months waiting for this deal to happen. He loves Christmas about as much as I do," he said.

"Best holiday of the year," I said. "Saddest, but the best."

"What's sad about Christmas?" he asked.

"My dad's gone. He isn't here to keep me company. It's not really fun unless you can share it with someone," I said. "But I still like it."

"And you said your mother's gone too, right?" he asked.

I nodded my head as I reached for my tea. My mother had a condition called placenta previa when she was pregnant. The placenta was positioned in such a manner that it covered the opening in her cervix making giving birth an impossible task without serious complications.

The main problem was that my father couldn't afford insurance at the time, and they were initially going to have me at home, naturally. When she went into labor, her placenta ruptured, and by the time the ambulance got there, she was barely alive. The paramedics did an emergency cesarean section, and delivered me alive, but my mother hemorrhaged, dying immediately after my birth.

My father raised me, alone. He never got married, nor did he so much as ever have another woman in the house.

I always admired him for his devotion to my mother, and I spent a lifetime wishing other men were more like him.

As I stared blankly at Vince, I realized he was like my father. Probably more than I cared to admit. I smiled again, wondering how much of the similarities I had noticed, and how many I didn't bother to notice, but let influence my feelings for him.

I shifted my eyes to my glass of tea and stared. "She died when I was little."

"I'm sorry," he said as he reached for my hand.

He hadn't done anything like that before, and I found it comforting and odd at the same time. As much as I wanted to perceive it as a comforting gesture of sympathy, my mind saw it otherwise.

For a fleeting moment, at least in my mind, Vince was attracted to me in a sexual manner.

"Listen," he said as he tapped his fingers against my palm.

I glanced up and forced a smile. "Yeah."

"I uhhm. I picked this place for a reason," he said.

"Oh yeah?" I asked. "Why's that?"

He pulled off his stocking cap and tossed it in the empty chair. After making a half-assed attempt to straighten his hair and a few strokes of his hand along his beard, he inhaled a short breath and shifted his eyes upward. After what seemed like an eternal pause, he exhaled and locked his eyes on mine.

"Well, I have a question," he said.

"Okay, let's hear it," I said cheerily.

"I uhhm. I was wondering if maybe you'd want to…like trying… you know. Adding…fuck. I don't know how to say it," he said as he shook his head.

He released my hand and cleared his throat.

"Sienna, do you want to try and be together? You know, try and see if we can be…like be a couple?" he asked.

Oh dear fucking God, thank you. I swear to fucking God almighty, I will not fuck this deal up, I fucking swear, I won't. Holy fucking fuck do I ever? Thank you, Lord.

"Yes," I said.

"You sure?" he asked as he reached for my hand.

My eyes began to feel swollen and my throat got tight. I knew enough to know not to speak. I bit into my bottom lip and nodded my head.

He stood from his seat and lifted my hand as he did so. On some pretty shaky legs I followed his lead and stood up.

Everything following that moment seemed to happen in slow motion. He leaned over the table and lifted my chin ever so slightly with his free hand. As I felt his fingers touch my face, my entire body began to tingle. With his hand now lightly gripping my jaw, I opened my mouth slightly in hope of what was to come. While he maintained eye contact with me, he continued to lean forward until our lips met.

The moment I had been waiting for finally arrived. My prayers had been answered. I closed my eyes…

And he kissed me.

It wasn't a sloppy kiss, nor was it aggressive, but it was our first. It was the kind of kiss a girl spends a lifetime dreaming about. A kiss that causes your palms to sweat and makes your heart stop beating until a few seconds later when you feel it racing to catch up. It was the kiss that stops time, causing your entire body to tingle during the process; the kiss that sets the standard for every other kiss that might follow it.

MONEY SHOT

Yeah, it was *that* kiss.
The money shot.
It was November 9th.
The happiest day of my life.

VINCE

November 9th, 2014

On the ride to Sienna's house, it dawned on me that her experience in reading romance, erotica, and BDSM books would more than likely cause her to have a broad range of sexual interests. Not knowing for certain what the night might bring, but fully realizing we were two adults, I suspected sex was on the forefront of her plans for the remaining portion of the afternoon.

The garage door was going closed as I pulled into the driveway, and instead of parking on the street, I pulled up the drive and parked on the sidewalk leading to the front porch. The front door opened as I got off the bike, and she stood in the opening with her hair twisted into a bun and a smirk on her face.

"Well, are you going to come in?" she asked.

"Suppose so," I said as I pulled the key from the ignition.

It had been five months since we met, and although my former wife and I had sex on the first date, I was glad Sienna and I had been friends for as long as we had without introducing sex to the relationship. There was no doubt in my mind that we were compatible in many ways, and I believed sex would do nothing but bring us closer together.

I stepped past her and into the living room. As I turned to face her, she gazed at me blankly, as if she was uncertain of what to do. Obviously

99

waiting for me to make the first move, she stood in wait, looking far more innocent than I suspected she truly was. As she twisted her hips to the side, I reached for her neck and pulled her into me.

The kiss that followed wasn't as special as the one in the restaurant, and I suspected none would ever be, but it was apparently enough to lead her to believe I had opened the door, sexually speaking.

She reached for my belt and fumbled with the buckle as we kissed. Quite sure she'd never get it unbuckled without my help, I reached down and pulled against the belt, freeing the leather strap from the buckle.

Now grabbing for the button on my jeans with one hand and rubbing my back with the other, she kissed me as if she believed it would be our last. Within a few seconds my jeans were unbuttoned, and she quickly shoved her hand deep into my pants.

As her hand wrapped around my swollen shaft, she pulled her mouth from mine, leaned away slightly, and widened her eyes.

"Holy crap," she said as she shifted her eyes toward her hand.

After a few tugs, she freed my now completely rigid cock from its confinement. She began to stroke it slowly, leaned forward, and raised herself up on her tip-toes. Within a few seconds we were well into an extremely sensual kiss, and I slipped my hand along her back and gripped her ass tightly. As I kneaded her butt in my hand, she began to moan wildly.

She pulled away, made eye contact, and exhaled a choppy breath. I either had my hands on one very one wild woman, or she was clearly as sexually frustrated as I was. Slightly confused and a little uncertain on which it may be, I dismissed her elevated sexual tension to a long period of abstinence, which was something I could certainly relate to.

As much as I wanted to perform for her, and as important as it was for me to satisfy her completely, I realized actually being with a woman, and especially Sienna, would be enough of a turn-on to cause me to reach climax pretty promptly.

Still slowly stroking my cock as she gazed into my eyes, she lowered herself onto her knees. There was no way I would last for any length of time if she was going to suck me off, and realized I should object to her doing so, but for some reason the words never came.

I eagerly watched her delicately wrap her lips around the swollen head of my dick. Fighting to pull my jeans further along my thighs as she moved her mouth up and down the shaft, she eventually became frustrated and pulled away. As she softly stroked my throbbing shaft in her delicate hand, she glanced upward and smiled.

"We're both adults, right?" she asked.

I gazed beyond my twitching cock and fixed my eyes on her. "I suppose so."

Her mouth was formed into a full-on pout, as if she was truly in need of assistance. "Can you help a girl out? Like maybe take off your jeans and boots?"

"Anything else?" I asked in a sarcastic tone as I pressed the sole of my right boot against the heel of my left one.

She released my cock, stood, and promptly removed her shorts. Before I got my other boot off, she was standing in front of me completely naked. As my eyes met hers, her mouth curled into a smile.

"Yeah, there's one other thing," she said as she turned and bent over the arm of the couch. "Make me scream your name."

Just remember, you asked for this…

SIENNA

November 9th, 2014

Reading a book on how to cook may assist with the preparation of dinner, and reading a book about landscape architecture might provide ideas on the development of a great looking flower garden, but no amount of MC Romance novels could have prepared me for being fucked by Vince.

A book hadn't been written yet to accurately describe how he was making me feel.

"Who's fuckin you?" he bellowed.

"Vince!" I shouted as he shoved his cock into me once again.

With each powerful stroke, I felt like I was being impaled. Not only was I well out of practice at having sex, but his dick was thick, long, and far beyond what I could describe as *hard*. As he held himself deep inside of me and ground his hips against my ass, his balls began to massage my clit.

I'm never going to make it. The head of his dick feels like it's pounding against the bottom of my heart. I'm going to die right here and collapse on the couch, death by a cock induced heart attack.

"And whose big fat cock is in that sweet little pussy of yours?" he asked as the palm of his hand came down sharply against my ass.

I gripped the cushion of the couch in my hand and squeezed it tightly as I opened my eyes and glanced over my shoulder.

We had been fucking for longer than I cared to guess, and my legs were weak and felt like rubber. Much to my surprise, he hadn't reached orgasm, and I wondered just how much longer he could make it.

He widened his eyes and raised his hand. As it hovered above my ass, I grinned and waited. My tingling clit provided all of the mental support I needed to stay right where I was for as long as he would allow me to.

"Whose?" he growled.

I blinked my eyes and silently studied his muscular torso. He was covered in sweat and every muscle was tensed. I was truly in heaven, and Vince was my big dicked biker angel. After a few seconds of eye contact, his face washed with faux anger and his hand came down.

Smack!

I winced in pain as his hand slapped against my butt cheek. I truly loved being fucked doggie style, but not being able to watch him was sheer torture.

"Say it!" he shouted.

I turned, lowered my head into the edge of the couch and bit into the cushion.

"Vince's," I said through my teeth.

"God damned right it is," he grunted as he began to fuck me again.

The sound of our sweaty flesh colliding was music to my ears. Something I had yearned to hear for almost six months, and now was quite sure I would never be able to live without, it provided me a reminder of just who was in charge.

And it was time he took charge and ended this escapade before he killed me.

"Fuck me, Vince!" I screamed into the fabric of the pillow.

His pace increased, pounding his hips into my ass and slowly driving the couch an inch or two across the floor with each thrust of his hips. The smell of his sweat, cologne, and the sweet scent of sex filled my nostrils, bringing me closer to orgasm, and undoubtedly closer to collapsing.

"Fuck me, Vince!" I shouted again, the sound muffled by the pillow my head was buried into.

As he continued forcing himself deep into me, I felt a slight tug against my hair. As I wondered if he was going to actually *pull* it, he began to. My one true weakness, at least that I was aware of, was having my hair pulled. If a man knew how to do it, and do it right, it was about as pleasurable as anything…

Oh dear God. Ding, Ding. Ding.

It was immediately obvious Vince knew how to do it right.

My back arched and my neck craned as he filled me with dick and continued to push the couch toward the wall.

"No, fuck me!" I wailed.

And that was all it took.

He began to powerfuck me, pulling my hair the entire time he did so. After a few seconds, there was no sound, no smell, only the feeling of him inside of me and our two bodies becoming one mechanical sexual machine. After a few more seconds of him fucking me and forcing me and the couch across the floor in the process, I was about to come loose at the seams. As my entire body began to shake and my legs began to tremble, the couch hit the wall.

And he continued.

"My little pussy," he grunted as he held himself deep inside of me.

My clit began to tingle and my nipples ached as I reached a level of climax I never knew existed. At the same time I felt myself contract around his shaft, his cock began to swell. I arched my back, allowed a moan to scape my lungs, and almost immediately felt him explode inside of me. His groans of pleasure confirmed he felt the same way I did.

The labored sound of his breathing continued for a moment as I attempted to collect my thoughts. Within a few seconds, his chest pressed against my back and he released my hair from his grasp.

I felt his mouth kiss along the back of my shoulder, up along my neck, and eventually reach my ear. His warm breath on my neck was a relaxing change to an otherwise intense sexual romp.

"Whose pussy?" he whispered into my ear.

"Yours…" I breathed.

And there was no doubt what I said was true.

My pussy, my heart, and my soul…

All belonged to Vince.

VINCE

November 14th, 2014

I knew from the first day we met that Sienna was different, but I had no real idea of how changing our level of commitment to each other would affect me. There was no doubt she was exactly what I had been missing in my life, and from what little she shared about her feelings, she felt exactly the same way about me. Her having changed how I felt about women was quite an accomplishment, but nothing or no one would ever change *who* I was.

After locking the door of my truck, I walked around the corner and studied the front of the house. Based on the size and the amount of windows, my guess was that there was one bedroom, one bathroom, a kitchen, and a small living room. The Sedgwick County property listing had it detailed as a residential one bedroom family dwelling, but accuracy by our state and county government was something that really didn't exist.

One late model Nissan coupe sat in the driveway, seeming clearly out of place in the rundown neighborhood. Dressed in jeans, a loose-fitting long sleeved pullover, and my boots, I looked the part of someone the homeowner might trust enough to open the door.

I tugged at the bottom of my untucked shirt, making sure it covered the pistol hidden in the holster on my hip. After checking the side of the house for additional cars and seeing nothing, I stepped onto the porch and knocked on the door.

"It's open," he responded.

It wasn't the greeting I anticipated, which led me to believe he was expecting someone; and there was no doubt in my mind the person he was expecting wasn't me. I glanced over each shoulder, cleared the pistol from the holster, and held it behind my right thigh. As I turned to the right, exposing my left side to the door, I gripped the handle with my left hand and pushed the door open.

The floorplan was pretty much what I expected. After a wide-eyed and more than likely drug induced squeal, he jumped from his seat at the dining table and started to run toward the small kitchen. He was half-naked, obviously scared, and skinny, but he was fast.

I took aim and barked out my demand.

"Freeze, Motherfucker. I'll drop you dead right where you stand," I shouted as I kicked the door closed with the heel of my boot.

He stopped, turned toward me, and narrowed his gaze. His shoulder length hair didn't look like it had been washed in a month. He was in his late twenties, obviously strung out on much more than weed, and may have tipped the scales at a hundred and fifty pounds if he was fully dressed and soaking wet. At my guess of six feet tall, he looked pretty fucking unhealthy. Barefoot, and dressed in jeans and nothing else, it was all I could do to look at his scab-covered malnourished body without offering him a much needed meal.

If I didn't kill him first.

"Fuck, I uhh…"

"Save it," I said. "I'll make this easy for you. I'm here to collect the debt you owe Jimmy Weed. Thirteen grand. I'm not leaving without it.

You got that much here?"

"Awwe, fuck, man. No. No, I got maybe five hundred," he responded as he began to dig his fingernails into the side of his neck.

"Five hundred? You sure that's all you got?" I asked.

"Uh huh," he responded as he continued to scratch along his lower jaw.

"I'll cuff your ass, stuff a sock in your fucking mouth, toss you in the tub, and tear this place apart," I said as I held the pistol rock steady, pointed directly at his chest.

He stopped scratching and began to stammer. "I got maybe...I mean...yeah... maybe...uhhm...five...oh, fuck, Dude, don't shoot me. Yeah...like five hundred *maybe*."

"You're sure?" I asked.

He started scratching again. "Yeah. Way sure."

"Sit down," I demanded.

"Where?" he asked as his eyes darted around the room.

"Right where you're fucking standing," I barked.

He dropped to the floor as if someone had kicked his legs out from underneath him.

"So how the fuck did you plan on paying this debt?" I asked as I pulled the vintage chrome legged chair away from the dining table.

"I uhhm...I was gonna...I...fuck, Dude, I dunno," he said.

"You reached an agreement with Mr. Weed, and he honored his part. You, however, didn't honor yours. Do you understand that?" I asked as I waved the pistol in his direction.

"Uh huh," he said.

I glanced around the house. Spongebob Squarepants played on the flat-screen television that was sitting on the floor beside the only couch in the small living room. The place was a disaster, and smelled like a combination of piss and pizza.

I shifted my eyes from the living room to where he was sitting. "And you understand thirteen grand is a lot of money?"

"Uh huh," he said.

"You also understand it really doesn't matter if it's thirteen grand or thirteen cents, you made a promise. And you broke it. You understand that?" I asked.

"Yeah, I guess. We were gonna…I mean I…"

"Shut up. Jesus fucking Christ. You understand you broke a promise, right?" I asked.

He scratched his face and stared blankly in my direction.

"You're never going to make it if you don't change the way you're doing things, kid. *Show respect, get respect.* Understand?" I asked.

He nodded his head.

"Where's your phone?" I asked.

He narrowed his eyes and wrinkled his brow. "Huh?"

"Your fucking phone, dipshit. Where's your phone? You're expecting someone, and I need to see who. Where is it?" I asked.

"Think I knocked it on the floor," he said as he pointed underneath the table.

I glanced down at the floor. A phone sat a few inches from the chair I was sitting in. I leaned down, picked it up, and attempted unsuccessfully to unlock the screen. Growing increasingly frustrated, and wondering when and if his friend or friends were going to show up, I stood from my seat and walked in his direction.

As I stepped to his side, I pointed the pistol at his head and held the phone in front of his face.

"Reach up, unlock the screen, and do it slowly. If you reach for this piece, I'll blow what little brains you have all over this fucked up green carpet. Understand?" I asked.

"Yeah, Dude," he said as he reached for the phone. "How'd you... uhhm...how'd you, oh fuck man..."

After he pressed a series of buttons on the screen and nodded his head, I raised the phone and opened the text screen.

After a quick study of his text messages, it appeared Lamar was on his way. I glanced at my watch, realized it was definitely not three o'clock like it depicted, and glanced at the screen of the phone. If Lamar was going to be on time, and most drug dealers never were, he was five minutes late.

"Lamar carry a gun?" I asked.

He stopped scratching his neck and glanced in my direction. "Huh?" he murmured.

"Does Lamar carry a fucking gun?" I asked as I walked to the table.

"Uhhm. No, Dude," he said.

"If he walks in here strapped, I'm going to shoot you first, and then I'm going to shoot his dumb ass. Does he carry a gun? I asked again.

He widened his eyes and shook his head from side-to-side. "No, Dude, I swear."

"When he gets here, you're going to tell him just what you told me, understand? No more, no less. 'It's open' is all you're going to say, understand?" I asked.

"Uh huh," he responded.

Some of the people I encountered through my day-to-day activities were more intelligent than others. A good portion of them were simply people who got caught up in trouble, and were incapable of meeting their commitments. Others were questionable, and some were just plain stupid. A quick study of the text messages on the phone provided enough information for me to believe the scab covered fool on the floor was the biggest idiot I had ever had the experience of encountering. It seemed every drug deal he made was detailed in the form of a text message on his phone for all to see.

"You know the government can read these messages without a search warrant, right?" I asked.

"Huh?"

"Neverfuckingmind," I said.

My level of respect for Jimmy Weed diminished slightly as I placed the phone on the table beside me. For anyone to trust such an idiot to return any amount of money did nothing in my opinion but clearly show their desperation of hope for another dollar earned. As the sound of a vehicle in the drive became apparent, I stood from the chair.

"Move your skinny ass over toward the couch and remember what I said," I said as I waved the gun in his direction.

I walked to the hinge side of the front door and stood. Three sharp knocks were met by the scab covered fool's authorization to enter.

"It's open," he said.

The door opened, and who appeared to be the walking skeleton's brother entered holding a small cardboard box.

"Don't move or I'll blow your fucking brains all over the wall," I said as I stepped from behind the door and pressed the pistol into his temple.

"Oh fuck, Dude. Don't shoot me. You can have it all," he said as he tried to hand the box to me.

"Put it on the floor," I demanded.

He dropped the box at his feet. It hit the floor with a solid thud. I shifted my eyes to dumbass number one, and back to number two. They appeared to be twins.

"Brothers?" I asked.

"Twins," dumbass number one responded.

Just what the world needs, two of these dumb fucks.

"Go stand by your brother," I said. "Don't reach in your pockets or do anything stupid, or I'll shoot both of you, understand?

"Yeah…I uhhm. Fuck…Don't shoot me. Yeah…I understand," he murmured as he walked toward the couch.

I picked up the box, opened it, and looked inside. To describe it as being full of money would be an understatement.

"How much is in here?" I asked.

"Uhhm, money or meth?" Lamar asked.

"Money," I responded as I peered into the cash filled box.

"It's uhhm. It's…there's…there's twenty-two grand…uhhm…in bills, and about thirty grand worth of…in there…uhhm, in meth," he responded.

I shifted my eyes toward dumbass number one. "You dipshit. So you had enough to pay your debt and keep your word, and you didn't?"

"Huh?" number two asked. "What debt?"

I shook my head in frustration as I alternated glances between the box and the two idiots. "Jimmy Weed."

"You didn't pay The Weed?" number one asked number two.

Number two shrugged his shoulders. "Dude, I was gonna pay him after we got the shit sold."

I waved the pistol toward the kitchen. "Both of you just shut the fuck up. Go sit in the kitchen in the middle of the floor."

Dumbass number one led the way, and number two followed close behind. After they were both sitting in the middle of the floor picking at their faces, I turned, locked the front door, and walked to my seat. I dumped the contents of the box in the middle of the table, and began to count the money, doing my best to stick with hundred dollar bills. The box was filled with every denomination of bill, including countless well-weathered one dollar bills. A few minutes later, I had two piles of cash.

One with thirteen thousand and one with three thousand nine hundred.

"We can do this one of two ways. You owe Mr. Weed thirteen grand. That's not negotiable. My cut is thirty percent. So, I can take the thirteen, leave the rest, and you'll be seeing Mr. Weed – or quite possibly me – again, for the thirty-nine hundred dollar fee I'm charging him, because that comes off the top of his thirteen grand. Or, you can pay the thirteen and pay me my cut now, and it'll be the last you see of either of us. So, do you two want to discuss it?" I asked.

"Take all you want," Lamar said.

"I want thirty-nine hundred, and not a cent more. Mr. Weed wants thirteen grand. I really don't give a fuck if you pay me, or if he pays me. I'm just telling you a way to keep him, or me, from coming back. So what'll it be?" I asked.

"Take it all now," dip shit number one said. "The thirteen and the three grand."

I shook my head. "Thirty-nine hundred."

"Yeah, whatever. Take it. And you're just gonna go? Like *that's it*?" he asked.

I stood from my seat and shoved my gun in the holster. "Yep. That's it."

"And you're leaving the dope and the rest of the money?" he asked.

I glared at him as if he was even more of an idiot than he actually was. "It ain't mine, why the fuck would I take it?"

He shrugged his shoulders and widened his eyes. "Because you have the gun?"

"You dumb fuck. Having a gun doesn't give a person the right to steal. A gun is a deterrent to crime and a means of protection, not a license to be a god damned thief. I fucking swear, that's what's wrong with society. No one keeps a promise, and people are too god damned quick to take what's not rightfully theirs," I said as I shoved the piles of money in my two front pockets.

"Good luck in your endeavors, Fellas," I said as I unlocked the door.

I stepped onto the porch, pulled the door closed behind me, and started to walk away. After pausing for a long second, I pushed it open and peered inside. The two dipshits were still sitting on the kitchen floor scratching their faces.

"You two fuckers can get up now," I said.

They both stood up and stared in my direction. I considered giving further instructions, but opted to simply pull the door closed and leave.

It bothered me that the criminal activities in the city were carried out by idiots like the two men I had just left behind. *There is no honor among thieves* was a saying I had always believed to be true. At least in my mind, a thief was the worst type of criminal to ever exist. A drug dealer, however, was nothing short of a businessman, choosing an illicit or illegal substance as his means of obtaining income.

Drug dealers weren't inherently bad people, nor did I assume they were irresponsible simply based on their chosen profession.

Furthermore, I didn't believe *all* drugs were bad, or that they should all be illegal, yet I refused to enter in the debates regarding their legality. I did, however, believe that a man should always honor his word when he gave it, regardless of his means of obtaining income.

A promise was no different than a contract, and when a man gave his word, he needed to honor it at any or all costs. If he didn't or wouldn't, he was as worthless as the promise he had broken.

If my father taught me one thing before he died, it was to be honorable.

I walked to my truck a member of a motorcycle club, a one percenter, a criminal, and without a doubt a man who could be placed in prison for his actions and choices.

But everything I did, I did with honor.

And I never made a promise I wasn't able to keep.

SIENNA

November 15th, 2014

I believed most people on this earth were living a life not of their choosing, but one of settling for what it was they were convinced they were entitled to. Their quality of life was directly tied to their belief in their self-worth.

It saddened me that a world full of women with minimal self-respect settled for substandard treatment at the hand of less than honorable men, and did so for the simple reason that they didn't believe they were better than what it was they were receiving.

I knew I had made some pretty poor choices in my lifetime regarding men, but my choice to wait as long as I had to for Vince to accept me as a lover proved to be the best decision I had ever made. Following my father's advice of being persistent had provided me with the best man I believed this world could or would ever produce.

I had always hoped one day I would find a man that would not only be handsome, but would share my views on life, love, and hopefully, books. After twenty-six years I had all but given up, realizing finding someone capable of pleasing me fully would be impossible. There was no doubt in my mind that a qualified man existed somewhere on earth, but I had all but decided he was on another continent somewhere and probably speaking a different language.

I was now living my lifelong fantasy with Vince, and he had proven to be everything I had always dreamed of.

And more.

He cocked an eyebrow comically. His facial hair was several inches long now, and I was quickly finding out just how well his beard length was directly connected to my pussy's *on* button. Each time I noticed his beard had grown a little fuller, I'd become a little wetter, and it would happen a lot quicker.

I loved doing things with Vince and spending time with him, but no differently than an alcoholic who had just came off a two year dry spell only to take that first drink and eventually go on a full-blown drunken bender, I felt if he was in my presence I needed to be fucking him.

And his beard stood as all the proof I needed.

As his mouth continued to move and his hands gestured in one direction or the other, my mind wandered to thoughts of him shoving me full of dick. I was convinced if the entire population on earth was getting fucked the way Vince was fucking me, world peace would only be a few strokes of a thick cock away.

There was no doubt in my mind if Lizzie Borden was being fucked by Vince, she would have never swung the fateful axe.

If a woman is being fucked *right*, happiness soon follows.

His mouth continued to move, but my mind was elsewhere. As his hand massaged his beard while he talked, I stared as if possessed by sexual demons. All I heard was *Fuck me, Sienna. Fuck me, Sienna...* regardless of what it was he was actually saying.

He really needed to shave.

Well, either that or crawl over the table and fuck me.

"Huh?" I said as I shook my head from side-to-side.

"What part didn't you get?" he asked.

"I uhhm. I think I had a spasm or something. I didn't hear anything. I was watching your mouth move, but I didn't hear anything," I said.

"Catch anything about the book I'm reading?" he asked.

I shook my head and shrugged an apology.

Leaning back in the chair, he slowly raised his hand to his chin. As he massaged his beard, he scrunched his brow and silently stared until it appeared he wanted more. With his eyes still fixed on mine, he leaned forward and rested his muscular arms on the edge of the table. His eyes were an odd color of green but were lightly sprinkled with little brown specks, and all but made me become a helpless and hopeful little girl each time he opened them wide. I gazed back at him blankly in admiration, all the while hearing my heartbeat and fearing he could do the same. I tried to turn away, but my eyes remained locked on his as if he was in control.

In all reality, he was.

"No shit?" he asked. "Nothing?"

"Sorry," I said with a smile.

"I'll be damned," he said. "Just went deaf for a minute, huh?"

I grinned at the sight of him and did my best to change the subject. "So what are you reading?"

"What's so funny?" he asked.

I attempted to wipe the grin from my face and remain in his good graces. "Nothing."

"What are you smiling about?" he asked.

"About? Uhhm, nothing. Not *about* anything. I dunno, maybe because of something, I guess. Sorry," I stammered.

He pushed his cup of coffee to the side of the table and turned his palm upward. "Because…"

"You really want to know?" I asked.

He relaxed into the back of his chair and cleared his throat lightly. "Enlighten me, sure."

"Because you're fucking me right," I said.

He coughed a laugh and leaned forward slightly. "Is there a wrong way?"

I flipped my hair over my shoulders and leaned forward, grinning the entire time. "Believe me, there are plenty of wrong ways, and it appears you don't know any of them."

"And being *fucked right* makes you smile?" he asked.

"You ever seen a girl who has CBF?" I asked.

He shifted his eyes down to the table and shrugged his shoulders. "Guess I don't know what that is."

"Chronic Bitch Face," I said as I pursed my lips and narrowed my gaze.

"See women like that all the time," he said with a laugh.

"Well," I responded as I raised my coffee cup. "They're not getting fucked right."

He nodded his head and grinned.

"And women like *this,*" I paused and grinned a big cheesy grin. "They're getting all the dick they need."

"And you?" he asked.

With each index finger, I pressed the corners of my mouth upward until it hurt, doing my best to create a smile like The Joker on Batman.

He raised his hand to his face, pressed his palm against his beard, and winked.

"That's good to know. So, what's the latest masterpiece or flop in the world of Independent authors?" he asked.

"Masterpiece? *Loving Mr. Daniels*, by Brittainy Cherry," I responded.

"Good?" he asked.

"Words can't describe it. I'm thinking I'm just going to take a few pictures of the tears I shed when I read it and post them. It's a fucking masterpiece," I said.

"It's about time you read a good one," he said with a nod.

"Did you finish the one about the guy with cancer?" I asked.

"Sure did. Same thing. A fucking masterpiece. In the end she was..."

He paused and shook his head.

"I'm not going to ruin it. You'll read it soon enough," he said.

"Started anything new?" I asked.

He nodded his head. "*The Girl With the Dragon Tattoo*. You know, I heard a lot about it, but never read it for some reason. I never really got into those kinds of books, but this motherfucker's good."

"It sure is. How far along are you?" I asked.

"Half," he said.

I nodded my head. "You'll love it."

"Have to beat anybody up this week?" I asked, coughing out a laugh as I did so.

He shook his head and started to laugh, almost choking on his water as he did so. "No. But I pushed a guy down some steps on accident."

"Really? By accident?" I asked.

He eventually stopped laughing and told the story. "I told him I was going to, and I grabbed his shoulders and acted like I was about to shove him. He was some Romanian dude, and he was wearing one of those shiny fucking track suits. So, I grabbed him, pushed him a little to add some incentive, and the fucker slipped out of my hands and fell down the steps. Those shiny jackets are slippery as fuck."

"Did he pay up?" I asked.

"Like a fucking slot machine. As soon as I got to the bottom of the steps, he was reaching for his wallet," he said.

"Well, I guess that's good," I said.

It didn't bother me that Vince did what he did for a living. In his own words, he forced people to realize the responsibility associated with making a promise. Most of the broken promises he dealt with had to do with money, and he simply made sure they met their part of the commitment they had already agreed to. In his mind he was teaching people to be moral.

"And yesterday, a couple of one hundred and ten pound twin meth heads who owed a guy thirteen grand and hadn't paid him a dime had a box with about thirty grand worth of meth and twenty-five grand in cash in it when I showed up. But they didn't make one phone call to try and pay for the dope that got them there. I fucking swear," he said.

"Drug dealers without morals," I said as I shrugged my shoulders.

"Men without a moral code. It doesn't matter the profession," he said.

I guess not," I said.

I waved at the waitress as she walked past. We had been at the restaurant long enough after dinner that we'd changed waitresses.

"I need coffee," I said as she walked up to the table.

"Make it two, please," Vince said.

"Cream or sugar?" she asked.

"Black on both," he responded.

Vince paid attention to all of the details. I liked it that he knew how I liked my coffee, noticed what perfume I was wearing, and remembered the year of car I drove. He recalled what jeans or outfits I wore on certain days, and made reference to them later, describing the time, place, and article of clothing. It was nice to think a man had enough interest in me to remember things about me. As with most things about Vince, his actions and his manner of living reminded me of my father.

The waitress quickly returned with two cups of coffee. After thanking her and sliding one of them toward my side of the table, Vince raised his cup to his mouth and took a sip.

"So, I have a question," he said over the rim of the cup.

He wasn't a very predictable man, but when he preceded a question with that particular statement, it meant that whatever he was going to ask was something he felt was significant.

"Let's hear it," I said as I reached for my cup of coffee.

"Well, Thanksgiving is coming up a week from this coming Thursday, and I was wondering if you'd like to spend the day at my mother's? I want you to meet her and she's been asking about you," he said.

Immediately, my heart felt swollen. "You told her about me?"

He lowered the cup of coffee to the table and pushed it to the side. "I told her about you six months ago, Sienna. She knows we're in a relationship now, and she's pretty excited. So yeah, she wants to meet you."

When my father went to prison my mother's sister came down from Ohio and stayed with me. At the time she was young, single, and felt sorry for me. Although I never met her before my father went away, we got along fine, but I always felt in the back of my mind that she blamed my father for the death of my mother. Why else would my aunt never take the time to meet her niece, I wondered? After my father was released, she left, and I hadn't seen her since.

For me, holidays were a thing of the past. Since my father's death, my music was my Christmas, and I enjoyed his favorite album, *A Very Special Christmas*, all year round. I hadn't celebrated a birthday, Thanksgiving, or a Christmas in the presence of anyone since he died, and although I hadn't told Vince yet, Christmas was not only Christmas as he knew it, but it was my birthday.

"I'd uhhm. Thank you. Yes, I think I'd love to. Do we get dressed up or anything?" I asked.

"Well, funny you asked. My mother's kind of old fashioned, and she would skin me alive if I dressed like this for Easter, Thanksgiving, or Christmas. It's just been in the last few years that she's come to terms with me having tattoos. So, if you could wear a dress, that'd sure be nice," he said.

Squeeeeee!

I tried my very best to hide my excitement. "Sure, I'll dig around in my closet and find something nice."

Sienna's going shopping…Sienna's going shopping…

"She cooks a huge meal, and she'll expect us to eat damned near everything," he said.

"Sounds great," I said. "I love Thanksgiving. Can I help? I mean can I cook anything?"

It was becoming more difficult to contain myself. The thought of it all was almost too much. My father had been gone almost five years, and to think I was going to share a holiday with Vince was almost too much to comprehend.

"We'll go see her maybe Sunday or something, how's that?" he asked as he reached for his coffee.

I leaned on the edge of the table and batted my eyelashes. "Uhhm,

Sunday's tomorrow."

"Okay, we'll go see her *tomorrow*. If you don't like her, it'll give you time to bow out of the Thanksgiving deal, how's that?" he said with a laugh.

"Sounds perfect," I said.

Before I met his mother, I needed desperately to get my nails done, go get makeup, buy a new dress, spend a few minutes in a tanning booth, and make a few adjustments to my ratty hair.

"What time?" I asked as I reached for my coffee.

"I don't know, noon?" he asked.

"How about a little later? I have a few things I need to get done first." I said.

He relaxed in his chair, sipped his coffee as he studied me for a moment, eventually placing his cup on the table and pushing it to the side. As he rested his massive forearms on the edge of the table and leaned forward, he grinned.

"What? Get your nails done, go fake bake, and hit the mall?" he asked.

Vince Ames may have been a biker, a criminal of sorts, and a debt collector for drug dealers, but to me, he was perfect.

And I deserved his perfection.

VINCE

November 16, 2014

Introducing Sienna to my mother required a level of commitment on my part not much different than marriage. In my lifetime, only one other woman had met my mother, and it was my ex-wife. In inviting Sienna into my mother's home, I was not only inviting her into my life, but into my mother's life. As far as I was concerned, this would make Sienna part of the family.

In a short period of time, I beat myself up about her meeting my mother, and cancelled the Sunday plans, and simply left Thanksgiving as the meeting day. Sienna was ready, I was afraid I was not so ready.

"So, you ready for this?" I asked. "Just a few more days. I can't wait for you to meet her."

He glanced upward and stared for a moment. It appeared he intended to be attentive, but eventually his eyes fell closed and he lowered his head. Apparently I was boring him with my subject matter, and he was about to fall asleep.

"You fucking prick. Don't you dare pass out before I'm done, you rude son-of-a-bitch. When I'm talking, you good and god damned well better listen, understand?" I seethed.

He shook his head violently, no doubt attempting to prevent himself from falling asleep. He slowly shifted his eyes to meet mine, blinked a few times, and lowered his chin slightly.

"So anyway, she's pretty to look at, but she's also pretty damned smart. She reads more books than Pop and me combined," I said.

He blinked his eyes again and stared, apparently waiting for me to continue

"Hard to believe, I know, but she reads half a dozen books a week. And, she's thin. Not one of the unhealthy skinny bitches like you see on television or in those fucking magazines, but just naturally thin, like a supermodel. And her hair? Wait 'till you see it. It's perfect. Her eyebrows are hit and miss, but don't you dare stare at 'em, got it?"

I paused and shifted my eyes to meet his.

Fast asleep and lightly snoring, it was obvious he had very little interest in knowing anything about Sienna before she made her grand entrance for Thanksgiving dinner.

I turned toward the sound of the front door opening, and met my mother's gaze as she peered toward the porch swing where we were seated.

"I can't believe this weather we're having," she said. "It's so nice out here. Now you two need to come in here for dinner, it's ready."

I stood from the porch swing and shrugged my shoulders. "He's asleep."

She shook her head lightly and sighed signature sigh of frustration. "He's going to be mad if he misses dinner, just wake him up."

"Bradley!" I shouted. "Dinner's ready."

He opened his eyes, jumped from the porch swing, and ran toward the front door.

"He was tired of listening to your stories, that's all," she said over her shoulder as she walked away.

"He's the only one in this house that pays attention to me. He just fell asleep," I said as I followed her into the house.

Bradley and I followed her into the dining room. As she pulled her chair away from the table she shifted her eyes toward me and sighed again. "I listen to what you say."

I pulled my chair away from the table, sat down, and placed my napkin in my lap. "You listen to what I say, but Bradley *hears* me."

"Who's saying grace?" she asked.

"I said it last week," I said.

"You sure did," she responded as she reached toward the plate of roast beef.

After picking up a piece of meat large enough to choke a horse, she held it to the side and shook it. Within a few seconds she had Bradley's full attention. Having performed this ritual no less than a thousand times, he knew just what to do.

He situated himself directly beside her, sat, and tilted his head back.

"It's your turn to say grace, Bradley," she said.

"Woof!" Bradley barked as he stared up at the roast beef.

"Amen," my mother said as she dropped the piece of meat.

"Amen," I said.

"So, finally. What's it been? A year? And you're finally bringing her to meet us," she said as she began to spoon mashed potatoes onto her plate.

"I met her in June. And we didn't start seeing each other until I took her those flowers, and I think that was in August," I said.

"It was July. The fouth," she said.

I shook my head as I loaded my plate with meat. "August."

"That's exactly why Bradley falls asleep when you talk to him. He gets tired of the fibs you tell," she said.

"He falls asleep because he's fat and unhealthy," I said, knowing what I said would irritate her.

She turned and glared at me over the top of her fork full of mashed potatoes. "Stephen Vincent! Take it back."

"It's true," I said.

"Every word out of your mouth is a fib. Bradley's not fat, he's muscular. And it was right after you got beat up, because you had those stitches in your face. It was July Fourth, and we were eating fried chicken. Right here," she said as she pointed at the table.

"I know where we were, Mother. Whatever, Okay, July. Fine," I said.

"So, six months ago you started seeing her, and just now I get to meet her. I think it's sad," she said.

"Well, you won't have anything else to complain about here in about ten days," I said.

She wagged her fork in my direction and cleared her throat. "They're not complaints, they're observations. Now, eat your dinner."

"Well, I'm excited to finally meet her," she said. "And if you've been seeing her all year, and if you truly love her, you should..."

She paused and took a bite of bread.

"I should what?" I asked.

She handed Bradley another piece of roast beef, glanced upward, and shook her head as we made eye contact. "Never mind. I'm excited to meet her, that's all."

I forced a sigh of sarcasm and continued to eat. I was pretty sure I knew fully what my mother intended to say. She was a master at hinting at what she wanted, expected, or believed she deserved, but not actually saying it.

And, in time, I was pretty sure I would grant her wish.

SIENNA

November 27th, 2014

Dressed in a new black V-neck pleated dress, 2" heels, and a black shawl, I felt as beautiful as Vince said I looked. Vince was dressed in dress jeans, dress boots, and a black button down shirt. Much to my surprise, he allowed me to drive, and we listened to Christmas music the entire way to his mother's house. I felt for the entire trip that my life was finally not only precisely where I had always wanted it to be, but exactly as I deserved it to be.

The neighborhood wasn't exactly what I had expected, and as we pulled into the driveway of the two-story brick home, I was immediately surprised at the size, perfect landscape, and southern appeal. The home clearly stood out as being different than all the others surrounding it.

A red brick home with wrap-around porch complete with porch swing, white shuttered windows, and a yard filled with huge trees in a middle class neighborhood wasn't where I expected Vince's mother to be living. Considering the fact that Vince's father was a biker who had died in prison, and Vince was an only child, I expected a little more modest – and much smaller – home.

"This place is huge," I said as I shut off the engine.

"Pop built this place," he said. "Bought three lots to build it on so he could have this huge yard."

"Seriously?" I asked as I admired the home.

He gazed in the direction of the house and nodded his head. "Yep, pretty cool place, huh? He was a biker, but being a construction contractor was his day job. Hell, he wanted a dozen kids and a place where they could always come back to for Sunday dinners. I grew up in this big fucker all alone. Lots of cool places to hide, though."

"Wow. That's crazy he built it. Good for him," I said. "And the yard is huge."

"Just remember, no cussing. Oh, and *you* can call me whatever, but she's going to call me Stephen," he said.

"Got it," I said as I reached for the door handle.

"And don't call Bradley fat," he said.

"Okay," I said with a laugh as I got out of the car.

Vince got the pies from the back of the car and we began to walk up the drive. I continued to admire the massive home as we walked up to the sidewalk leading to the front steps. Growing up in such a place would be heaven for a child, especially with the yard as large as it was. As we stepped off the sidewalk and onto the steps, the reality of it all hit me. I had never met a man's parents, at least not a man I was in a relationship with. I suspected Vince felt the same way, but as far as I was concerned, this was a huge step toward securing our relationship as being one that was solid and secure.

"After you," Vince said as he opened the door.

I nervously stepped into the home. The very large living room was decorated as I expected a home to be in the south, and although it wasn't ornate, it was pretty close. Camel back couches, arm chairs with carved wood, and various coffee and end tables were scattered about the room, and very plentiful. There was no doubt the home could easily be used to

134

entertain dozens, but from what Vince said it was never more than him and his mother who occupied the home.

As I inhaled the aroma of the Thanksgiving meal, all of the emotions associated with the holidays I had at home as a child filled me. We rarely had a large crowd, and frequently ate alone, but the holidays were special nonetheless. From time to time my father would invite a less fortunate friend, and I remember times when I had friends from school visit during the holiday season, but the holiday meals were typically only my father and me. Although the holiday dinner table was less than full, the love that filled the dining room was immense.

My father loved to cook, and his recipes for the holiday meals were always traditional. Although we often ate meals which were more customary in his actual home land, Ukraine, he never introduced any of his family recipes into our holiday meals. He was proud of being a U.S. citizen, and proud of adopting the traditions and policies of the country, recipes included. His sweet potatoes were my favorite; he put big marshmallows in with the potatoes, and because it was only him and me eating, I always got plenty of marshmallows with my sweet potatoes.

"Oh my word," his mother said as she walked out of what I expected was the kitchen.

According to Vince, she was in her early fifties, but she looked to be in her forties. She was petite, dressed in a burgundy dress, had long brunette hair with highlights, and was absolutely beautiful. A white apron was tied around her waist, and contrasted completely with her beautiful dress, but clearly showed how much time and effort she had placed in the preparation of the meal we were about to eat.

As she stood in the doorway and gazed in our direction, she slowly raised her hands to her mouth and pressed the tips of her fingers to her lips.

"Sienna, this is my mother, Anita," Vincent said. "Ma, this is Sienna."

She lowered her hands from her face, opened her arms, and curled her fingers toward her palms repeatedly as if she was trying to coerce a small toddler to come see her.

"Go give her a hug," Vince sighed in the form of a light whisper.

I walked across the living room toward where she was standing, and as I stepped directly in front of her, realized she was softly crying. I felt an odd sense of pride that Vince adding me to his life provided her with such joy, but also felt guilt for some reason. As she wrapped her arms around me and pulled me into her, I realized the guilt was more a feeling of responsibility.

"I love him very much," I whispered in an effort to comfort her. "And it's nice to meet you."

"Where do you want the pies?" Vince asked.

"You know where to put the pies," she said in a sarcastic tone as she released me. "Now, go play with your brother, Stephen. We have work to do."

"Follow me," she said as she turned toward the kitchen.

I glanced over my shoulder, grinned, and winked at Vince. As I followed his mother into the kitchen, an adorable – and obviously overweight – English bulldog ran past us and toward the living room. As he ran, slobber flipped from his lips.

"That's Bradley," she said as he ran past. "He's Stephen's brother."

"Hi, Bradley," I said jokingly even though he was long gone.

"Stephen was right, your hair is perfect," she said as she stepped to the side and studied me.

"Why, thank you," I said.

I glanced over my shoulder and upon confirming we were alone, lowered the tone of my voice to a whisper. "He told you about my *hair*?"

"Honey, I've been hearing about you since the day you met back in June. He tells me bits and pieces at a time, but that hair of yours…he just won't stop talking about it." She said.

"He's silly," I said.

She pulled the oven door open slightly and peered inside. "He sure is. And just so you know, he's been known to tell a fib or two. Now, back in July, what happened to his face? Someone beat him up, didn't they?"

I pointed to my cheek innocently. "When he got the stitches?"

She glanced up and nodded her head. "Mmmhhhmm."

I shrugged my shoulders. "I thought he wrecked his motorcycle."

"Well aren't you cute," she said. "Sticking up for him already."

She opened the oven again and pulled out a sheet of dinner rolls sufficient to feed a small army. After placing them on the counter beside the rest of the meal, she sighed.

"Stephen's always prompt, and so am I. I think that's about all of it," she said as she glanced around the kitchen.

"It smells wonderful," I said.

"So do you, Honey. I absolutely love that perfume you're wearing. And that dress? It's beautiful," she said.

"Thank you," I said with a smile. "I just got it."

She walked past me, peered through the doorway, and turned to face me. "He's in there talking to Bradley."

She walked back into the kitchen, picked up the platter of turkey, and nodded her head toward the sweet potatoes. "Honey, grab the yams and follow me."

I glanced in the dish. The sweet potatoes were covered in marshmallows. As I inhaled the sweet aroma, a rush of emotions washed over me. Other than in my father's home, I had never seen them prepared in the same manner, and although I never assumed my father invented the recipe, I had yet to deal with such a strong reminder of him. I bit into my quivering lip, picked up the sweet potatoes, and followed her into the dining room, my mouth watering the entire way.

A table large enough to seat eight with a large chandelier over it sat in the center of the room. She placed the turkey on the table and reached for the potatoes. After situating them in what I suspected was her perfect place, she turned away. After a few steps, she paused.

"Do you want children?" she asked.

I was slightly shocked by her question, and wondered how I should respond. It was something Vince and I had yet to discuss, but I was sure we would at some point in time. Talking to her about it first seemed strange.

Still facing away from me, she turned her head and gazed at me over her shoulder. "Just between you and me."

I grinned and nodded my head eagerly. "I do."

"How many?" she asked as she turned away.

"Just between you and me?" I asked.

"Honey, everything we discuss is between you and me. It's what mothers and daughters do, they keep secrets with each other," she said.

Her response didn't immediately sink in, but as I responded, I felt flattered and considerably more welcome in her home. Whether she intended to or not, she made me feel wanted, and almost as if I was already truly a part of the family.

"Enough to fill this house if I got my say in it," I said.

She blinked her eyes, smiled, and quickly turned toward the sink.

"Grab the green beans, honey, I think I've got something in my eye," she said as she turned away.

I carried the remainder of the food to the table as she walked to the bathroom and tried to get something out of her eye. As I gazed down at the table and wondered if she would be mad about my placement of the food, I heard her yell at Vince.

"Bradley, Stephen! Dinner's ready, you two," she shouted.

"It's perfect," she said as she walked into the dining room.

"I didn't know where to put everything," I said as I shrugged my shoulders. "It looks wonderful."

"So, we're ready?" Vince asked as he walked into the room.

His mother shifted her eyes toward me and grinned. "We sure are."

"You been crying, Ma?" Vince asked as he walked into the room .

"No, I got something in my eye, didn't I, Honey?" she responded as she shifted her eyes toward me.

I nodded my head.

"Yeah, and I wrecked my bike," Vince said with a laugh.

"Just be quiet and sit down," his mother snapped.

We all took a seat at the large table, Vince and I sitting on either side of his mother, and Bradley on the floor beside Vince.

"Who's saying grace?" she asked as she alternated glances between Vince and me.

"Well, according to your rules, it's Sienna's turn," Vince responded.

His mother tilted her head to the side and batted her eyelashes.

"I'll say it," I said with a nod.

I closed my eyes, bowed my head, and inhaled a shallow breath. As I began to pray, Anita rested her hand on my knee.

"Heavenly Father, we are gathered here today to give thanks. There are so many, Lord, who are less fortunate, and for them I ask you to give special consideration on this day, and throughout the holiday season. Bless them with understanding and a willingness to continue, for one day they, just as we have, will find their calling in life and see the world through clearer eyes, through your eyes, and through you they will pave the way to a brighter future. Today, Lord, I thank you for Anita, I thank you for Vince, and I thank you for Bradley, but most of all, I thank you for providing all of us with something as sacred as the ability to love. I give these thanks in your name, Lord, amen."

I opened my eyes, lifted my head, and glanced around the table.

"Pass the potatoes, Ma," Vince said.

His mother stood and patted me on the shoulder.

"Hand him the potatoes, Honey," she said as she turned away. "I've got something in my eye again."

I did wonder when she walked away the first time if she was crying or if she had something in her eye, and now the answer was pretty clear.

But I'd never tell.

Because that's what mothers and daughters do, they keep secrets with each other.

VINCE

December 15th, 2014

It was apparent Sienna was quite fond of Christmas, and obviously more so than any other holiday. Her constant listening to Christmas music and her inability to hide her excitement as the day approached caused me to ask more questions, and in due time I learned that her birth, her mother's death, and the holiday all shared the same day on the calendar. Throughout her childhood, she and her father spent the day celebrating not only the holiday and her birthday, but her mother's sacrifice, which ultimately provided Sienna with the gift of life.

I knew there weren't many people who would maintain such a positive outlook on life after forfeiting their entire family at such an early age, but Sienna wasn't like everyone else. She was grateful for what she had, appreciative for the time she was able to spend with her father, and had no reservations admitting that although she wished she would have been able to meet her mother, she blamed no one for her loss.

Christmas had always been a holiday I enjoyed, but on this particular year, I was enjoying it just a little bit more.

Even if it was difficult to admit.

"What's the options?" he asked nervously.

"You're out of fucking options," I responded. "He saved you from a dime piece in the joint. The fucking charge was manslaughter. You remember the not guilty verdict, right? I bet you had a huge fucking fiesta for that, didn't you?"

He glanced around the restaurant and leaned toward the center of the table. "I remember. But check this out…"

I shook my head and raised my left index finger in the air. "Check *this* out. You owe him eight, and my cut is thirty percent. That's ten thousand four hundred. Not negotiable."

Sitting in a restaurant with a gun in the pocket of my coat made me slightly uncomfortable, but this guy had proven to be impossible for me to find. After paying $500 to an informant a few weeks prior, the call finally came. I learned Hector was eating at one of his favorite places in the barrio, and if I hurried, I could catch him there. As I walked in, he was paying his bill and preparing to leave.

Now sitting at the table trying to negotiate a payoff in the presence of a hundred Spanish speaking patrons, I was beginning to feel like the center of attention. In this crowd, I stood out like a turd in a punch bowl.

"Look, Hector. You and I both know you were in the game then, and you're in the game now. Ten grand isn't going to kill you. I know enough about you to know you're aware you need to pay the debt. It's been six months, and it was due in 30 days. You know enough about me to know if I have to, I'll drag your ass out of here and it'll get real ugly real quick. I don't want that, and I know you don't either. Solve this problem for me," I said.

"Navidad's a bitch, and I got six kids. It creeped up on me this year. And I'm out of the click. You see any of my homies in here?" he asked as he motioned around the room. "Yeah, me neither."

"I'm stretched thin as fuck 'till I get another gig," he said. "Can we reach an agreement?"

"Like what?" I asked.

"I know exactly what I got at home in the safe. It's like $7,800. I can maybe scrape up a few more and make it eight," he said. "That's all. But I need it squashed."

"Eight leaves your attorney fifty-six hundred. He won't settle for that," I said.

"It *could* pay him off," he said.

I wasn't sure he had the money, but I suspected he did. It seemed every time I had to collect money from a member of the Hispanic community I entered into a bargaining agreement, and there was always an expectation of me forfeiting my cut, which I *never* did. The negotiating process seemed to be part of their culture, which I tried to respect, but eliminating my cut was not an option.

I wasn't in this business for my health.

"Ten thousand four hundred," I said as I shook my head. "Borrow what you don't have."

"Look, my wife took the kids and went Christmas shopping. She left me off here to eat. I don't want any trouble when she gets back, not around my kids. So let's make it eight and be done with it," he said.

"I ought to put a bullet in your ass and take that gold fucking watch. As many people as you've fucked over, I doubt anyone in here would say a fucking word. What's it worth? I asked.

"Maria got me this," he said as he pulled his arm away from the table.

"Hell, I need a watch. Mine's fucked up, anyway. Take it off," I said.

"I can't do that," he said.

I leaned into the center of the table and narrowed my eyes. As he shifted his eyes to meet mine, I gave my demand.

"Actually, you *can*. Give me the fucking watch or I'll drag your ass out on the sidewalk and pistol whip you into a bloody fucking pulp. And *that,* Hector, is a fucking promise," I said through my teeth.

"She'll kill me if I give you this watch," he said.

"And I'll kill you if you don't," I said.

He studied me for a moment, and eventually reached for the clasp of the watch. One thing I had developed over the many years of doing what I did was a reputation. My customers always ended up with their money, merchandise well worth in excess of the money, or I delivered their client to their doorstep.

And, as a local attorney wouldn't be able to make much use of me delivering Hector – and he knew it – he further knew I wouldn't let him leave my sight without the money or an equivalent.

He unclasped the watch, extended his arm, and handed it to me.

"Good choice," I said as I shoved the watch into my coat pocket.

"Tell that to my wife," he said. "So what now?"

"We'll wait for your wife and kids. Tell her we're old friends. But you're riding in the truck with me to your house. And I'll wait till you get the money out of the safe, or wherever you have it. Then, I'll be gone," I said.

"I got some brand new 22" rims for a Chevy truck, and a 60" flat screen. Take that shit instead of the watch, homie," he said.

"Do I look like I need a fucking set of rims? Or a fucking TV? I'm keeping the god damned watch," I said. "And I'm not your fucking homie, remember that."

After a few long silent stares and two glasses of water, I watched as a little girl struggled with the front door for a minute, and then finally pulled it open. Dressed in a bright orange colored coat, black leggings, and little black buckled shoes, she was adorable. After scanning the restaurant for a recognizable face, she locked eyes with Hector and smiled.

"Papi!"

Speaking Spanish faster than I was able to understand, she ran across the restaurant and directly toward our table. As she jumped into his arms, it was apparent she was one of his many children.

What seemed to be a small argument ensued, and after a little negotiation, Hector turned to face me.

"She wants to know if she can ride with us in the truck?" he asked.

I cocked an eyebrow and glared at him. "Are you fucking kidding me?"

"Show me some respect," he said as he nodded his head toward his daughter.

Although having children in my presence wasn't something I was used to, it didn't take me a matter of a split-second to realize I had cursed in front of his child. Cursing in my mother's home cost me a lot of money over the years, and as much as I hated to admit it, I needed to show him and his daughter respect regardless of the debt he owed.

Show respect, get respect.

"Lo siento por mi elección de palabras," I said.

The little girl smiled.

"Listo?" I asked.

He nodded his head.

As we stepped out of the restaurant and onto the sidewalk, I noticed a Suburban in front of the front door. Filled with kids who were all waving in our direction, it was apparent the story he told of his wife taking the kids Christmas shopping was true. As we began to walk toward the vehicle, a boy in his teens stepped out of the vehicle and grinned.

"We got you some presents, so don't be trying to look all in the back and see what they are," the boy bragged.

The remaining children, all much younger, beat their fists against the windows and made faces as his son stood outside talking about the presents they had purchased. .

In ten days, Christmas would be upon us all.

"This is Vince," Hector said to his son as he motioned toward me with his free hand.

"Emilio," the boy said with a smile.

I nodded my head. "Nice to meet you."

I alternated glances between the boy, Hector, and the Suburban full of excited children. Memories of being a boy at Christmas, and opening presents with my mother and father were some of my fondest memories, even as an adult.

Christmas would be upon us in a matter of days.

"Come here for a minute?" I asked Hector.

"Take your sister and get in," Hector said as he motioned toward the SUV.

"You know where our shop is?" I asked as the children crawled inside the car. "Our clubhouse?"

"Couple blocks east of the pizza place?" he asked.

I nodded my head. "You have me the eight grand buy January 15th? No bullshit, can you?"

"I can get the eight to you tonight. It'll be tight, but I can do it," he responded.

"Here," I said as I handed him the watch in my cupped hand.

He shook his head and raised his hands as if he wasn't going to accept the watch. "I can't get you $10,400. I can't even get you $8,400. I wasn't bullshittin'. Just keep it. I'll tell her something."

Based on what I knew about people, I was pretty sure what he was telling me was true. I shook my cupped hand in front of him.

"Keep the watch. Get me $8,000, and we're straight. Merry Christmas," I said.

"No shit?" he asked as he took the watch in his hand.

I nodded my head and extended my hand. "Bring it to the shop by the 15th, just put it in an envelope with my name on it."

"You have my word," he said as he shook my hand. "Merry Christmas, Vince."

"Merry Christmas to you and your family," I said. "And this didn't happen. I've got a reputation to uphold."

"What didn't happen?" he said as he clasped the watch on his wrist.

"Exactly," I said as I turned away.

And, just like that, I was out of the mood to collect debts and in the mood for Christmas. I got in my truck, glanced at my watch, and realized it was nowhere close to the three o'clock time it depicted.

This fucking watch.

As much as I needed a new watch, I knew it would be a cold day in hell before I broke down and bought another one. I would have no problems spending money on Sienna for Christmas, though.

Because there was no doubt in my mind that she was a necessity.

SIENNA

December 25ᵗʰ, 2014

Christmas was so much more than a holiday for me. I was born on Christmas, my mother died on Christmas, and according to my belief, Jesus was born on the same day. After my father's death, I made it a point to remember my father's and my memories of the day by enjoying the music he graced me with when he gave me the special CD, and I did so on a daily basis.

I typically didn't tell people when my birthday was, because if they knew about my mother's death, it made the holiday and my birthday both seem sad. It wasn't a sad day as far as I was concerned, and in fact, I considered it to be the best day ever.

In the last five years, the holiday had been a difficult one for me. Celebrating it with Vince and Anita would not only bring back so many fond memories, but would without a doubt develop new ones that we could spend a lifetime sharing together as a family.

"Open it," I said as I pushed the gift in his direction.

"Don't be jumping around, I want a clear picture," Anita said.

"I'm not six years old, Mother. I'm not going to jump around like a fucking idiot," Vince said.

Uh oh.

I widened my eyes and glanced in Anita's direction. She pointed

149

over her shoulder toward the kitchen, cleared her throat, and after not gathering Vince's attention, did it again.

"The jar, Stephen," she said.

He glanced in her direction, sighed, and stood. "It's Christmas," he said.

She pointed toward the kitchen and grinned. "All the more reason to be respectful."

He lowered his head and began walking toward the kitchen slowly.

"Let me see it," she said.

He reached into his back pocket, pulled out his wallet, and removed a $1 bill. "Here," he said as he waved it in the air.

She raised the camera and took a picture of him as he held the bill high in the air. After a minute, he returned to the room and sat down beside his gift.

Incapable of containing myself, I began to clap. "Open it, open it, open it."

We had stayed all night at his mother's home, and I was still wearing my pink pajamas. After hot chocolate, coffee, and his mother's Christmas breakfast, the morning was just like I remembered it being with my father. There's nothing on earth like waking up Christmas morning with the one you love.

He slowly peeled the wrapping from the package while his mother sat back and took pictures with her digital camera. After carefully pulling all of the paper away from the box, he turned toward me and scowled.

"Really?" he said sarcastically.

I shrugged my shoulders. "Sorry."

"See this?" he said as he held the box in the air. It was covered in clear packing tape.

"Take a picture of this shit," he said.

Uh oh.

He cussed again.

I glanced at Anita. She lowered the camera, cleared her throat, and glared. Without speaking, Vince stood, pulled a $1 bill from his wallet, and waved it in the air. After being photographed as he walked to the kitchen, he returned, sat down, and quietly began peeling the tape away from the box.

As he opened it I held my breath.

"Oh my god," he said as he peered into the box.

I hope you like it.

"Well, let's see it," his mother said.

He picked the book out of the box, held it in the air, and turned it toward his mother. A hardbound first edition, first printing of *Pride and Prejudice*, I hoped he would take great pride in having it. I had bid on two of the books on eBay, hoping to buy the first one, but I lost out on it at the last minute. Although the one I purchased was in much better condition, the first one was five years older, and I was interested in it for that reason alone.

He stood, held the book at his side, and grinned. After a dozen or so pictures, his mother turned toward me.

"It was his favorite since high school," she said. "He might try and act tough, but he's a romantic at heart."

I grinned and mouthed the words "I know."

Vince walked over to me, hugged me, and kissed me as he released me from his arms. "I love you, Sienna."

"I love you," I said. "Merry Christmas."

"Open this," he said after reaching under the tree and handing me a gift.

It was the first Christmas gift I had been given since my father died. I had several gifts, but they were all purchased by me, wrapped by me, and opened by me. And, speaking from experience, I can say they're never as much fun when you know what's in them.

"I don't open them like you do," I said.

"However you like," Anita said as she raised the camera.

"Well, if you're going to take pictures, you better hurry," I said as I tore into the paper.

Within a few seconds, the wrapping paper was in shreds and an untaped box remained. I quickly opened the box and looked inside. As much as I didn't want to, I began to softly cry.

"You didn't," I said as I wiped the tears from my face.

"I did," he said.

The book I wanted to buy for him, a first edition, first print of *Pride and Prejudice* from 1850, lay in the box. I not only had been outbid by my lover, but we both had the same ideas for what we believed the other would cherish for a lifetime. Our each having purchased the other the exact same gift spoke volumes of not only our love for each other, but for our love for books.

With glassy tear-filled eyes, I glanced around the room. The camera sat in Anita's lap as she wiped tears from her cheeks. I lifted the book in the air.

"He…" I paused and bit my lower lip.

I realized if I continued, I would be in a full-fledged sob. It was too much. Vince was too much. Spending Christmas morning with a family was too much. I turned toward Anita and held the book close to my chest. With tears rolling down her cheeks, she raised the camera and took a picture. I turned toward Vince and shook my head.

"I love you," I said.

He shrugged his shoulders. "I guess we think alike," he said.

"It's all the proof I need. You two are made for each other," Anita said.

For the next hour we opened gifts, some large, some small, but none as meaningful as the book Vince bought for me. The day, as far as I was concerned, was best day of my lifetime. I wished my father could have been there, but realized his departure from the earth wasn't something he had planned, but something that had simply happened. I didn't know if my belief in matters was correct, but in my belief he was witnessing everything that was happening while enjoying a glass of his favorite wine.

"There's one more for each of you," I said as reached behind the tree and removed a two small gifts.

"There sure is," he said as he reached behind the couch and produced a large box.

He kicked the box with his boot, sending it sliding across the floor. It came to a stop at my feet. I stood, stepped around the big box, and handed him the small one. After giving Anita hers, I walked to the couch and sat down in front of the big box.

"I'll go last," I said.

Anita opened hers, turned toward me, and smiled. "Bombshell?"

"Yep. The day we met. You said you liked it. It's what I was wearing that day, on Thanksgiving," I said.

"Thank you, Honey," she said. "I'll wear it with fond memories."

"Open it," I said as I motioned toward Vince.

He tilted his head toward the large box in front of me, "Open yours."

"I'll go last," I said.

He removed the wrapping paper, took his knife from his pocket, and made a huge production as he cut the tape from the box. After removing the outer cardboard covering, he stared down at the hard plastic case.

After studying the case for a moment, he opened it.

"I knew you didn't want something fancy, but I really wanted it to be dependable. The jeweler said it was a good one," I said.

Sitting and gazing at the box, he simply nodded his head and continued to stare into his lap.

He removed the black Tag Heuer Formula watch from the box, studied it for some time, and unbuckled the watch from his arm without speaking. The process seemed more like a ritual than simply replacing a watch. He hadn't so much as made eye contact with me since opening the box.

Anita sat down beside me on the couch and began to take pictures.

"His father gave him that watch when he was a kid," she whispered. "It's a cheap watch, and it hasn't worked right for years."

I turned to face her and chewed my lower lip. "I'm so sorry. I didn't mean to…"

"Let him be," she interrupted as she nodded her head toward Vince.

Slowly and methodically, he removed his watch, strapped the new one on his arm, and placed his old watch in the presentation box. After studying the watch for a moment, he turned toward where we were sitting.

"What time is it?" he asked.

"9:10, Dear. And the date is the 25th," Anita said.

He nodded his head, glanced down at the watch, and made the adjustments. I was humbled that he replaced his father's watch with the one I had purchased for him. From what the jeweler said it would keep time better than any other watch I could buy.

After studying the watch for a long moment, he shifted his eyes toward where we were sitting. Without speaking, he raised his clenched fist in the air and extended his thumb, giving me the "thumbs up" sign.

I returned the gesture.

He reached into his lap, pulled out his knife and shook it in the air to get my attention. As I noticed what he held, he slid it across the carpet toward me. As it came to a stop at my feet, he motioned toward the big box. It was almost as big as the ottoman sitting in front of the couch.

Curious as to what may be inside the box, I flipped the knife open, set it at my side, and tore into the wrapping paper with my hands. After exposing the large box, I cut the tape from the seam and opened the flaps. A smaller box sat inside. I removed it, slid the large box to the side, and cut the tape on the smaller box.

I opened the box and gazed inside.

Another smaller box was inside the box between my feet. I turned toward Vince and cocked an eyebrow. "Really?"

He grinned and shrugged his shoulders.

"Scoot back, Honey," Anita said. "I need a picture."

I turned toward her, smiled, and pointed to the boxes. A few pictures later, and I was back to the box opening routine. Six boxes later, and I held a small box in my hands. I glared at Vince and shook the box.

"Was all of that necessary?" I asked.

"Probably not, but it was fun," he said.

I opened the cardboard box. Inside, a slightly smaller box with a name I recognized from the jeweler I had visited.

Rolex.

I opened the box and removed the gold watch. Much smaller than the one I had purchased Vince, it was gold and had small diamonds that circled around the face. Back to wiping tears from my face and fully realizing just how much my father's saying of *the unexpected result of the natural development of life* was applicable to us, I turned toward Anita and held up the watch.

With tear-filled eyes and a heart full of what I was sure was pride, she took several photographs.

"You're always one minute from being late. Now you'll never have to worry about the clock in your Continental crapping out. Turn it over," Vince said. "Look at the back."

I wiped the tears from my cheeks, turned over the watch, and gazed down at the back of the case. Delicately engraved, but easy to read, the inscription was perfect.

The Money Shot.

November 9th, 2014

The fact he remembered the date came as no surprise, Vince's memory was almost photographic. He remembered almost everything, and seemed to remember anything with numbers in it.

Sitting on the couch in the living room of the big house that I hoped to one day fill with grandchildren for Anita to enjoy, I realized that particular day was far more than special.

It was the…

Best.

Christmas.

Ever.

VINCE

January 13th, 2015

January 13th, 2015

I sat patiently and waited for him to arrive, thinking of Sienna the entire time. Love drunk and feeling completely different than I had ever felt before, I realized Sienna was exactly what I had hoped Natalie would have been. It had also become painfully obvious I wasn't actually ever in love with Natalie, and it took my having met Sienna to realize it. Since I was eighteen years old, I was in love with the idea of who I wanted Natalie to become, but not who she was. With Sienna, there were no changes I wanted to see made, nothing I hoped she would do differently, nor was there anything about her I either despised or even lightly questioned as being in need of adjustment. In summary, Sienna was the woman of my dreams, and I was now filled with thoughts of her every waking moment of the day.

In many respects I felt as if her presence had become nothing short of a necessity. Having experienced her in my life for the last six months, imagining living without her was something I couldn't force myself to do. Her being a permanent fixture in my life undoubtedly made me a much better man. Not completely convinced she wasn't making me a softer more subtle version of my former self, but realizing it really didn't matter, I allowed my days to simply include her, silently hoping she didn't turn me into a twat.

Parked across the street from where he lived with me slumped down in the reclined seat, the vehicle I was in appeared to be empty, at least to a passerby. The neighborhood wasn't at all what I expected, and I wondered how a man who could afford to live in a $600,000 house couldn't afford to pay a $30,000 attorney's bill.

I felt odd in the rental car I was using, but trying to blend in while driving my old truck or riding my motorcycle would have been impossible. Being dressed in my button down shirt and dark blue jeans did very little to make me comfortable, but again, in this particular neighborhood I realized the importance of fitting in. With my line of employment, the fewer people who witness my activities the better off everyone was. After what seemed like an eternity, but was only an hour and a half according to my new watch, an Audi sedan pulled into the driveway.

After the garage door closed, I patiently waited a few minutes and proceeded with my ritual. I confirmed there was a round in the chamber, secured the Glock pistol in my holster, and began to open the car door. The sight of him walking down the sidewalk was a surprise, but a welcomed one. I turned and glanced over my shoulder as he continued down the walk. Apparently, he was walking to his mailbox, which was only a matter of ten yards behind where I was parked, but on the other side of the street.

Dressed in jeans, a pull over camouflage sweatshirt, and military style boots, he didn't at all appear like I had expected him to, especially after studying his photos at the attorney's office. Obviously a physically fit man, I suspected he may put up a hell of a fight or try to run, but there was no way he was going to outrun a bullet.

As he removed mail from the mailbox and inspected each individual piece, I quietly pulled open the car door and took a few steps in his direction. Half way between the car and where he was standing, he turned and looked over his shoulder.

"Something I can help you with?" he asked in an obviously aggravated tone of voice.

"Come on, Rudy. I'm Paul. *Paul*, you're acting like you don't remember me." I said as I turned my palms upward and continued to walk in his direction.

In the decade that I had been employed in my profession, I had collected debts from all walks of life including businessmen, criminals, the accused, the convicted, drug dealers, drug users, and everyone in between. Although neighborhoods like the one I was in were uncommon and lower class areas were more frequently the hiding places of my targets, I never changed my defensive posture regardless. A man willing to walk away from a $30,000 debt and tell his attorney to *fuck off*, knowing all the while I was eventually going to pay him a visit was a threat regardless of where he chose to reside.

The difference for me was not where Rudy Vallencio lived, but that he was known to be a collector of firearms, and more than likely would be armed if he was in the home. I needed to keep him outside for our negotiations if possible.

With his back still facing me, he turned his head toward the house as if I hadn't even spoken. Assuming I was going to need to say something else to keep him within earshot, I took a shallow breath and prepared to continue our one-sided conversation.

As I saw the mail fall to the ground in front of him, I realized he wasn't planning on talking.

Everything went into slow motion. The sound of a vehicle's squeaky brakes behind me, the fluttering of the mail to the ground, his pivoting toward me, and the pulling his pistol from the waist of his jeans were all as clear and precise as if they were a scene from a movie. The sound of his gun firing and a scream from behind me were equally – and unmistakably – clear, and everything happened before I was able to clear my Glock from my holster.

My fear was now a reality.

I had become a twat.

I cleared the Glock from the holster, instinctively dropped into a defensive crouch, and fired the weapon twice. The sound of three gunshots rang echoed, and Rudy fell to the ground.

Fuck.

I ran the thirty or so feet which separated us, picked his pistol up, and searched him for additional weapons. The two gunshot wounds – one in his abdomen and one in his chest – were each bleeding profusely. The sound of shouting from behind me caused me to turn around, and I was shocked to see a US Mail Jeep, complete with a bleeding mail delivery person inside.

Fuck.

Rudy wasn't dead, but he would be in a short period of time. The woman in the Jeep appeared to be shot in the leg. I ran to the vehicle and gazed down at her leg.

Fuck.

I pulled my knife, cut the sleeves off my shirt, and tied them together. After tying a tourniquet to her upper thigh, I asked if she had a phone. Relatively alert, and surprisingly calm for having just been shot, she pointed to her purse.

"In…in my…purse. Thank you…for…saving…me," she said.

I reached into the purse, removed the phone, pulled out her pack of cigarettes, lit two, and handed her one.

"Thank you," she said.

I took a long much needed drag on the cigarette, inhaled, and let the smoke fill my lungs completely. I exhaled the cloud out into the winter air, inhaled another long drag, and held it deep in my lungs. As the smoke burned against my lungs and I felt the pressure build, I made the call no one percenter ever wants to make.

I called the police.

SIENNA

January 13th, 2015

Police cars, crime scene tape, and a firetruck aren't the things a woman wants to see when her respective other calls and tells her to come and *come quick.*

"They may charge me with murder" wasn't very comforting to hear, either.

I pulled the car right up to the edge of the crime scene tape, got out, and shifted my eyes toward the *crime scene.* Countless police officers, police cars, firemen, and what seemed to be an off-duty ambulance were all forced into a one hundred foot square area. It looked like what my father often described as a *Mongolian clusterfuck.* I shook my head, scanned the area for Vince, and ducked under the yellow tape.

"Ma'am, you're going to need to step behind the tape, this is a crime scene," an officer said in a demanding tone as he gestured toward the tape with his hand.

I disregarded his demand and continued walking toward Vince as if I was a crime scene professional.

"The dead are incapable of demanding justice, Ma'am, but it's my responsibility to see to it that you stay out of my crime scene so I can see to it that justice is served," he said as he puffed his chest out.

The officer narrowed his gaze and glared. I wondered how many times he'd rehearsed the cheesy line waiting for an opportunity to use it. Dressed in jeans, Ugg boots, a sweatshirt, and Victoria's Secret hoodie, I didn't quite look the part, but I really didn't care. As far I was concerned, Officer Responsibility needed to fuck off. I'd read enough books I could fake my way through some yellow tape, and I was sure of it.

I placed my hands on my hips and gazed up and into his eyes. "Well, in 1879 James Madison drafted a little document I like to refer to as the Fourth Amendment to the Constitution of the United States, and it's *my* responsibility to my client to see to it that justice is served in respect to unreasonable search and seizure, and it's further *my* responsibility to remind him to exercise his right to remain silent and make every effort to avoid any police coerced self-incrimination in what is undoubtedly a stressful time. Now, with all due respect to you and *your* crime scene, excuse me, Officer," I said as I stepped past him.

"Counsel," he said with a tip of his hat.

Standing beside a police cruiser talking to an officer, Vince stood in a sleeveless black shirt with a cigarette dangling from his lips. A habit he had given up two years prior, the stress associated with shooting someone had probably caused so much mental anguish that he had to have a cigarette just to keep his sanity.

"Not another word," I said as I walked up to where he was standing.

Vince turned to face me, glanced at my boots, shook his head, and grinned. "We're done here."

I turned toward the officer. "I'm his legal counsel."

He glanced down at my boots, slowly shifted his eyes up along my frame, and locked them on mine when our eyes met.

"Is that right?" he asked.

I nodded my head. "Sure is."

"Well, doesn't look like he's going to need any," the officer said with a light laugh. "He clearly shot this shit bird in self-defense."

He turned toward Vince, nodded his head, and extended his hand. "Appreciate your help with the report."

Vince tossed the cigarette at his feet, blew out a cloud of smoke, and shook the officer's hand. I was thoroughly confused. From what Vince had said when he called from the mail lady's phone, he was involved in a shoot-out with a guy he was trying to convince to pay his debt. He was, at least at that time, worried he may be charged with murder.

Seeing his smiling face, jovial mood, and lack of overall concern made me immediately feel comfortable that something must have changed drastically. The officer clutched his notepad, turned, and walked toward another officer. After he was far enough away from where we stood that he was incapable of hearing us, I shrugged my shoulders and shook my head.

"What's going on?" I asked.

"Self-defense, I'm free to go," he said.

"Nice shirt," I said as I nodded my head toward what I could now see was formerly his nice black dress shirt.

He glanced at each tattooed arm, flexed his biceps, and grinned as he did so. "Cut off the sleeves to make a tourniquet," he said.

"I fucking love you," I whispered.

"I love you," he responded.

"So we can go?" I asked.

He glanced around the chaotic scene and nodded his head as he turned toward me.

"The mail lady gave her testimony to the officers before they got her hauled away and it matched mine perfectly. Hell, they're calling me a fucking hero. The dead guy had a few outstanding warrants, the gun he used was stolen, and I fired in self-defense. I told them why I was here," he said with a shrug of his shoulders. "And they didn't give a fuck."

I nodded my head and forced a smile. I was far from happy, but very relieved he was unharmed and wasn't going to be arrested.

"My gun's registered and I have a permit for it. His was stolen. He shot the mail lady, and only after he shot the mail lady did I even pull my gun. I'm free to go," he said.

"He shot at you first?" I asked.

He widened his eyes as he shook his head lightly. "Actually he got two shot off."

I stood and stared. "You said you always shoot first. *Always*. You said there was nothing for me to worry about, ever. You said *ever*, Vince"

"Yeah, we probably need to have a talk," he said.

"About?" I asked as I turned toward the Continental.

"Fucking," he said. "We need to slow down on the fucking. It's making me soft."

"Not an option," I said over my shoulder. "I'll just buy you a bullet proof vest."

"I'm being serious," he said.

"So am I," I responded as I began to walk toward my car.

So am I.

VINCE

February 14th, 2015

Sienna and I had continued our ritual of eating out on Sunday's for lunch, and often went together to my mother's house in the late afternoon for dinner. When the weather was nice, we typically met at the establishment because I was on my motorcycle, and even though the warm winter days were warm enough for me, they were never warm enough for her. On this particular day, the forecast had called for cold enough weather that my bike was locked in her garage, and we intended to ride in her car.

I stepped from the shower, wrapped myself in a towel, and walked toward the vanity to shave my neck. My beard was now pretty long, and according to Sienna, was the best aphrodisiac ever. I never understood the fascination some women had with beards, but I wasn't one to argue with her, especially after she described herself as *weak* when it came to having sex with me while I had a full beard.

She had proven to be the best possible sexual match for me, and although my deep sexual desires were never met – or even discussed – with Natalie, I had no deep desires with Sienna, everything was a reality.

After shaving my neck, pulling on a pair of jeans, and grabbing a white tee shirt, I walked from the bedroom and into the living room while unfolding the shirt. Sienna appeared comfortable on her back with

167

her Kindle held in the air, still dressed in a pair of pink plaid pajamas and matching pink plaid house shoes. Hanging over her shoulders and draped onto the couch, her hair looked perfect, as always.

Engrossed in her book, and unaware I had even entered the room, she continued to read as I walked across the room. As I pulled the shirt over my head, I paused and said what I was thinking.

"You're pretty," I said.

She lowered her Kindle onto her chest, draped her head over the side of the couch, and cleared her throat. "I'm always prettier with your big dick in my mouth. You know that, right?"

There was no doubt Sienna was different than most women in almost all respects, and sex certainly wasn't excluded from the differences. She didn't care much for me making slow, kind, caring passionate love to her.

Sienna liked being fucked.

And, as fate would have it, I liked fucking her.

I pulled my shirt over my head, unzipped my jeans, and admired her for a short moment. The mid-day sunlight made her hair even more beautiful than it was in its absence. Impatient, as always, she released the Kindle from her grasp, opened her mouth, and extended both her thumbs in the air.

"Do it," she said.

I really didn't need any more of an invitation to stick my cock in her mouth. My only problem, if it was truly a problem, was that I was incapable of lasting more than a few minutes while watching her suck my dick, and for whatever reason, I was incapable of closing my eyes while she did so. It simply felt too damned good and she looked great doing it. As a result, almost immediately following her performance on me orally, I would pull out of her mouth and start fucking her. I suspected she was well aware wrapping her soft lips around the head of my dick wasn't a prerequisite to having sex, but her doing it always seemed to lead to me fucking her.

Her consistent offering to suck my cock stood as a pretty solid indication that she used her oral skills to coerce me to have sex with her.

Either way, the process was something we both seemed to enjoy immensely.

I kicked my jeans to the side, gripped my cock in my hand, and began to stroke it while I walked toward her. Laying on her back with her head dangling off the side of the couch, I knew not only that I'd be able to force myself deep into her throat with her in that position, but that I wouldn't last a matter of minutes.

As I watched the head of my dick slip past her lips, I considered closing my eyes and face fucking her into a whimpering little pile, but I couldn't force myself to either shut my eyes or turn my head the other direction.

She was right.

She *was* prettier with my cock in her mouth.

After a few seconds of her sucking and licking masterfully, I began to buck my hips back and forth. Within ten seconds, I was burying my cock deep in her throat, and she eagerly accepted every inch of it.

Watching my shaft disappear into her mouth provided a sense of satisfaction that was not only sexual, sensual, and fueled my dark and dirty inner being, but provided confirmation of just how compatible we truly were. Sienna liked having my cock in her mouth just as much as I liked it there.

And I *really* liked it there.

169

A few more slow strokes into her mouth, and I felt my scrotum begin to tighten.

"Time to switch it up," I said as I pulled myself from her mouth.

"Fuck my mouth," she said as she turned her head to the side and blinked her big brown eyes. "Please."

"You little fucking tease," I said. "Get up."

"I'm not a tease," she said as she stood, wiping her mouth free of saliva with the back of her hand.

"A tease teases. I want that cock in my mouth," she said as she kicked her shoes to the side and pushed her pajamas and underwear off in one effortless motion.

"I want world peace, and eighty degree median temperature, and gas prices to plummet below a dollar a gallon," I said. "But we don't always get what we want."

She huffed out a sigh, bent over the couch, and acted as though I was cheating her out of something she was truly entitled to. With her cute little ass sticking up in the air, and her pussy right in front of me for the taking, I stroked my cock with one hand and slapped her ass with the other.

"Sorry, but I'm not fucking you from behind," I said.

She glanced over her shoulder and puffed out a pouty lip. "Why?"

I rubbed my beard with my left hand and continued to stroke my cock with my right. "Because I love you."

Her eyes shifted back and forth between my cock and my beard. After glancing at each a few times, she sighed heavily. "If you truly loved me, you'd just shove that in me right now."

I released my cock, reached around her waist, and lifted her from the floor. "When we're done, tell me if you hated this."

"Hate what?" she asked.

I lifted her into my arms fully, walked into her bedroom, and lowered her onto the bed, facing up. As she peered up and into my eyes, I crawled on top of her and began to kiss her deeply. With our lips pressed firmly against each other and our tongues intertwined, she began to moan in pleasure.

Purposefully making sure there was no penetration, at least not yet, I moved my mouth along her jaw and began to kiss her neck while grinding my hips against hers. A quick glance toward her face produced an image of her biting her lip and writhing in suppressed sexual agony.

My mouth slowly slid along her skin from her shoulder to her chest, kissing along the surface of her skin the entire way, and eventually came to a stop at her breasts. Kissing her nipples and massaging her breasts in my hands, I pressed against her firmly and ground my hip bones against hers. In a show of her sexual satisfaction, or quite possibly her frustration, she arched her back and pressed the backs of her shoulders deeply into the comforter. With her perky breast now pushed fully into my mouth, I squeezed the other in my hand and twisted her nipple between my thumb and forefinger.

"Please…" she moaned.

I lifted my free hand to her mouth and covered her lips with my index finger. "Shhh."

I raised myself slightly and worked my way along the length of her body until my mouth met her waiting swollen mound. I slowly began to work my right finger in and out of her wet folds as I sucked and licked her clit with precision.

She bucked her hips against my face and I continued to lick her pussy and suck her clit as if my life depended on it. My tongue as deep as I was able to force it while my finger rhythmically continued to work her into a sexual frenzy quickly proved to be too much for her. A loud wailing sound silenced by a pillow against her face confirmed her satisfaction and having reached climax.

I raised my head in enough time to see her remove the pillow from her face and toss it aside. Her eyes met mine and remained fixed for a moment, but not a word was shared. I admired her beautiful face and allowed her a moment to regain her senses.

Sienna's beauty wasn't simple.

There was no disputing Sienna was a beautiful woman in her outward appearance. Often times, I found myself simply standing and staring at her, incapable of believing she truly existed in the sense she did, and that she did so with such ease.

Her willingness to eagerly participate in the act of living life was testament to her inner beauty. A woman who refused to allow the unfortunate events in her life to bring her down in spirit, she held her head high and lived life completely and to the fullest. Always giving those around her a smile, if for no other reason but to confirm her position on life, she exuded her beauty from her very being.

But nothing Sienna did, believed, or participated in was quite as beautiful as the scent of her having reached climax on my face.

I slowly inhaled a deep breath through my nose, savoring her aroma as I did so. As her head collapsed onto the bed, I carefully crawled on top of her and began to kiss her sensually.

Our mouths pressed against each other and our bodies chest to chest, I continued to kiss her as I guided my stiff cock inside her wetness. As I slowly and silently began to work my hips back and forth, she bit into my lower lip and held her bite, moaning as I continued the steady rhythmic pace.

I slid my hands under her shoulders and held her chest tight against mine, working myself in and out of her warmth in a balanced and predictable motion. Each stroke of my cock was full and forceful, but not abrupt.

After five minutes of my body grinding against her, and our mouths encompassed in a kiss the entire time, she released my lips and tilted her head rearward. As I continued my long, full strokes, I lifted my body from hers, arched my back, and worked my long shaft in and out with a forceful grace.

As I released every drop of my love into her, she relaxed and howled into the room, providing all she needed to confirm she loved me as deeply and as permanently as I loved her. I collapsed on the bed, drained of every ounce of energy, and satisfied completely that I had provided her a powerful message of my love. Eventually her breathing became less intense, and slowed to a steady pace. After a few minutes of silence, she turned toward me and smiled.

"You were right," she said.

I raised my head from the bed and turned toward her as I rested my jaw in my palm. "About what?" I asked.

"I didn't hate that," she said. "Not one bit."

I nodded my head and didn't say a word. I'd proven my point. I didn't hate it either. I knew I wouldn't.

It was the first time we actually made love.

And I tricked her into doing it on Valentine's Day.

Score: Vince 1, Sienna 0.

SIENNA

March 16ᵗʰ, 2015

The routine I had developed over the last nine months not only provided me with a sense of security, but gave me great satisfaction. My adult life, finally, was exactly where I had always hoped it would be. To have everything I had always dreamed of after spending five years doubting it would ever exist made the taste of it all so much sweeter.

I had read half a dozen books a week for as long as I could remember. The count was well into many thousands, and almost all of them had been romance novels. I had never, however, read a book that depicted a relationship or romance as sweet as the one I was living with Vince.

Having been raised by a father who instilled tremendous moral value, a mother who stressed the importance of loyalty and love, and a motorcycle club who required he be strong, fearless, and selfless, Vince was the perfect mixture of what made the perfect man the *perfect* man.

His mother was exactly as I pictured a mother should be; loving, caring, nurturing, demanding at times, sentimental when she needed to be, and funny. At this juncture in our relationship, my friendship I had developed with his mother was almost as important as the relationship I had with Vince.

"Bradley, you know better. Don't 'snatch', it's not polite," she said as she waved her fork in Bradley's direction.

Bradley had just aggressively taken a bite of tamale from Anita's fingers before she told him he could have it. Now sitting on the floor beside her chair trying to decide if he wanted to chew the food and eat it or spit it on the floor, Bradley wallowed the tamale around in his mouth as if he'd been given a rubber ball to eat.

"That dog is going to explode. Who feeds their dog Mexican food? I'll tell you who. Nobody, that's who," Vince said as he grabbed a tamale from the platter.

I shifted my eyes from Vince to Anita and waited for it…

"He wanted a bite," Anita said. "He asked for it."

I bit into my taco and shifted my eyes back to Vince.

"He's a dog, Ma. A *dog*. He didn't look at a menu and see we were having Mexican food and ask for a bite of tamale. He knows we're sitting here eating, and he wanted some of what we were eating, because he's fat and he's always hungry. If he'd have known it was Mexican food, he wouldn't have *asked*," Vince explained.

And, back to Anita.

She pointed her fork at Vince and wagged the end of it up and down. "You know, for as smart as you are, and for as many books as you've read, sometimes you surprise me, Stephen. He knows it's Mexican food, he sat in the kitchen and watched me make each and every bit of it. Long before you were here I might add."

I glanced at Vince.

Vince poked a bite of tamale into his mouth, chewed it, and before he swallowed, spoke over his mouth full of food. "Oh, now he can recognize ingredients, huh?"

"Don't talk with your mouth full, Stephen. I swear, your father would have smacked you for that, and you know it," she said in a scolding tone.

"He knows better, Honey. I'm sorry," Anita said as she patted her hand against my knee.

I turned toward her and smiled. "The food's so good. I love it."

"Why, thank you," she said.

"Watch this," Vince said.

After we both shifted our eyes toward Vince, he reached for the bowl of homemade salsa, scooped out a large spoonful, and held it to his side.

"Bradley!" he said.

Bradley turned, realized he was being offered food, and ran to Vince's side. After flopping his butt down on the floor, he looked at the spoon, looked up at Vince, and barked.

"Come on bud, it's good," Vince said as he wiggled the spoon.

Bradley glanced at the spoon, tilted his head back, and barked again.

"He doesn't like salsa," Anita said.

"Come on bud, *look*," Vince said as he raised the spoon and pretended to eat some of it.

He lowered the spoon to his side again.

Bradley barked.

Vince raised the spoon, dumped the salsa on the side of his plate, and shook his head. "His stomach's bothering him after that tamale."

"Bradley!" Anita said.

Bradley turned, studied what she held in her hand, and upon recognizing it, ran past me toward Anita. As he reached her side, he quickly sat down and tilted his head back slightly. She tossed the piece of tamale in the air and Bradley caught it in mid-flight. After gobbling it up and licking his lips, he glanced toward Vince and me.

"See?" Anita said. "He knows what he likes."

"Tamales," I said with a laugh.

She patted her hand against my knee. "That's right, Honey. He loves the tamales."

"Stephen, you're picking again. Did you eat with those boys before you came?" she asked.

"Ma, how many times do I have to tell you? Sienna and I eat every Sunday. And we ate at noon. It's 5:30 now. So, to answer you, no, I didn't eat with the boys. And I'm not picking, I've had two tacos and two tamales," he said as he poked his fork in his half-eaten tamale and raised it in the air.

"Well, what did you eat for lunch? Maybe you're still full," she said.

Vince sighed and bit into the tamale. "We do this every week, Ma. I'm not full. I'm hungry, and I'm eating."

"You're talking with your mouth full again. That's what you're doing. If that's the type of manners those boys are teaching you, you need to just quit that little club," she said.

Vince swallowed the tamale and took a drink of tea. "I'm not quitting the club, and they're not a bunch of manner lacking pigs."

"How would I know? You never bring them over for dinner. It makes me wonder, Stephen," she said. "I've always wondered."

"Keep wondering. They're *not* coming over," he snapped back. "Not now, not ever."

Uh oh, time to change the subject.

Although Vince was in the MC, and was an active member, he wasn't at all what I expected a member of an MC to be. He went to all the meetings, rode in all the mandatory runs, and sometimes I was convinced he loved his motorcycle more than he loved me, but he wasn't really friends with any of the members. He didn't hang out with them, ride with them, or do anything with them that wasn't mandatory or sanctioned by the club.

He told me he didn't trust them, and I silently wondered why he was in the club with 30 members he didn't trust. He explained the trust of the brotherhood was much different than trusting someone as a friend, and even though they were each his brother, none were his true friend.

It made sense, but it didn't make *perfect* sense.

I suspected, like with all things Vince, he simply didn't want to set himself up for a failure by being misled, lied to, or develop and expectation and have it unmet.

"It's warming up outside, huh?" I said.

"It sure is, Honey," Anita said.

Vince stood from his seat. "I've got to go to the bathroom, excuse me."

"You're excused, Dear," his mother said.

After he walked away, Anita patted me on the leg. I turned toward her and grinned, assuming she was going to say something about Bradley eating tamales, but that wasn't the case. What she chose to share with me provided considerable insight to Vince, and why he was the way he was about *some* things. As she covered the side of her mouth to speak, I knew what she was going to say was about Vince, but only after she proceeded to speak in a light whisper, did I realized the significance of what she was telling me.

"When Stephen was a little boy, he had very close friend. He was the cutest little boy, and so polite, his name was Jackson. They were inseparable. The little boy had a heart condition, and we all knew it, but it wasn't something we ever *discussed*. You know, as parents we think those things will always work themselves out. Well, he lived down the block," she said, pausing and pointing over her shoulder.

"Three houses down. They started kindergarten on the same day, and were together until third grade. The bus picked them up at the corner. I think Stephen was nine and Jackson was ten at the time." She lowered her fork to her plate, leaned forward, and peered through the doorway to confirm Vince wasn't coming.

"He died that summer. Vince hasn't had a friend since. Not a single one. And when *that woman*…when she cheated on him? I thought he'd never be the same. The two people he opened up to and chose to let into his life had both let him down. I guess they were each for separate reasons, but he didn't see it as different. You know, he looks at things differently than most, and I blame it on him losing Jackson," she said.

Vince hadn't told me about his friend. As with many things from childhood, I suspected it may have been something he chose to forget, but I doubted that was the case. More than likely he remembered it, and the memory of losing a loved one and a cherished friend at such a young age not only affected Vince then, but still affected him today.

"That's so sad," I said. "I'm so sorry."

"So were we, Honey. They moved out right after. We lost them all. The Smiths. A wonderful couple and a wonderful little boy," she said.

As soon as she finished speaking, Vince walked back into the dining room. I turned toward him and forced myself to smile the best I was able.

"I love you," I said.

It wasn't all I could offer him, but it was the best I could do. I meant it, and I wanted him to know it. He needed to know it, understand it, and hopefully believe it.

"I love you, too," he said with a smile as he sat down.

I told myself as I watched him prepare another taco that regardless of how bad things ended up, or how difficult life became that I would always be there for Vince. I would be the one person in his life that would never let him down.

And all I could hope was that one day he would be able to realize my devotion, my sincerity, and my need to have him as my significant other.

At that moment, and forever.

VINCE

April 7th, 2014

Never let your guard down. I have no idea how many times my father had told me that, but it was a phrase not only that I remembered, but something I applied in my day-to-day activities, and it proved to be some of the best advice I ever received.

"How bad?" Axton asked.

I shrugged my shoulders. "Pretty bad."

"Well, fuck, Vince. Your definition of 'pretty bad' and mine might be different. Let's hear it," he said as he sat down.

I pulled the chair away from the edge of the table and hesitated. Although I was proud that I wasn't hurt, and thankful I was aware enough of my surroundings to recognize what was happening at the time, I wasn't proud of what happened.

"Broke out most of his teeth, at least the ones you can see when a guy smiles, anyway. Said I broke his jaw in a couple places, and broke his ankle," I said.

Axton stood from his seat, crossed his arms in front of his chest, and shook his head from side-to-side. After inhaling a long breath, he exhaled a whistle. "God damn, Vince. And how in the fuck did you break his ankle?"

"When he came up behind me. I flipped him over my shoulder. He landed pretty bad on the table and all," I said.

"Right there in the restaurant?" he asked. "Broad fucking daylight? This fucker just comes up behind you with a gun and tries to rob you?"

I shook my head. "Wasn't really a robbery. He was mad about me taking the money I took from him on a deal from about a year ago and was trying for a little *get back*. Little more than ten grand, and he sure didn't want to give it up at the time. He kept going on and on about how if I took the money it was going to cause the whole snowball effect and shit. Goes without saying I took it anyway. Guess he just saw me and recognized me."

"And that girl? She wasn't there?" he asked.

I shook my head. "Nope. Actually I was in there looking for someone else."

"Work?" Axton asked.

"Yep," I said with a nod.

"So in three months you've shot some prick, killed him, and beat some other poor bastard half to death, leaving him in intensive care in the hospital. And, to top it all off, when this shit happens, nobody can help you, you can't help yourself, and the club's got our pants around our fucking ankles and our asses in the breeze..." he said.

"Is that what this is about?" I said through my teeth as I stood from my seat.

"I haven't said shit yet, Vince. Now sit the fuck down!" he demanded.

I stood for a moment, glared at him, and eventually sat down. Axton had called me to the clubhouse to have a talk, and although I suspected he wanted to talk about the incident, I had no idea he was going to make it *club business*.

"So what are you trying to say?" I asked.

"I'm not *trying* to say a damned thing. What I *was* saying was this; the business you're in is *your* business, at least until it becomes a problem for the club. Your business isn't a problem for the club…" he paused and lowered his arms as he sat down.

He locked eyes with me and leaned forward, resting his forearms on the table. "Yet."

"At the rate you're going, you're going to be on the news more than Bret fucking Baier, and it's going to become a problem if the club's brought into it," he continued.

I kept my eyes locked on his and leaned into the edge of the table. I respected Axton, but no one was going to intimidate me, including him. "Anybody named the club yet? Ever?" I asked.

He shook his head. "That's not the point…"

"It sure as fuck is," I interrupted.

"Slow down, Vince. God fucking damn, we're on the same team here, you hot-headed prick. Jesus H. Christ," he paused and pulled the rubber band tight, released it, and snapped it into his wrist.

After snapping it again, he fixed his eyes on mine. "Here, let me say this before you fucking explode again. Don't wear your cut when you're *working*. And, it goes without saying, nothing with the club name on it. Just while you're working," he said.

He leaned back in his seat and glared.

"I don't," I said.

"Ever?" he asked.

"Never. Not fucking once," I said.

"Well," he said as he raised his hands in the air. "Looks like we're all good."

"That it?" I asked as I stood from my seat.

He shook his head from side-to-side and rubbed the few days of growth on his face. "No. There's one more thing."

I gazed down at him and widened my eyes. "And?"

"A phone. I know you got rid of your phone after Natalie and you split up, but…"

"We didn't *split up*. I divorced her," I said.

"I swear. You're one difficult motherfucker. Nobody here is out to get you," he said.

I crossed my arms in front of my chest and shook my head. "Never said anybody was out to fucking get me."

"Sit down. You make me nervous looming over me like that," he said.

I sat down and glared in his direction.

"You didn't have to say you felt like anyone was out to get you. You fucking *act* like it. Now this brings up *another* thing. Answer this. When was the last time you did *anything* with *anyone* in the club that wasn't mandatory?" he asked.

I shrugged my shoulders and glanced around the room. After a moment of calming down, I turned my eyes toward Axton.

"When was the last time you did anything with anyone except with the five or six motherfuckers you run with? Fucking *never*. You gonna tell me who I got to run with now?" I asked.

"That wasn't what I was…" He paused and shook his head, obviously frustrated. It made two of us.

He glared at me as he responded. "To answer your question, no I'm not going to tell you who to run with. Who you run with is your business."

"That it?" I asked as I pushed myself away from the table.

"Get a phone," he said.

"Excuse me?" I asked.

"You tossed your phone in the bon fire after you found those text messages from Natalie on it. We all figured you'd get one after a while, and we're coming up on two years here pretty quick, and you still don't have a god damned phone. What if someone needs to get ahold of you?" he asked.

I stood from my seat, turned toward the door, and took a few steps. After exhaling what little breath I had in my lungs, I turned to face him.

"Anybody I care about needs anything from me, they know how to find me," I said.

And I walked out the door.

SIENNA

May 8th, 2015

Vince and I had known each other for almost a year. The last eleven months had flown by – quicker than any other time in my life – and I wondered if a life with Vince was just going to whoosh past, leaving me with many memories and no real recollection of where all the time had gone.

Spending time with Vince was like watching an action packed movie or reading a fabulous book; it passed at three or four times faster than any other time. I loved the watch he bought me for Christmas more than anything, but if we were out on a date all I had to do was look at it, and I was immediately reminded that the night was all but over.

It was apparent the satisfying things in life caused my mind to relax, and the passage of time was immeasurably fast when my mind was less resistant to what was being processed. Life's stressful events made me tense, and when I was stressed out the clock seemed to stand still, making my shitty days last forever and my great ones over before they ever got a good start. Life would be so much more enjoyable if the tables were turned; and the memorable times seemed to last forever, leaving the tension filled days to blow past like speeding freight train.

As I heard the rumble of the motorcycle's exhaust, I grabbed my purse and ran to the door. I pulled the door closed and turned toward the street just in time to see him come around the corner and accelerate toward my house.

Riding on Vince's motorcycle was one of my favorite things ever, and even though it was ugly to look at, it was delightful to ride on. Mentally, I compared his motorcycle to oatmeal; something grotesque to stare at, but one thing I clearly couldn't imagine life without.

As he pulled into the driveway I jumped off the porch, hurried down the walk, and stood by the garage door waiting. He slowed down, turned around in the drive, and faced the street. With the change of weather from winter to a very warm spring, his thick beard was long gone, and he was back to having nothing but short stubble on his face. Sad that my beard porn winter was over, but enjoying his new look, I lifted my leg over the seat and got on.

"Glasses," he said over his shoulder.

Shit.

I opened my purse, grabbed my glasses, and put them on. Remembering all of the things I had to do when riding the motorcycle didn't come naturally to me, because I didn't ride on it often enough. I did always remember that I needed to hang onto him to keep from falling off, but each time Vince pulled out of my driveway, I made it a point not to, because it felt like riding a rollercoaster when I teetered back in the seat as he pulled away. And he always pulled out of my driveway slowly, which allowed me to enjoy the feeling each time.

After placing my feet on the rear pegs, I tapped him on the shoulder and kissed his cheek.

"Ready," I said as I lifted my hands out to my side and closed my eyes.

He pulled out of the driveway slowly; causing me to rock back in the seat and making me feel as if I was riding an amusement park ride. As I opened my eyes and grabbed him around the waist, he accelerated up the block, leaving me to wonder if he realized I enjoyed coming out of the driveway slowly, and he purposely did so for a that reason alone.

It seemed Vince knew everything, so I chose not to ask, deciding he did what he did for a reason.

As we rolled to a stop at the end of the block, Vince tilted his head to the side. "There's this cool little place in Andover. It has a pretty small selection, but it's great food. Guy started out on one of those little street vendor grilles with fucking wheels on it."

He glanced in either direction, and pulled away from the stop sign gradually. "Maybe fifteen minutes to get there, sound good?"

I didn't ever care what I ate with Vince, simply being with him was enough. Hell, he could starve me, and as long as I was starving with him, I really wouldn't care.

I leaned forward and rested my chin on his shoulder. "Sounds great."

"Andover it is," he said, twisting the throttle a little more after he spoke.

I gripped him a little bit tighter and pulled my chest tight to his back. Feeling my body against his provided a level of comfort I had not previously known. It didn't matter if he was hugging me, making love to me, or we were riding on the motorcycle, but when our bodies were touching and I was positively held in place, I felt as if nothing could harm me.

With Vince as my lover, I felt the only person who could harm me was me.

What seemed like five minutes and very little traffic later, we pulled into a small and rather sparsely occupied strip mall. At the far end was a small restaurant with a nice unoccupied covered seating area outside. As Vince came to a stop in a parking stall adjacent to the restaurant, I envisioned us sitting alone in the outdoor patio, talking and eating while enjoying the warm western evening sun.

We walked to the door side by side, and Vince pulled against the handle. The door rattled, but didn't open. He pulled against it again, rattling the windows of the storefront.

We both gazed through the tinted glass into the restaurant. Everything was in place, but it was obviously closed. It seemed odd on a Friday night that the restaurant would be closed, but that sure seemed to be the case.

I studied the sign positioned above the door, grabbed my phone, and Googled the name of the restaurant.

"Closed. Says it right here. All of his restaurants are closed, this one was the last, it closed just yesterday," I said, pointing to the screen of my phone.

"Motherfucker!" he shouted as he kicked the frame of the door.

From the force of his kick, the glass door flexed inward terribly. As it bowed back outward, it opened.

"Oh my god," I said as I glanced over each shoulder. "Did you break it?"

"No," he said as he kicked it again playfully. "These aluminum framed doors are pieces of shit."

He gripped the door frame in his hand and pointed to the latch, which was still in place. "The slightest flex in the frame and they open, it's a bad design."

"Oh," I said, as I studied the door.

I turned to face him and shrugged my shoulders. "So now what?"

He pulled the door open and peered inside. A quick glance over his shoulders later, he stepped inside the vacant restaurant. "Come on."

I gazed the length of the parking lot. The half a dozen or so shops, which included a nail salon, a gaming store, and a frozen yogurt shop, all had very little business. A few passing cars were in the street, but no one was actually in the parking lot, only a few parked cars and Vince's bike.

Not wanting to say no, and rather intrigued by the abandoned restaurant, I followed him through the door. With my heart beat steadily increasing with each step; I gazed around the empty establishment, staying a few steps behind him. The restaurant consisted of one large room, filled with eight booths, eight tables, and a small kitchen which was exposed and open for the patrons of the restaurant to view while dining. It was more upscale than I suspected it would be, considering its location. As I turned and looked at the artwork still hanging on the walls, I couldn't help but wonder if the location was part of the reason it closed. Such a nice place in a small town outside of the city, and in a rundown shopping mall, it seemed a strange choice for the location. I glanced toward a few of the tables, their chairs askew, wondering if people left in a hurry or were ushered out after a grand closing complete with wine, live music, and streamers dangling from the ceiling. It seemed strange having full access to the place, knowing at one point it was a thriving business filled with lovers, businessmen, and the occasional debt collecting biker.

"Well I'll be damned," Vince said, causing me to shift my focus daydreaming to him.

He pointed to a single bottle of wine below the wine rack, sitting in a wine cooler. "There's one bottle…"

"What is it?" I asked.

He shrugged his shoulders, opened the door of the small cooler, and handed it to me.

"It's a 2006 Schiopetto Pinot Grigio," I said. "Most wine connoisseurs wouldn't admit to *loving* this, but it's a great wine."

He pulled two glasses from the overhead rack, blew away what little dust may have been inside, and began to hunt for a corkscrew. After a short search, he found one and uncorked the bottle.

After pouring the wine, he lifted a glass and gazed into it. "Want a taste"

As I chuckled at his question, my mouth began to water. "Really? You're asking me if I want some wine?"

Dressed in his cut, a snow white tee shirt, jeans, and his leather boots, he seemed out of place standing in the end of the kitchen with a glass of wine in his hand. Truth be told, we both seemed out of place in the closed restaurant. We seemed like criminals.

After sip of the wine, it really didn't seem to matter much. The wine was chilled perfectly, and was quite tasty. Somewhat disappointed we didn't at least have an appetizer or something to nibble on while we drank it, I fixed my eyes on the small stainless steel refrigerator a few feet to Vince's right.

"What's in the fridge?" I asked. "Anything?"

He took a sip of wine, walked to the refrigerator, and opened the door. "Looks like some white cheese, some leafy shit, a bag of tomatoes and that's about it. Maybe something left over from an appetizer or something."

He slammed the door of the refrigerator and turned to face me.

"Let me see it," I said as I stepped around him.

I opened the refrigerator. Fresh Basil, Roma tomatoes, and a few pounds of fresh mozzarella were on the bottom shelf of the refrigerator, just as Vince said. No doubt left over from the previous nights closing, it appeared fresh and seemed like a great idea.

A few seconds later, and I had found appetizer plates, a sharp knife, and balsamic vinegar. While I sipped my wine, I prepared two plates and walked to where Vince still stood.

"Viola!" I said as I handed him a plate.

"Does this shit even go together?" he asked.

"Try it," I said as I picked up a piece of the appetizer I had prepared.

"All together?" he asked.

"Just like they're layered," I said as I lifted mine in the air.

I ate the cheese, tomato, and basil leaf in one bite and after swallowing it, took a drink of wine.

"Heaven," I sighed.

Vince did the same. "Damn, pretty good stuff. You're handy as fuck."

"Blind luck they left that stuff there," I said.

We carried our plates, the bottle of wine, and the glasses to one of the many empty tables. Although it might not have appealed to just any woman, having wine and an appetizer with Vince in a restaurant we had broken into was romantic.

We were alone, the place was only lighted by the indirect sunlight, and it was quiet. As we sat and talked, drinking our wine and sharing cheese, a few cars came and went in the parking lot, but as far as I was concerned, we were alone in a perfect sense.

As the bottle of wine produced its last drop, I glanced at my watch, well aware we would need to leave soon. Three hours had passed since we had left my house, further proof of my belief that time with Vince passed at a drastically rapid rate.

"I've got to pee," I said as I glanced around dining area.

"The hallway in the rear," he said as he tossed his head to the side.

I walked to the rear of the restaurant and into the hallway. The first door I reached was the men's restroom, and although I fully realized I never would have considered doing it in any other circumstance, I always wanted to see what the inside of the men's bathroom looked like.

Fully expecting to have to hover over the dirty toilet, but far too curious not to go inside, I pushed the door open, knowing no one was going to come inside.

Surprised at the cleanliness of the restroom, I peed, washed my hands, and pulled out a towel from the dispenser. I tossed it toward the trash can receptacle, missed, and walked toward the corner to pick it up.

A small brown bag lay on the floor beside the trash can with my wadded paper beside it. I picked up both, tossed the tissue in, and began to wad the bag into a ball. As I smashed the brown paper sack, a receipt fell out onto the floor.

Naturally, I picked it up, and even more naturally – at least for me – I looked at it. The receipt was date and time stamped, and from a local upscale grocery store close to Vince's mother's home. I stared down at the receipt and did the math for military time, which never quite came natural for me.

16:44 5.8.2015

The receipt was for the bottle of wine, basil, tomatoes, and cheese. And the items were purchased at 4:44 pm, roughly a half hour before Vince showed up to pick me up.

The entire night wasn't happenstance, he had planned it.

I folded the receipt, shoved it into the pocket of my shorts, and looked at myself in the mirror. The woman who looked back was happy, beautiful, and very much in love. I grinned at her, opened the door and stepped out into the hallway.

Still sitting at the table, holding his half-full glass of wine under his nose, Vince didn't look the part of a romantic, at least not in the big picture. He looked like he wanted the world to see him.

Like the bad ass, take no shit, don't fucking look at me or I'll rip your head off, tattooed biker that he was.

He was those things, but he was so much more.

He was kind, sincere, and filled with devotion to the woman he loved.

And that woman just so happened to be me.

VINCE

May 8ᵗʰ, 2015

I watched as she walked down the hallway toward where I was seated. A firm believer that she was without a doubt the most beautiful creature God had ever created, I sat and admired her without trying to bring attention to the fact I was doing so. Watching her simply meander from point "A" to point "B", for me, had to be comparable to what most men experienced watching a Victoria's Secret runway show.

"I love you," she said as she stepped to my side.

I leaned forward, kissed her lightly, and gazed at her admiringly as I pulled my lips from hers.

"I love you," she said. "Very much."

"So, you ready to get out of here?" I asked as I picked up the glasses and plates from the table.

She placed her hands on her hips and arched her back slightly. "I don't think so," she said.

"Oh no?" I asked as I walked toward the kitchen.

I placed the dirty dishes in the sink, turned to face her, and shrugged my shoulders. "I think it was a great evening here. Kind of romantic, if you ask me."

"It was," she said. "It was *very* romantic."

"What are we going to do now?" I asked as I motioned around the room. "Here?"

She twisted back and forth on the balls of her feet, her hands still pressed against her hips. "Well, I'm going to suck that big cock of yours. I don't care what you do."

"Oh are you?" I asked.

She nodded her head, reached behind her head with both hands, and tightened her ponytail.

"Yep. Sure am," she said as she lowered her hands.

With her eyes fixed on mine, she began to walk in my direction. The entire twenty or so feet, she maintained eye contact, walking slowly and gracefully. She stopped mere inches from where I was standing, still gazing into my eyes, and lowered herself onto her knees, her eyes locked on mine the entire time.

By the time she reached me, my dick was fighting against the fabric of the denim jeans, aching to be released.

Without speaking, I unbuckled my belt, unzipped my pants, and pulled out my cock, gazing into her eyes as I did so.

She took me in her hand, and while still looking up at me intently, licked the pre-cum from the tip of my dick, leaving a small strand of it connecting her tongue to the head for a long second before it finally fell, only to be caught by her hand and lifted to her mouth.

As she licked her hand, it was over for me. I couldn't take it any longer. Seeing her doing what she was doing was far too much for me, and on this particular night, although I wasn't drunk, I was well aware I wouldn't make it a matter of minutes.

Sienna was much too sexy of a woman.

I bent my knees slightly, reached down and slipped my hands under her armpits, and as she began to encompass the swollen head in with her lips, I lifted her from her knees and to her feet.

"What?" she asked innocently.

"Don't even start," I said. "You know *what*. You do that shit on purpose, you sexy little bitch."

She pressed the tip of her index finger to her lips, doing her best to look innocent, but appeared to be as guilty as she truly was. "I just love that big cock of yours, that's all," she said.

"And I love that tight little pussy of yours," I said as I lifted her in the air.

Her eyes met mine as I hoisted her above the floor and held her in the air, her feet dangling six inches from the floor.

"What are you going to do to me, you big mean biker?" she asked in another effort to be as innocent as she could in appearance.

"Whatever I want to," I said as I held her in place.

"Please don't fuck me," she whispered. "I just wanted to suck your cock. Please don't fuck me."

"You afraid?" I asked.

She gazed down at my cock, feigned a gasp, and covered her mouth quickly. "It's too big. It won't fit in my little pussy. I'm scared."

I lowered her to the floor. As her feet made contact with the concrete, I began to stroke my cock. Her innocent routine had me so worked up I'd be lucky to last a matter of minutes. I unbuttoned my cut, took off my shirt, and draped them over the back of a chair.

"You're so muscular. Oh *no*, you're not going to make me fuck you, are you? Please, don't make me fuck you. You're so big and muscular," she said as she widened her eyes and stared at my chest.

"Get undressed," I said as I pointed toward her shorts.

"But my pussy, it's so tight, you'll hurt me," she said in a high-pitched whine as she turned away.

"I'll hurt you if you don't get undressed," I growled.

"Yes, Sir," she said. "I'll do whatever you say."

I shook my head at her innocent little girl efforts. "Toss your clothes on the table and bend over," I said.

"Anything you say, just don't hurt me," she said softly as she pushed her shorts down her thighs.

"Leave on the shoes," I said as I pointed to her sneakers.

"Please let me take them off, I don't want you to fuck me in my shoes," she whimpered. "I'm so scared…"

I shook my head, pointed at the table, and cleared my throat. "Bend over."

"Please, please don't fuck me from behind. Pleeeaaaaaase, I'm begging you. It'll go too deep," she whined as she pulled down her panties and tossed them on the table.

"Bend over," I said in a demanding tone.

"But you're too big. You'll hurt me. You'll tear my little pussy up," she said as she bent over and pressed her tits into the top of the table.

My jeans had been around my thighs the entire time. As she turned to face away from me, I kicked off my boots and dropped my jeans to the floor. Now standing naked with the exception of my socks, I was well beyond ready to start fucking.

Without warning, I swept my foot against the inside of each of her feet, spread her legs apart slightly, and guided the head of my stiff cock inside of her at the same time. With the feeling of her tight wet pussy surrounding the shaft, I slowly pushed myself into her until I bottomed out.

"Oh, god," she gasped. "You're way too big."

I pulled my hips back, revealing my glistening cock one inch at a time. As I watched it slide free of her wet folds, I realized I had no business watching. Keeping my eyes open while I fucked Sienna was becoming a huge problem. She was turning me into a twat in more ways than one, the primary being I was far too deeply in love with her, and the secondary was without a doubt the fact she was more beautiful than any other woman on earth. Hell, I couldn't even give her a good fucking and enjoy seeing it. Frustrated at the thought of me becoming soft, and feeling the need to give her a good hard fucking, I needed her to stop with the "I'm a tight-pussied little girl" routine.

It was just too much.

"Just stop it," I sighed.

She turned and glanced over her shoulder. "Stop what?"

I leaned forward, gazed down toward her ass, and watched my cock disappear into her tight hole.

I should have turned away.

"Oh, god. You're too big, please, please, Sir. Let me go. Don't fuck my tight little pussy any more, I'm begging you," she pouted.

You really need to stop that.

I grasped her waist in my hands, pulled my hips back, and as soon as I felt the head clear her pussy lips, pushed my hips forward again. As I felt her warmth surround the shaft, I pulled back again.

I can do this. I can do this.

I pushed myself inside her until I felt myself bottom out.

"Please, let me go. Your cock is way too big, you're going to rip my little pussy to shreds," she whimpered.

You ornery little bitch…

I reached down, grabbed her ponytail in my hand, and pulled against it tight. As her back arched slightly, I pressed my hips against her ass, held them in place, and began to grind my cock in and out of her. With my free hand, I reached around and cupped my palm against her mouth.

Fucking her deeply with her hair pulled tight, I tightened my grip on her mouth, preventing her from saying a word. Her muffled grunts against my hand, our fucking each other in an abandoned restaurant, the setting sun, and the fact her pussy really was tiny and tight was slowly working against me. I needed to close my eyes.

Fuck it.

I love this woman, what's it really matter.

"Take that big cock, little girl," I bellowed as I pounded it deep in her pussy.

She grunted against my hand.

"That's right. You're getting that big biker dick now, aren't you? And there isn't a god damned thing you can do about is, is there?" I grunted.

I pressed my chest to her back and moved my face beside hers. She turned her head to the side and widened her eyes. I pressed my hand against her mouth, continuing to muffle her voice into nothing but grunts.

"Fuck no there isn't. You're fucked. I'm taking that pussy whether you like it or not," I growled into her ear.

"Because I can," I whispered.

I began to fuck her hard, fast, and without reservation. The sound of my hips slapping against her ass echoed down the empty corridor. With each stroke *in*, I pulled her hair back, causing her to arch her back even more.

"You helpless little girl, what are you going to do to stop me? Huh?"

I barked as I continued to fuck her.

"Nothing. That's what I thought," I said through my teeth as I worked myself in and out of her tight twat.

And I released her mouth from my grasp.

"Holy shit," she wailed.

Instantly, her breathing became irregular and she began to grind her hips against me. Within a few seconds I felt her pussy contracting around my swollen shaft. I felt the tension building within me with each stroke, and I knew it would only be a matter of time…

"I'm going to come in you," I said.

"Please don't," she breathed. "Please…let me…let me go…"

And that was it.

I arched my back, held my cock deep, and as she began to cry out into the room in pleasure, I erupted inside of her, filling her with all the proof I could that I felt the way I felt about her.

After we both collapsed onto the table and lay side by side breathing like we'd just finished a marathon, she turned her head to the side and gave her best pouty face.

"You don't play fair," she said, her bottom lip pushed out as far as she could push it.

I raised my head slightly and gazed down at her. "And you do?"

"I'm just a little girl," she said with a laugh. "With a really tight pussy and a willing throat…"

I gazed down at my twitching cock. Just like that, she made me want more of her tight little pussy. She was clearly in control of my cock.

There was no doubt I was a big mean motherfucker in the eyes of the fellas and in the minds of all who encountered me. There weren't a handful of men on earth who I believed could beat me in a fist fight, and none could handle a knife better than me.

But Sienna was turning me into a sexual twat with little stamina and no self-control, and there wasn't a damned thing I could do about it.

Damn I love this woman.

SIENNA

May 10th, 2015

Throughout our relationship, I continued to one-click and read romance novels like an addict, my actions mirroring a meth-head hitting the pipe. I had always wondered if anyone on earth had the same problem with buying and reading books that I had, but at this point in my life I doubted anyone was as bad as I was.

I believed I initially started reading love stories to dream. The books were like fuel for my internal fire; giving me hope, providing me an outlet, and allowing me to live through the characters in the books in a manner I was incapable of living without them. Through the books, I was able to live in various places, experience exposure to a very diverse group of people, and do so in the comfort of my home without fear, worry, or ridicule. To me books were like magic, and the authors were nothing short of genius.

After I met Vince, I knew I was living a dream and had no real need to continue to read about it, so I wondered if my reading pace would slow. It didn't. Reading the books now, I didn't dream as much, but I made comparisons.

And none of the men in my love stories could compare to the reality of Vince.

But it was still fun letting them try.

I lifted the bottle to my lips, held it in place, and stared at the monitor.

Inside Vera, by Claire Puckett, is nothing short of a masterpiece.

I began the book and quickly found a down to earth relatable hero, and a heroine who didn't whine, bitch or do dumb shit. With my interest piqued, I continued.

The story unfolded at a quick pace, following each of them through their respective lives in a first person alternating POV format.

Finding a different voice for each character must be a difficult task, because many authors simply change the name of the character at the beginning of the chapter, but in the absence of that one declaration, the characters seem to be the same. The personality, the speech, and the characteristics mimic the character in the previous chapter. Many male authors writing female leads are unaware of the female mind's differences, and many female authors write male characters that seem feminine.

Claire hits it out of the fucking park.

A boxer running from his past meets a girl who should be running but isn't (at least physically). She doesn't realize it, but she is running farther and farther with each passing day, convinced she is loyal to her spouse.

She is loyal, but she's fading fast.

The problem is that her husband is an abusive dick. Not the type of abuse that a woman soon recovers from; more the type that requires sunglasses to cover up.

The ancillary characters in the book are almost as interesting as the mains, with the exception of one. The best friend of the boxer needs a book of his own (Claire, I'm begging you…)

The book continues to follow the life of the boxer and the life of the abused woman, until their lives collide one day.

And collide they do.

I cheered, I screamed, I hid under my covers. I almost pissed my pants. I cheered again. I actually stood in the boxing ring. Yes, in the fucking ring; sweat dripping from my chin, my muscles aching, and waited for the opening to swing the perfect right cross into the jaw of my opponent.

The book detail sheet said three hundred pages. I was certain it was more like fifty pages. Hell, I'd finished it in thirty minutes, I was sure. I glanced at my watch and eight hours had passed.

And, as satisfied as I was, I wanted more.

swallows heavily and takes drink of wine

I grinned, took a long drink from the bottle, swallowed it, and took another. I hoped Claire herself would read the review and appreciate it, but I doubted that would be the case. What was more important to me was that everyone on Goodreads was able to understand my position on the book, and consider reading it. Hopefully, if they did they would enjoy it as much as I did.

I took another drink, set the bottle aside, and stared down at the keyboard. After a moment of thought, I continued.

So, I'll close by saying this. The author made me fall in love with a bald-headed 220 pound hot-tempered thug who uses pruning shears to resolve his frustrations (read the book). I would have never guessed anyone could have caused me to feel this level of emotion for such a man, but she did.

For her ability to tell a story such as this, keeping my interest and making me cry the entire trip, all the while using characters that are clearly unconventional, I give five stars.

For making me fall in love with aforementioned bald guy, two more.

For the perfect ending, two more.

And, for taking me into a sport I know nothing of and making me feel like I know everything about boxing, another.

So….

On a five star scale, I give ten.

Thank you, Claire.

Thank you.

I stopped typing, studied the screen for a moment, and pressed the button to publish my review. Half a bottle of wine and two reviews later, and I was down to my last review. Of all the books I had read in the last year, I wanted to review this one the least. It was an awful book, terribly disturbing, and not something I would have ever continued to read had I not been persuaded to do so by the author. The thought of writing the review made me feel ill, hence saving it for last.

As much enjoyment as I got out of writing reviews, and as entertaining as I found drafting them to be, one thing I always felt terrible about was when an author asked me personally to read and review a book, and the book ended up being awful. Typically, when I received a book I simply couldn't get interested in, or if I found it to be poorly written, or something I simply felt I would be incapable of reviewing honestly, I would attempt to get the author to allow me to *not* review the book.

No harm, no foul, so to speak.

Well, on this particular book, the author refused my request to not review the book, stating that he wanted the book reviewed regardless. In fact, even after I reluctantly finished the book and *still* didn't want to review it, he insisted on it.

I want your opinion, he said.

Believe me, you don't, I responded.

Yet, he insisted.

I walked to the kitchen, realized I was just north of a drunken mess, and opened bottle number two. I fully realized I didn't *need* any more wine, but I wanted more. I removed the cork, poured a glass, and re-corked the bottle.

That'll make sure I don't overdo it.

I slid the bottle to the side, took a sip from my glass, and stumbled toward the room.

After drinking half the glass of wine in one slurp, I pushed it to the side and began to type.

A Man, a Woman, and a Knife, by Alton Parsons was a book I would not normally read. At the insistence of the author, I went against the grain of my comfort zone and read the book for review.

And.

I can't brush my teeth enough or drink enough wine to get the foul taste out of my mouth.

bile rises in throat

Thinking about this book is making me sick, which is typically okay, but there was no real reason for the scenes that are making me sick to have been in the book. They served no purpose whatsoever.

Don't get me wrong, I like dark reads. I like books that make me check and double check my front and back doors to make sure they're locked. I like books that make me cringe, and I love books that make me cough up matter that I wish would have stayed in my stomach.

But.

I despise books that have subject matter randomly inserted into them for no reason, and were clearly done for shock value alone.

In considering what to type next, I began thinking about the book. Thinking about the book caused me to get angry, and my anger immediately turned to thirst. I finished my glass of wine, walked to the kitchen and poured another. Half a glass later, and I was back to writing my review.

"Show, don't tell", is good advice to all authors. I have always felt the author should allow the reader into the mind of the character, to some degree. But. Don't tell me he's angry, have him cross his arms and kick a rock. Don't tell me "it was a terribly hot day in Atlanta", tell me "my breath was nearly sucked from my lungs as we walked out of the airport, and the sun bore down on us like a heavy weight as we walked what seemed like a mile and a half to the parking garage..."

This book is so full of purple prose that it made reading it feel as if I was being told a story in detail in lieu of seeing it happen in my mind.

And, it was full, and I do mean FULL of two hundred pages of graphically detailed violence that need not be in it to tell the story.

After the first chapter I fully understood Barton Sole was an animal, a psychopath, and that he had a temper like a human Tasmanian devil. But to continue to beat a dead horse (or in this case, beat a dead prostitute) in the manner the he did (through, of course, the author's tale) until her skull was in pieces on the floor and brain matter was on the walls...

I lifted my glass and took another drink.

And another.

And then it was gone. I half crawled half stumbled to the kitchen, poured the last of the wine into my glass, and zig-zagged back to my room. After pouring half the wine on my pajamas and the other half down my throat, I began typing.

Fine.

The first time, I felt it was okay. A little graphic, but I lived with it because it allowed me to FULLY understand the man was a fucking lunatic.

But, the sixteen additional chapters telling detail upon detail of "I'm so angry I think the only way to diffuse this situation is to bash in the skull of another prostitute" is taking it a bit too far.

The story told could have been done in eighteen pages (I highlighted each one). Three hundred and three pages were useless graphic bullshit. In short, the book could have been edited down to roughly twenty pages at most, including the ridiculous preface and prologue.

Bottom line?

This book was nothing short of a disaster.

One star.

Because I have to give it something to get this review to post (you asked, Alton)

I did my best to read the review, and as the monitor's screen began to sway back and forth in my field of vision, published it.

As I stood from my chair and reached for my wine, I fell against the desk, almost tipped over, and eventually ended up lowering myself to the floor rather gracefully, considering all things. After crawling to my bed and climbing up on it, I relaxed into a spinning room.

I hate that fucking book.

I covered my eyes with my pillow...

VINCE

May 10th, 2015

One thing I never expected to happen with Sienna was to be stood up. Not in a million years would I have thought I would have been left looking like a fool, but then again…

It had only been a year.

It took me fifteen years to determine my wife was incapable of keeping her promises. Learning after a year should be considered a blessing.

I left my mother's home after an embarrassing one-sided conversation which lasted all evening. After fidgeting with the food for an hour and a half only to force myself to swallow a few small pieces, I finally left and rode my bike to Sienna's home, praying I would find an answer.

What I found was an empty house free of any signs of life. All interior lights were off, the porch light was off, and although I spent nothing short of a half hour beating on the front and rear doors, no one answered the door.

Two women had been allowed into my life. In return for my loyalty I received two broken promises.

And one broken heart.

Bile rose in my throat. I raised my hand to knock again and realized I was shaking terribly. I inhaled a deep breath through my nose, gazed down at the toes of my boots, and exhaled. The bile rose again. I turned toward the driveway, walked to my bike, and lifted my leg over the seat. As I sat staring out into the street, I knew if I left it would be the last time I would ever pull away from her house.

She had done the unthinkable.

In Sienna's own words, what had happened was the *unexpected result of the natural development of life.*

At least now, when it came to women, I would know what to expect.

Broken promises.

I started the motorcycle, pulled in the clutch lever, and kicked the lever into gear. After a long hesitation and a more than ample amount of time, I released the clutch and pulled out into the street.

Alone.

SIENNA

May 11, 2015

I opened my eyes, rolled onto my side, and tried to make sense of why my mouth felt like I had someone else's tongue in it. My mouth was dry, I felt like I'd been ran over by a truck, and I could feel my heart beating in my eyes.

I drank way too much wine.

With the room illuminated naturally by the setting sun, I narrowed my eyes and studied my surroundings as if they were unfamiliar. A quarter of a glass of wine sat on my desk beside my monitor, which had the screen saver zooming back and forth across the screen.

Fuck, I must have fallen asleep.

I stretched, walked to the kitchen, and took some Tylenol for my aching head. After finishing my glass of water, I walked to my bedroom and sat on the edge of the bed. After a few seconds, I lowered my head into my hands and prayed for it to stop throbbing.

Son-of-a-bitch.

After a considerable amount of time, my head felt good enough to stand, and I walked to my desk. The black screen indicated I had been asleep for long enough that my computer shut down, which happened after fifteen minutes. I rubbed my eyes and stared at the monitor. Although I vaguely remembered writing a review, I didn't really remember writing all of the reviews I was supposed to write, or exactly where I left off or what happened.

I wiggled the mouse, cleared the screen of the wiggling blurry ball, and stared at the review. It didn't look familiar in the least. After a moment of staring blankly at the monitor, I refreshed the screen and stared. The review still seemed strange, as if it was written by someone else, but the time stamp at the side left me slightly puzzled.

14 hours, 38 min ago

Fourteen hours ago? How can that be?

I glanced at my watch. 7:22. I stared blankly at my watch, tried to make sense of what was going on, but couldn't.

If it's 7:22, the sun wouldn't be setting. It would be totally sunny.

I walked to the bedroom window, opened it, and peered outside.

Fuck.

I ran to the kitchen and looked at the microwave.

7:21

Fuck. It can't be.

After a frantic search, I found my purse, got my phone, and looked at the screen.

7:23 AM Mon, May 11

No…no…no, please God, no.

***

After repeated calls to his home went unanswered, I finally left a message, which was not at all what I wanted to do. Three hours later, and still having received no phone call from him, I was scared I had disappointed him much more than I expected.

I sat in his driveway frustrated that I had passed out from being drunk and missed dinner. I not only that I had I down Vince, but Anita as well. She took so much pride in her preparation of the meals, arrangement of the table, and found such value in our conversations that my having missed dinner would have disappointed her greatly. I was sure of it.

"*Gabriel's Message*," by Sting played over the stereo as I sat and waited for Vince to return.

I can fix this.

Two and a half complete plays of the CD later, while "*Do You Hear What I Hear*," by Whitney Houston played, I hoped Vince would understand, but I had spent enough time playing ideas over and over in my head of how he *may* react, that I feared he would overreact.

As gentle as he seemed to be, and as kind as he was, his temper was beyond what most would describe as *hot tempered*. His ability to forgive was minimal, and his ability to forget was nonexistent.

Fuck.

I covered my head in my hands, realizing fully that my actions got me into the predicament I was in, and no matter what his reaction was, I could get through it one way or another.

An hour and a half later, and I had convinced myself that I fucked up and fucked up bad. As I sat in the silent car, I heard the unmistakable sound of his motorcycle coming down the street. A quick glance over my shoulder confirmed my suspicion, and I saw him coming up the street.

Breathe, Sienna, breathe…

His motorcycle slowed, he glanced to the side, and upon what appeared to be his recognition of my car in his driveway, he accelerated past the driveway and up the block.

Oh no you don't.

I started the engine, shifted the car in reverse, and backed out of the driveway. As the car came to a stop in the street, he was a block away at the intersection at the end of the block.

Think you can outrun this motherfucker?

I shifted the car in drive and stomped the gas pedal to the floor.

Think again, Vince.

The car lunged forward, and the tires began to spin. As the smoke bellowed out from the rear fenders and the car continued to race forward at a very rapid pace, Vince pulled away from the stop sign and crossed through the intersection.

I released the gas pedal, frustrated that he hadn't waited on me, and slowed down for the stop sign. Upon seeing no cars coming from either direction, I opted to stomp the gas pedal again and run through the intersection without stopping. Within a few seconds, I had caught up with Vince and was following close behind him.

After a slow-paced cat and mouse game that included covering half of the city and consuming no less than another hour of time, it appeared Vince was riding back toward his house. Fifteen minutes later, and I followed him into the driveway and parked the car.

He parked the bike in the middle of the drive, shut it off, and sat on it staring at the garage. Upon realizing he had no intention of walking up to the car and talking to me, not only did I realize that he was angrier than I hoped he would be, but I knew that I was going to have to get out and talk to him about what had happened.

So much for having the comfort of my music and my car.

I pushed the car door open, cleared my throat, and walked alongside his motorcycle. "So, I was doing book reviews and I guess…"

"Save it," he said flatly.

Still staring at the garage, he held his gaze for a moment. As his eyes shifted down toward the gas tank, he spoke again, and as he did, he closed his eyes.

"Just go," he said.

Oh shit. He's really mad.

"Do you want to come over later? Or maybe I could bring some pizza over here, and we could…"

He turned his head to the side and glanced upward. "No, Sienna, I don't want to come over. You broke a promise. You left me sitting at my mother's house like a god damned fool, and I had no idea…"

"Wait, I'm sorry, I just fell asleep…"

He raised his left hand in the air and held it between us. "Like I said, *save it*. I can't do this."

"Do what?"

He pointed his finger at me, and then wagged it back and forth between us. "This. You and me. It's over."

A lump rose in my throat and I felt hot all over. My throat constricted and I fought to breathe. This couldn't be happening. As I fought for each choppy breath I was able to eventually take, I was sure he didn't mean what I felt like he meant.

"Wait. Over? What?" the words came out as if someone else had asked them.

He reached for the handlebars, started the motorcycle, and shook his head.

"Yeah, *over*. Don't call, don't come over, don't write, don't fuck with me. You broke a fucking promise, Sienna. I can't do this again," he said.

My eyes welled with tears, and as much as I wanted to say, to scream, to grab him, to apologize, to hug him, or just stand and talk, I was paralyzed.

He released the clutch, slowly pulled forward, and turned around in the yard. As I heard the sound of his motorcycle's exhaust fade down the block, I realized he was gone. I stood in the driveway staring down at my feet and crying, incapable of doing anything else. It seemed like a terrible dream. As I cried and shook from the heartfelt pain, I prayed for answers. Answers never came because I believe there weren't any; but eventually, through the many tears, it began to make sense.

In Vince's mind, I was no different than Natalie. To him, the circumstances didn't matter. The depth or the latitude of the broken promise, as far as he was concerned, was irrelevant. I had unknowingly done the unthinkable. I had broken a promise.

And I had done so to the one man who would probably never be able to forgive me.

VINCE

It had been two weeks since Sienna didn't come to dinner, and I hadn't been back to my mother's house since. Partially embarrassed, somewhat disappointed, and totally heartbroken, I felt there was no way I would ever be able to face my mother again. I realized in time I would probably change my mind and be able to one day return, but I had no idea when that might be.

"I can remember when you said you'd never do anything with a bitch but shove her full of cock, remember that conversation?" I asked.

Axton crossed his arms, glared at me, and sighed. "What's your fucking point?" he asked.

"I just made it," I said. "Never thought I'd see the day you had an Ol' Lady on the back of your bike."

"She isn't my Ol' Lady, she's a friend," he said.

I shrugged my shoulders and turned away. "Doesn't matter to me. You'll learn your lesson sooner or later."

"Hold up, I wasn't done…"

"*I'm* done," I said as I walked out of the office.

"God damn it, Vince, you can't…"

I pushed the door closed, walked out into the shop, and fired up my bike. There was nothing I wanted to listen to about him trying to justify some chick who had been hanging off the back of his bike for the last two weeks. As I sat on the bike and waited for it to warm up, I lit a cigarette and took a long, slow drag.

If there was one thing I couldn't stand, it was a hypocrite.

My parent's had proven to be the only people who mattered to me that hadn't eventually let me down. The two women in my life, one who I mistakenly thought I loved lied to me and broke a vow. The other, the only woman I *truly* loved, broke a promise and left me looking like a god damned fool.

Axton seemed like a hypocrite, talking out both sides of his mouth about women. One day he was talking shit about how *if the MC wanted a man to have an Ol' Lady they'd have issued one to all new prospects*, and the next time I saw him he had an Ol' Lady hanging off the back of his bike.

Axton may have been the president of the club, and I might have respected him, but he was no friend of mine. I had one friend, and only one, in my entire life.

We made a pact. A promise to each other. *Best friends forever.*

That's what we said.

We walked down to the railroad tracks and put pennies on the tracks. Sitting in the row of trees along the tracks we would wait for the train to come smash the pennies, talking about our futures. He was going to be a doctor and I was going to be a fireman; at least when we talked about it the first time. For me, at least, each time we talked my desires changed. But he always wanted to be a doctor.

He said doctors saved lives.

To be able to take a dying person and redirect the hand of fate, allowing someone to live – when in the absence of your actions they

224

would die – would be miraculous. As a young boy of six his desire to save lives didn't make as much sense as it made when I was an adult, but the older I got the more I respected him for standing firm in his wishes.

A fireman, a police officer, a tree trimmer, and an ice cream man were a few of my childhood dream careers. I found it funny that as I grew older my view on what was important changed. In my opinion, at least as a boy of six or seven, an ice cream man was much better than a doctor. Although a doctor may be able to save lives, an ice cream man could make everyone happy, the sick and healthy.

We lived our lives convinced that a bank robber rode the train through town as a means of escape, and that during his way out of town, he had tossed a bag of money from the railcar. Convinced all we needed to do was find it, we scoured through the weeds and along the edges of the trees to find it. From when we were six until we were ten, we searched along the tracks almost every day, but never found anything.

One day, right before his tenth birthday, we were both convinced *that* was the day we would find the bag of money. With expectations running high, we searched like never before. As the day unfolded and the money was undoubtedly under the base of the very next tree, I asked what he was going to do with his share of the riches.

Walking along the edge of the wooden railroad ties while dragging his stick behind him, he shifted his eyes upward and in my direction. Three weeks older, and much wiser in my opinion, I walked along the top of the steel rail, towering above him. I continued to walk slowly, being careful not to lose my balance as I waited for him to respond.

After a few steps, he paused and began to tap his stick against the tracks. When he finally stopped tapping the rail, he responded. As he spoke, I continued my balancing act.

"Buy a new doctor," he said.

I stopped and attempted to turn around without falling off the edge of the rail. Eventually I felt the need to speak more important and jumped down.

"Why would you need a new doctor?" I asked.

He cleared his throat, stared down at the tracks for a long moment, and shifted his eyes out toward the tree line. "A cardiovascular pathologist. He's in Texas."

I'd never heard words that sounded so important, even out of an adult's mouth, let alone a kid my age. Impressed at his intellect, but now concerned with why he would need an out of state doctor with such a name, I pressed him for more information.

"Why?" I asked.

He turned to face me and shrugged his shoulders. "He's the best."

It made sense. Who would want anyone that wasn't the best at what they did? Satisfied with his answer, and knowing nothing of the real reason why he needed a doctor, I stepped onto the railing and waited for the command he always gave before we started our journeys.

"Lead the way?" he asked.

"Follow me," I said.

We never found the bag of money, and Jackson never got to go to Texas. His heart stopped two weeks later, just before he turned ten years old.

The school shut down for his funeral, and it seemed the entire city attended. We searched for a spot to park the car for what seemed like forever, and after finding a place, walked along the sidewalk for much longer than Jackson and I ever walked along the tracks. In that time I thought of him, our friendship, the permanency of death; and about losing the only friend I ever had.

I wondered if the pain I felt in my heart was similar to the pain Jackson felt from the disease I learned he had. I decided as we walked into the funeral home that if I never befriended another person, I would never be forced to feel the pain again.

As the sound of my motorcycle's exhaust echoed throughout the shop and I stared blankly out into the street, I realized I was wrong.

And I suspected this new pain, no differently than the pain I felt from the loss of my best friend, would only be able to be temporarily suspended and not totally eliminated. As an adult, I had learned it wasn't a doctor or the ice cream man that caused the pain within me to subside, it was a machine.

And that machine was between my legs.

SIENNA

I had waited a year for the day to arrive. Instead of a celebratory dinner and discussions of our fond memories as a couple, I sat alone under a blanket of pain. A month had passed since I last saw Vince, and although I hoped the pain would eventually stop, it hadn't so much as decreased.

As severe on this particular day as it was the day he rode away, it was apparent living with the pain was something I would be forced to deal with. Over the course of the last month I prayed a lot. Not for Vince to return or for the pain to diminish, but for the ability to continue to be myself and not to fall prey to the evils of anger or hatred.

The same fate that brought Vince and me together broke us apart, and for me to reserve gratitude for one and misery for the other would be to second guess the hand of God. I could never claim to fully understand life or all of the rewards, gifts, complications and losses associated with it, nor did I feel I needed to.

Living, it itself, was my gift; and I felt it was my responsibility to do so to the best of my ability. Keeping my chin up and my spirits high, despite the pain I was feeling, was not only in my best interest, but mandatory to me keeping my sanity.

Attempting to grow from the situation I had put myself in, I developed my own opinions of pain and healing. I convinced myself the process of healing brought along with it pain; the more difficult the healing process, the more severe the pain. The pain acted as a reminder of the damage done, and in the mind of the wise, a deterrent to repeat the process which brought about the pain in the first place.

It made perfect sense, at least to me. A runner with a torn muscle felt pain until the muscle had healed, and the process took weeks. A broken bone was painful until the fracture mended itself, requiring a few months to heal. A burn victim with severe burns over half of their body might take an entire year to heal, the pain requiring a morphine drip to be manageable. Seeing the differences in these damages, the healing processes, and the severity of the pain allowed me to believe one day I would no longer hurt.

But I knew the healing process would be a long one.

Although I continued to review books over the last month, I hadn't had a drink of wine since the day I passed out drunk and missed my date with Vince. I didn't swear off alcohol, or convince myself I had a drinking problem, but I did realize my having drank too much wine on that particular night caused a problem that I wouldn't have had in the absence of the wine.

Coffee, however, was a different story.

"So, is that your Continental?" he asked.

I turned toward the voice and nodded my head. "Sure is."

"Mid-sixties?" he asked as he pointed to the seat beside me.

I nodded my head at his guess of the year, not at his request to sit.

"1965," I said.

He sat down and smiled.

I did fully expect to one day heal, but in the end I knew I wouldn't forget Vince, stop loving Vince, or ever be able to love anyone else. My love for Vince wasn't something I had developed; it had been inside of me for a lifetime, waiting for the person who was entitled to it to come along and claim it.

I believed there were many women, who in the absence of finding the *right* person, convinced themselves the person standing before them *was* the right person. I didn't have to convince myself of anything with Vince, all I had to do was be in his presence. Long before the first kiss, I was well aware he was somehow special to me, and although I wasn't sure why or to what degree, the first kiss was all it took for me to fully understand what it was he provided to me.

He, through his actions, words, wisdom, and expression, provided proof that he was entitled to receive the love which had been reserved within me for a lifetime, and without my expressed consent, he received it.

I initially found it odd that I didn't make a conscious decision to give Vince my love. I almost felt cheated that I didn't have to convince myself what it was I was feeling at the time, I simply knew, and allowed it to happen. It was natural, it was simple, and it required nothing on my part to exist. It was not developed, nor did it happen over time. I had always felt I would allow someone to have my love, or that I would *give* it to them, but that wasn't the case with Vince.

Something in me simply snapped as if a switch had been flipped. My love was his and he merely took what he was entitled to.

It was then that I knew the love I felt was true.

The day of the money shot.

"Would you mind sitting somewhere else?" I asked.

He ran his hand through his hair, shook his head lightly, and his hair fell down along his forehead. "I just thought you might want some company," he said.

I shook my head and grinned. "I'm in love. I have all the company I need."

VINCE

July 21ˢᵗ, 2015

The Sergeant-at-Arm's Ol' Lady had a brother who had been in prison for some time, and according to Axton's Ol' Lady, who was a paralegal for a local attorney, he was wrongfully convicted of a crime. The legal firm she worked for requested a new trial, received one, and a mandatory meeting had been declared to attend the trial. It was the opinion of the club that a strong presence at the trial would provide support not only to the man who was being dragged through the court, but to the patched member of the club and his Ol' Lady.

I didn't dispute the benefits of attending the trial, but I had a man in another state who had skipped bail, and needed to travel with a bail bondsman to attempt to extradite him. After discussing my work requirements with Axton, I was given permission to work in lieu of going to the trial.

So, while all of the other members of the MC attended the trial, I rode shotgun in a truck to Omaha, Nebraska.

"So the other day, I had this kid that skipped out on bail, and I got a tip on where he was. Kid was 19 years old, and it was a conspiracy to distribute cocaine charge. Kid was facing five years, but since he skipped out, was probably looking at six or so. Anyway, so I go to this house and knock on the door, and this little fucker answers," he said.

He was about my height, had a shaved head and was covered in tattoos, but weighed an easy fifty pounds more than me, all of which was muscle. He owned his own bail bonding company, and had hired me over the years to assist him with difficult clients. Through the course of doing business, we developed a good business-client relationship, he being the walking intimidation, and me being his physically persuasive partner. It was a good cop bad cop routine we played, and played well.

"And?" I asked.

"Well, his eyes get all big, and he looks at me and says, 'Biggs, I was meaning to give you a call.' Now I fucking know better, and I tell this little fucker we can do this the easy way or the hard way and I ask him to pick." He paused, lit a cigarette, and offered me one.

I shook my head and pulled my pack out of my cut.

After we each lit a cigarette and exchanged glances, he continued.

"So, he says the easy way and asks me to wait a second. Says he wants to grab something. I tell this little fucker if he tries to run, I'll shoot his little ass with a Taser, and he agrees. Now this house is a little one bedroom crack house, and it's nasty as fuck and smells like death. But this little fucker just steps aside, opens a drawer on an end table beside this piss stained sofa, and pulls out a wad of cash." He paused and puffed on his cigarette.

"How much?" I asked.

"Hundred grand. In hundreds. Motherfucker says 'Here, just act like we never saw each other.' I took a look at the money, took a look at him, and I shake my head. 'What you gonna get if you take me in?' he asks me. 'Damned sight less than that,' I tell him. Finally I tell this little prick to turn around and let me cuff him or I'm gonna shoot him in the neck with the Taser, and he lets me take him in. But you know what?"

he asked.

I took a drag off the cigarette, inhaled the smoke, and tossed the butt out the window of the truck. After I exhaled the smoke, I turned toward him and responded.

"What?" I asked.

He took another long drag from the cigarette and blew the smoke around the cab of the truck. "I thought about taking the money. I mean, I think I never would have *really* took it, but I'll be damned if I didn't think about it. Weird, if you ask me," he said.

I shook my head. "Good, evil. Right, wrong. It's just temptation, it happens. Acting on it is what matters."

"You think?" he asked as he flicked the ashes from his cigarette out the window.

I nodded my head. "Everyone is tempted."

"I told my pop a lie once when I was a kid, and I tell you what I felt like a damned shit head for about six months. Finally came clean and told him the truth. Fucker beat my ass to a pulp. Not for chewing the tobacco, but for lying to him," he said.

I laughed and shook my head at the thought. "That's not temptation, that's just telling a fucking lie."

He exhaled another cloud of smoke and flipped the cigarette butt out the window. "I know the fucking difference," he said.

"Well, I never told my pop a lie, he'd a skinned me alive if I did," I said.

"Not even a little one?" he asked.

I shook my head. "Nope."

The thought of telling anyone a lie, especially my father, was incomprehensible. My father was a man of tremendous moral value, and taught me to be the same. Living as a man of my word, being honorable, and always making decisions I felt he would have made himself allowed me to live a life that I was sure would make him proud if he were here to witness himself.

"Knowing you, you're probably right. You're a weird fucker, you know it?" he asked.

I turned to face him, narrowed my eyes, and glared. "What the fuck you mean by that?"

"Well, for one, you don't carry a phone. Who the fuck doesn't have a phone? You, that's who. I don't know one more dude that ain't got a phone. And when you go on your debt collecting deals, you always act like Samuel L. Jackson in that fucking movie," he paused and pulled a cigarette from his pack.

After he put the cigarette between his lips, he continued, the cigarette flipping up and down as he spoke.

"*Pulp Fiction.* You give 'em some speech about right and wrong and breaking promises like you're some fucker living on the moral high ground. I ain't trying to say you're some hypocrite, you're just fucking weird," he said with a laugh.

He reached for his lighter, lit his cigarette, and glanced at me as if expecting a response. As the smoke rose from the glowing tip and spread over the headliner of the truck, I considered what he said.

After a moment's thought, I lit a cigarette, inhaled a long pull, and held it in my lungs. I turned my head, exhaled the smoke out the window, and turned toward Biggs.

"I'm not a hypocrite. I practice what I preach," I said. "So if you want to call that weird, fucking whatever. I think I'm the last of a dying breed."

He pulled the cigarette from his mouth and lifted the end close to his face and stared at it as if something was wrong. "I'll give you that. You sure are a stubborn prick."

I shrugged my shoulders and flicked my cigarette out the window. "Now I'm a stubborn prick?"

He shook his head and sucked on his cigarette. The ashes fell into his lap as we hit a bump in the road, but he didn't seem to care. "No, you've always been a stubborn prick. Like the phone deal. You're just a hot head, that's all."

"I get along fine without a phone," I said.

"Don't doubt that. Like anything else, you don't miss what you're used to being without, and you've been without for a couple years. Hell, there's fuckers who ain't got teeth, don't mean they wouldn't be better off with 'em," he said.

He took another drag from his cigarette, flicked the butt out the window, and took a drink of his soda.

"Ninety more miles," he said.

I nodded my head in affirmation, but didn't speak.

"So what? You think you'll find another that's better?" he asked.

I turned toward him and stared, feeling as if I must have missed part of something he said.

"Another what?" I asked.

"Girl," he said.

I turned and stared out the side window, thinking about how to respond. As the fields and farmhouses swept past, I considered my life, living it in solitude, and the benefits of doing so. I loved Sienna and I was incapable of changing it, but unwilling to expose myself to the pain and suffering associated with allowing myself to actively love her. It had been almost three months that we were apart, and it seemed like an entire separate lifetime. Soon, my mind drifted off to thoughts of her and what fun we'd had while we were together.

As the fields and farms changed to the skyline of a fast approaching city, I wondered where the time had gone. Ninety miles passed in a matter of minutes.

"We're here," he said.

And although I could clearly see we had physically arrived, I realized in spirit, I was elsewhere.

SIENNA

August 2nd, 2015

I sat, baking in the sun in my shorts. No differently than any other sunny August day, it was difficult to breathe the thick humid air, but the warmth of the sun felt good on my bronze skin. Under the cover of sunglasses, a messy bun, and a tee shirt I had spent all day doing yardwork in, I drank my iced coffee and listened to my iPod.

As *"Come Back to Bed,"* by John Mayer played, I closed my eyes and hoped to become one more shade darker by the time I decided to get up and go home. Over the course of the summer I had become quite a fixture at the coffee shop, often spending an entire day relaxing in the warm summer sun. I pulled my feet from my flip-flops, propped them on the chair beside me, and took a sip of my coffee.

The song ended and *"Modern Age,"* by Eric Hutchinson began to play. I closed my eyes and did my best to sing along with the fast-paced song, but quickly found out that I knew only about half of the words and was left in the dust by Eric's ability to keep up the pace. I had spent my entire life without an iPod, relying on my CD player in my room, car, and living room for music, but after purchasing one, found downloading music and using the shuffle option to be quite enjoyable.

A live version of *"Daughters,"* by John Mayer caused me to open my eyes, stand from my seat, and sway back and forth on the concrete patio.

Certain the patrons in the store and the handful of people outside thought I was absolutely insane, I imagined being at a John Mayer concert with my father listening to the song, and in a short time, wondered if he had ever had an opportunity to hear it before he passed away.

As the song came to an end, I pulled the earbuds from my ears and dropped them onto the table. I took a sip of coffee, gazed out into the street, and wondered what Anita was doing, thinking, and most of all, feeling. I truly missed her, Bradley, and the dinners I had become so accustomed to having.

It was easy for me to slip into a period of self-pity, but as soon as I recognized what I was doing, I made every effort to change my way of thinking and do my best to become grateful for what Vince and I had for the period of time we shared, and not dwell on what happened or what I lost.

I decided what happened was another case of nothing but the *unexpected result of the natural development of life,* and attempting to call it anything but fate would be to fall back into the state of self-pity.

So far, considering the depth of my love for Vince, I was doing rather well, at least in my opinion. I knew I would never recover, and my lifetime would be spent without something I was well aware I needed to be my true self. Living without Vince in my life was much different than living without my father.

When my father passed, I quickly came to an understanding of how much I loved him, missed him, and how deeply I wished he was still with me, enjoying time together as a family. In losing Vince, I realized I lost not only a lover and a person who was important to me, but I truly felt I lost a part of myself.

Now feeling as if I was incomplete and knowing the feeling would never fade, I wondered if Vince felt the same way and was simply either too stubborn to admit it, or chose, as I did, to accept it. If he accepted it, in a strange sense, it would almost be as if we were still together in spirit, but separated physically. In my odd way of thinking, I liked to believe that was the case; and we were together, but separated by space and nothing else.

As I stood in place attempting to cool the concrete with the shadows from my bare feet, the rumbling sound from an approaching group of motorcycles caused me to glance in their direction. Four motorcycles pulled into the parking lot, one behind the other, and parked directly in front of where I was seated.

They weren't one percenters, didn't wear colors, and seemed like some friends who were just out riding together, but they reminded me of Vince nonetheless. In being honest, everything reminded me of Vince, but it wasn't surprising to me at all.

There was no doubt in my mind that if Vince allowed someone into his life, be it a lover or a friend, they would immediately be intrigued by him, and never be able to replace him with anyone comparable in quality, diversity, or genuine kindness.

Vince was big, mean, tough, and willing to walk into the depths of hell; alone and without fear. Considering this made it difficult to admit, but Vince's only real fault in life was a fear of being hurt.

Not physically, but emotionally.

And I had no intention of causing him any additional pain.

I loved him far too much.

VINCE

Present day

I hopped off my bike and stared down at the carburetor. Fuel dripped out of it at a rapid rate onto the floor of the shop, not only making a stinking mess, but causing a fire hazard, and quite possibly preventing me from leaving if it continued.

And I had no idea of what to do to make it stop.

I lowered myself onto the floor and peered up at the bottom of the carburetor, only to get a face full of gasoline.

Fuck.

As the pace of the stream seemed to steadily increase, I ran around the shop like a complete and utter idiot, searching for a gas can. Engines, transmission, wheels, frames, and fenders littered one side of the shop, but a gas can wasn't to be found. The search of a trash can produced an empty beer can, and after some handiwork with my pocket knife, I cut off the top and was using it to catch what little fuel I could.

I exhaled a sigh of relief as I heard an approaching bike, only to realize whoever it was I didn't recognize as being a Sinner.

Fuck.

The bike came to a stop outside the door of the shop and a very muscular man in a *Sinner's* cut got off the bike and sauntered over to where I was. His hair was short, he had a few days growth of beard, and his odd manner of walking wasn't something he did, it seemed to be a part of who he was. He walked like he'd served time in the joint, and his walk made a clear statement. It was a *don't fuck with me* walk.

"Mikuni?" he asked.

I turned to face him and shrugged my shoulders. "Excuse me?"

"It's leaking like a motherfucker. You planning on watching it pour out until it's empty, or fixing it?" he asked.

"I don't know where it's coming from," I responded.

Without speaking, he turned and walked to his motorcycle, removed the seat, and unrolled a tool kit. After a few seconds, he meandered back to where I stood, knelt down, and tapped something against the bottom of the carburetor.

"There," he said.

The gas fumes were atrocious. If someone would have lit a cigarette, the entire shop would have gone up in flames.

"There what?" I asked.

"It's fixed," he said. "But I'd push that fucker in the drive before I started it. You try and start it over that puddle it'll go up in flames."

"You fixed it?" I asked as I shifted my eyes toward the carburetor.

The leak had clearly stopped.

He nodded his head. "That's what I said, wasn't it? Hell, I didn't think I was stuttering, anyway," he said with a laugh.

I shifted my eyes to the patch on the front of his cut.

Big Jack.

"Vince," I said as I extended my hand. "I appreciate it."

"Jackson," he said as he shook my hand.

The hair on the back of my neck stood. I hadn't heard that name since I was a kid.

"You alright, Brother?" he asked as he slapped his hand against my bicep.

"I uhhm. Yeah, yeah, I'm good. So, what'd you do to fix it?" I asked.

"It's a Mikuni. Someone took the old Keihin carb off and replaced it with a Mikuni, which was a pretty good call if it's not a stock motor," he said.

I shook my head and grinned. "It ain't stock," I said.

"Well, Mikuni's are pretty finicky when it comes to dirt. How long you had the bike?" he asked.

"Long god damned time. Fifteen years," I said.

"Surprised it's the first time. Just smack the bottom of the float bowl with a screwdriver. The gas is coming out the overflow hose. It's like a bowl vent. Smacking it'll fix it every time. Don't beat on it, just tap it," he explained.

"Appreciate it, I really do," I said.

"No problem. Good looking Shovel, though," he said.

I nodded my head. "I appreciate it. Let me buy your lunch?"

"No need for that," he said. "Seen Slice?"

"Axton? Yeah, him, Biscuit, Toad, and the big fucker, Otis. They headed out to Benton to the airport," I said.

He nodded his head and glanced around the shop.

"So, you're that fella that got out of the joint a month or so back, huh?" I asked.

"You got it," he said with a nod. "Still getting used to being out in the free world. Just making decisions on my own seems fucking surreal."

"How long were you down? Sorry, I missed the trial. Voted for you to get your patch and all, but I wasn't here when you showed up. I kind of do my own deal, you know," I said.

"Understand that for sure. Been a little of a lone wolf my entire life. I was locked up ten years on a fucking conspiracy to commit murder charge. Got set up by the ATF. Cocksuckers. Slice's Ol' Lady wrote an appeal, got my case reheard, and I'll be god damned if they didn't let me go," he said.

I felt like I was talking to a ghost. My father was charged with a conspiracy to commit murder charge by the DEA, which in my mind, was no different than the ATF. Feds were feds. The odds of his name being Jackson, spending time in prison on a conspiracy to commit murder charge, and then to be set up by the feds just seemed...

It seemed strange to even think it, but it was almost as if he was an angel.

"My pop was in the joint on the same charge, the fucking DEA set him up. It was bullshit. He could have talked, but he sat in there, refused to snitch, and they tried to prove a point by keeping him locked down. Only reason they did it was because he was a biker, and was hanging around a bunch of one percenters. They tried to use him to get to the club," I paused and shook my head.

"He ever get out?" he asked.

I crossed my arms in front of my chest and shook my head. "Died of pneumonia in the joint. This is his old bike."

"Cool that you kept it. Your pop sounds like a good solid dude. Respectful what he did," he said.

"Show respect, get respect," I said.

He turned toward me and cocked an eyebrow. "You been reading my mail?"

I coughed a laugh. "What?"

"Prison saying. Just seems funny. That's one of my mottos. *Show respect, get respect.* Been saying that for a long bit," he said.

"My Pop's saying, I got it from him," I said. "He raised me like that. So many of these young fuckers get patched in and don't give respect. Then they wonder why no one'll run with 'em."

"Damned truth. You'll never get it if you don't give it," he said.

"So, you want to grab a bite?" I asked.

He grinned, nodded his head, and glanced down at the beer can under my bike. "Remember what I said. Move that fucker out first."

I looked at the stain on the concrete, the half-full can of gas, and realized had he said nothing, I would have hopped on the bike and started it.

"Appreciate it," I said with a nod.

"Lead the way?" he asked as he walked away.

I couldn't believe my ears.

I pushed the bike forward, nodded my head, grinned from ear to ear, and responded.

"Follow me."

SIENNA

I opened the door to the car, got out, and walked up the driveway. I felt out of place without Vince, but I didn't feel that I was doing anything *wrong*, it just seemed odd. As I stepped onto the porch, the front door opened.

She stepped onto the porch, wiped her hands on her pants, and opened her arms.

"Come here, Honey," she said. "Come give me a hug."

I rushed to her and wrapped my arms around her. "I don't know what to say."

"Don't say anything, just let me hold you," she said.

After a long moment of standing there in her embrace, she released me, took a step back, and studied me. "You haven't changed a bit."

I grinned and wiped the tears from my eyes. "You know, I never used to cry."

"Neither did I," she said. "But I've learned those things change over time."

I nodded my head and tried to force another smile, but ended up beginning to cry again. Seeing her was just too much. I should have just stayed home.

"So what happened?" she asked as she turned toward the door.

I wiped my hands on my shorts, and shook my head. "I probably shouldn't come in, he might…"

She paused in the doorway and turned around. "He might what?"

I shrugged. "Come over."

"Honey, he hasn't been here since the night you missed dinner. I haven't spoken to him. This is what he does, he shuts down. Especially when he's embarrassed or hurt," she said.

I was shocked. From what Vince had said, he came to his mother's house every Sunday for dinner. It had been three months since we were apart, and to think I played a part in him severing his relationship and routines with his mother was difficult to accept.

"Come on," she said as she walked into the living room.

With some reluctance, I followed her inside. Feeling nervous and slightly guilty, I sat down on the couch and crossed my legs. She sat down beside me a few feet away, straightened the wrinkles from her pants, and turned toward me. As I stared down at my sneakers, she cleared her throat and began to speak.

"So, that night, what happened?" she asked.

"I reviewed a few books, drank too much wine, and fell asleep until the next morning. When I woke up, I thought it was Sunday night, but after I looked at my phone, I found out it wasn't, it was Monday," I said, turning to face her as I finished speaking.

"That's it? *That* is what happened?" she asked.

I nodded my head and shifted my eyes to the floor. "Yeah, that's it."

"I knew it was something, but I didn't know what. He left that night to go looking for you, and he called me later and said it was over between you two. I tried to talk to him, but he wouldn't have it. He never went into detail, and that night was the last I saw of him. He needs his hind end kicked," she said.

I shifted my eyes toward her and narrowed my gaze. "I can't believe he hasn't been back," I said.

"I can. It's Stephen," she said. "The most stubborn human being on God's little green earth."

"I just wanted to see you. I miss you," I said. "I'm sorry."

"Don't you dare apologize," she said. "Would you like some tea?"

I glanced at my watch as if I had something else to do.

"No, I really need to go," I said as I stood.

"So soon?" she asked.

I shrugged my shoulders. "I uhhm. I have to get home, I have some things I need to get done."

"I understand. Come back any time," she said.

I tried my best to smile, but only managed a crooked grin.

"I will," I said.

But I knew I wouldn't.

Not without Vince.

VINCE

I'd been running with Jackson on an almost daily basis, and riding with Axton, Otis, Toad, and Biscuit more than I ever had since joining the club. Jackson was what I expected my childhood friend would have been had he not died at such an early age. Stubborn, opinionated, and someone who immediately made me feel as if he would always have my back, regardless.

"So you're telling me you loved this woman? Truly loved her?" he asked.

I took a drink of my beer and nodded my head. "Yep."

"Bullshit," he said.

I shook my head. "Sure isn't."

"You still love her?" he asked.

I shook my head. "Nope. Can't do it. She fucked me over."

After hearing the inspirational story of Jackson and Emily, and how she waited for him for ten years without hearing a word from him, it lifted my spirits enough to tell him about Sienna. He questioned my love, however, because of my ability to walk away after she didn't show up for dinner. It was without a doubt something he would have never done, and as much as he was harassing me about it, I couldn't quite figure out what his angle was. All I knew was that the more we talked about it, the guiltier I felt for feeling the way I felt and doing what I had done. Having him give me advice was more like getting it from my father, which made it almost impossible to dispute.

"Have my doubts," he said sarcastically.

"Doubt me all you want, I know how I feel," I said.

"Jesus jumped up Christ," Axton hollered.

"What?" Jackson said over his shoulder.

"Have a fucking look at this, would ya?" he said as he held his cell phone at arm's length. "Jaye Campbell's daughter works with this chick. Girl says she wants to suck a biker's cock and ride on his bike. Wants some of the fellas to go to her tattoo shop and see if there's any she likes. It's the place where that kid I was telling you about gave me the tattoo without an appointment."

"Crazy bitch," Jackson said with a laugh. "That'll start a fight for sure."

"No bullshit. Girl says she wants to meet a few of the fellas." Axton paused, cleared his throat, and gazed down at his phone. "Take five or six with ya and run over there, would ya?"

"Sure thing, boss," Jackson said as he turned to face me. "And you're going to be one of 'em."

"Don't have any business going," I said.

"You're going for me to prove a point," he said.

"What's the point?" I asked.

"Just do this," he said. "Come with me and act interested. We'll have a talk after we get out of there. Don't worry, I won't ask you to fuck her."

"Well, I wouldn't even if you did," I said.

"You're coming whether you like it or not," he said.

After a few minutes, six of us were all saddled up, and headed across town to a tattoo parlor. After passing it, we cut a u-turn in the street, and parked out front at the curb. I got off the bike, turned to face the shop, and stared at the neon sign.

Blurred Lines.

"Cool name for a shop," I said.

Jackson nodded his head. "I'm gonna get a quote while we're in here. Come on."

We all followed him inside, and immediately after going in, the owner noticed Jackson from his childhood. Oddly enough, they grew up together, and hadn't seen each other for almost twenty years. It seemed Jackson's presence back in the city was something meant to be, because not only was he helping me deal with many issues and problems, he was clearly making this guy's day.

The girl from the picture on Axton's cell phone walked up to the counter where Jackson was standing and raised her hands in the air.

"Listen up," she hollered. "I don't ever fuck with anyone but bikers, and I'll only fuck with a biker if he's got a big dick. I've got a foul mouth, a shitty attitude, and an insatiable desire. I'm no whore, and I won't be treated like one. If you're looking to hit it and quit it, you can forget it. I'm not your girl. If you want an Ol' Lady who'll out drink ya, out fuck ya, and probably out cuss ya, I'm your girl."

I stood and stared, half shocked she was so brash. It seemed almost out of character. If I was the type of man to be attracted to someone based on looks alone, she would definitely work for me. She was drop dead gorgeous, had a fabulous body, but it seemed odd hearing her say what she was saying, because she was so damned beautiful.

"How many's that leave?" she asked.

"Vince?" Jackson said.

I reluctantly stepped to the front and stood with my arms crossed in front of my chest.

"What's your road name?" the girl asked.

I pointed to my patch. "Vince."

She started laughing. "That's your *road name*?"

Why you little bitch.

"Yep. Name's Stephen. They call me Vince," I said.

"You qualified?" she asked.

It was all I could do to keep from smiling. As my mouth curled into a smirk, I responded. "Look, I came up here after Slice showed us your pic at the bar. Thought you were a cute little fucker. Seem a little crazy for my taste now that I'm here."

She stood and stared, and after a moment, her face washed over with concern. I hated to make her feel bad or that I felt like she was unattractive or something, so I tried my best to make her feel better. "I ain't lookin' to add a bunch of drama in my fucking life. Shit, I just got rid of an Ol' Lady for bein' a drama queen. Well, that and a whore. Nice to meet ya, though."

She placed her hands on her waist, cocked her hips to the side, and glared. "I'm not a whore, and I'm not crazy. I'm just some chick that loves bikes, appreciates the freedom of riding, and appreciates one-percenters for being who they are. I'm a lot of fucking fun, really."

It was apparent she wasn't going to take no for an answer. "What's a one percenter mean to you? Who am I?" I asked.

"Well, being an outlaw. Fuck the man, fuck society. Riding isn't a fucking hobby, and it's not really *a way of life*, it *is* life. You see that mountain bike outside?" she asked.

I tilted my head toward the door. "Chained up by the door?"

She nodded her head. "I rode that motherfucker six miles here instead of taking a ride in a cage."

I nodded my head. "Is that so," I asked.

She cocked an eyebrow and stared. "So…"

"We'll go for a ride or something," I said. "I'll be back, don't worry."

She nodded her head.

"How long you gonna be?" I asked Jackson.

"Gimme ten," he said.

"Come on, fellas," I said as I turned toward the door.

We walked outside, stood beside the entrance, and waited. As I leaned against the wall and joked with the fellas about the girl with the purple hair, Jackson walked out.

"Give us a minute, would ya?" he asked the other four men.

They nodded their heads and each got on their bikes.

"So, you think she was pretty?" he asked.

I nodded my head.

"Why didn't you take her for a ride?" he asked.

I crossed my arms in front of my chest, sighed, and shook my head. It seemed foolish to even discuss.

"I'm not like that," I said.

He nodded his head. "Only been with two women, right?"

"Yep," I responded.

He chuckled and shook his head. "Remind me of me, you fucking weird prick."

"So, answer me this. After seeing this girl, don't you dare try and tell me a lie, either. What are you…no *who* are you thinking of?" he asked.

I really didn't have to give it much thought. "Sienna."

"And she's the girl who you say fucked you over?" he asked.

I nodded my head.

"And you don't love her anymore? You feel nothing?" he asked.

I uncrossed my arms, pressed my hands into my hips and glared at him. "Why in the fuck are you so gung fucking ho to get into my love life?"

"Call me a hopeless fucking romantic or whatever, I don't give a fuck. I just know this. After going through what I went through and seeing all the shit I've seen, only to find out that my Ol' Lady waited ten fucking years without me even speaking to her? Well, it kind of makes a motherfucker humble. If you don't love this girl, well, you don't love her. But if you're being a stubborn prick, and you really do love her, but won't admit it, I want to try and break you," he said.

"Well, I can't be broken," I said as I reached for my pack of cigarettes.

"We'll see about that," he said.

I nodded my head and lit my cigarette.

"I suppose we will," I said.

SIENNA

I had never been much for having girlfriends. Women seemed too competitive, and much too quick to judge, argue, fight, and lay blame. As a result, during high school most of my friends were male, and eventually most of my male friends ended up being my boyfriend, although some only lasted a few weeks.

I attributed some of my reluctance to be friends with girls to my relationship with my father, and a desire to fill a void in my life I felt my father left when he went to prison. Living with my aunt seemed weird at the time, and having my father gone was difficult to say the least. Having a male in my life minimized conflict, filled a void, and more often than not, provided me with someone to have sex with.

My patterns of behavior as a high school girl continued into my adult life, and over time, became second nature. As an adult, I ended up with no female friends to speak of, and really never wanted any. The few men who came and went out of my life provided companionship, and my friends on Facebook and Goodreads who followed my reviews provided a constant flow of communication and often gave advice.

But now I felt I needed more.

I wanted my father, and I needed a friend.

I sat at my parent's gravesite with a fresh arrangement of flowers and swept the dust from the base of the gravestone. After cleaning what little dust had settled into the etching of the headstones, I squatted down and placed the flowers on the stone base.

"You know I love you, but I sure hate coming here to see you," I said.

"Nothing's changed, we're still apart. I hate it, but I can't change it. I went to see his mother, and that was enlightening, but a disaster for me. You know I will never do anything to try and replace mom, but I really like her, Dad. She's so cool. She's like what I wish girlfriends were like, but she's a mom. Heck, I don't know, maybe that's what moms are like."

I leaned forward and smelled the flowers. As I moved back to my squatting position, I continued.

"But with her it's hard. She's so nice, and she makes me feel, I don't know, kind of like you did. She's just really fun. And she doesn't take any shit from Vince, either. But he's shut her out, and hasn't been there since. And just so you know, I still haven't had a drink of wine since that day. Maybe one day I will again, but I don't really know. So there's that. Uhhm, let's see," I paused and contemplated what else I should say before I said my departing remarks.

"I guess I just hope one day we can work things out, but I'm beginning to have my doubts. I think maybe it'll take a miracle or an angel. Yeah, an angel is probably a good idea, so if you know one who isn't busy, you can send one my way, you know, being as you're up there with all of 'em."

"I wish you could meet him, I really do. And you know what's funny? I was there for a while wondering if we got married, who'd give me away. So yeah. Not wondering about that so much anymore."

I stood, stepped to the left, and squatted.

"I love you, too, Mother. I'll keep you posted on the progress, but

I imagine dad will fill you in. Same goes to you, if you know an angel, send one, I could sure use one. I'll be back to see you before you know it, and maybe one day I'll have some good news."

I stood, blew a kiss in the direction of the gravestones, and turned toward the car.

If you're still listening, I wasn't kidding about the angel.

VINCE

As I sat in my driveway mentally preparing my morning, I heard the unmistakable sound of Jackson's bike coming up the block. The cams he added to the engine gave it a very distinct sound, but the *way* he rode it was what made the sound of it being ridden stand out as different.

He rode it like he stole it.

Within a matter of seconds, he was sitting in my driveway beside me.

"What's shaking?" he asked.

I shrugged my shoulders. "Trying to decide what to do. Got to meet a guy at eleven, but that's not for three hours."

He hopped off his bike and straightened the bottom of his cut. After going through a ritual of popping his neck, back, and shoulders, he stood and glared at me.

"What?" I asked.

"Can't be broken, huh?" he asked.

I shook my head.

"I'm going to ask you some shit, and I need you to be one hundred percent honest with me, and with yourself," he said.

"Always honest," I said.

"We'll see," he said with a nod.

"You need to just give up," I said as I got off my bike and lit a

263

cigarette.

"Yeah," he said with a laugh as he pointed to my cigarette. "Have you a smoke."

I took a long drag, nodded my head, and blew a cloud of smoke into the still morning air.

"So, you and your pop were pretty tight?" he asked.

I nodded my head and took another long pull on the cigarette.

"You ever make New Year's resolutions?" he asked.

"What the fuck?" I asked, coughing out smoke as I did so.

He folded his arms in front of his chest and grinned. "Just asking," he responded.

"Yeah, make 'em every year," I said.

He grinned and nodded his head. "Finish that smoke and fire up another, you might need it."

"Get on with it, Doctor Phil," I said.

"You ever go visit your Pop's grave? You know, go see him or anything, and before you ask, no disrespect here. I'm just saying, I know a lot of fellas whose pop has passed, and a lot of 'em go to the grave and just sit and talk. You know, some leave notes, and stuff like that. So do you do any of that?" he asked.

I nodded my head. "Sure do."

"Okay. Now. You said yesterday when we were at that donut place that the only reason you dropped this girl was because she agreed to meet for dinner, and she never showed up. It's undisputed you don't carry a phone, but she could have called your mom's place, because she's got her number, and she could have called your place, even though you were gone, but she didn't until the next day. You went by that night, and you thought she was gone, but she left you a voicemail the next day explaining that she got drunk and passed out. You see all of this as a broken promise, and how can you trust her if she breaks promises, right? Sound about right?" he asked.

"Sounds about right," I said.

He uncrossed his arms and clapped his hands together.

"When did you start smoking again?" he asked.

It shocked me that he knew I had even quit. The entire time I knew Jackson I had smoked, and was never around during the time I had quit. As far as answering the question, I didn't even have to think about it.

"When we broke up," I responded.

"Figures. Okay, and before that, did you smoke at all? You know, maybe an occasional cigarette?" he asked.

I nodded my head. "When I was really pissed."

"Alright. Now, here's a few questions I want you to either answer, or just stand and stew on for a minute. Let me ask them all," he said. "And then you can chew on 'em."

I shrugged my shoulders, pulled out another cigarette, and lit it. "Okay."

He held his clenched fist in the air and extended a finger each time he asked a question.

"Did you ever make a New Year's resolution to quit?"

"Did you ever tell your pop you quit? When he was alive or after his death?"

"Did you ever go to his grave and talk to him about it, you know, out of pride?"

"Did you ever tell your mom you weren't smoking when you were?"

"Did you…"

I held my hand in the air, spit my cigarette on the driveway, and stepped on it. "Stop."

"Something wrong?" he asked.

Almost everything he had asked, I had done. I gave up cigarettes, at least initially, as a New Year's resolution. Before and after doing so, I had gone to my father's grave, and told him that I intended on quitting, and after having done so, that I had successfully quit.

I had also told my mother on a few occasions when she said I smelled like smoke that I wasn't smoking.

I felt sick.

Somehow, someway, I had become exactly what I despised.

I was a hypocrite.

And there was no other way of looking at it.

I had made promises that I didn't keep; to myself, my mother, and to my father.

"You look sick, Brother," he said as he slapped his hand against my bicep.

"I feel sick," I said.

"Probably that cigarette. Those things'll kill ya," he said. "So, you didn't answer, you going to?"

"Don't think I need to, you already know the answers," I said. "How'd you know?"

He shrugged his shoulders. "Most people who smoke actually smoke their cigarettes. You take a couple hits and toss it. It told me you either felt guilty or you wanted to quit. I picked the former. Asked a couple of the fellas, and Axton told me you'd gone without for about five years as far as he could remember. And almost everyone who quits makes a resolution. The rest was just a good guess."

I felt as if my entire world had been turned upside down. My entire life had been lived under the premise that I was the one person who had never made a promise he didn't keep, and I expected everyone who befriended me to do and be the same.

And I used my ex-wife's shortcomings against Sienna, the only woman I truly ever loved, based on my belief that she had broken a promise.

"Think I'm going to be sick," I said.

"You already said that. You'll be fine. Oh, I got one more question," he said.

I gazed down at the toes of my boots. "I don't think I want to hear it," I said.

"Don't rightfully give a fuck, I'm asking anyway," he said.

I shifted my eyes to meet his and nodded my head.

"You still love that girl?" he asked.

I nodded my head. "Sure do."

He turned toward his bike, threw his leg over the seat, and fired the engine.

"Saddle up," he said.

"To where?" I asked.

"Sienna's place," he said.

I shook my head. "I'll go alone," I said.

"Not an option," he said.

I furrowed my brow and glared at him. "What's that mean?"

"Means it's not a fucking option. I've got a plan. You'll see," he said.

"I don't know if I want to," I said.

He revved the engine and grinned. "Don't give a fuck. Get on, and believe me, you'll be fine. I'm your friend, Brother, I won't do anything to disrespect you."

I reluctantly got on my bike, fired the engine, and shook my head in disbelief. After turning around, I pulled alongside his bike.

"Follow me," I said.

As I pulled out of the drive, I felt in many respects like I was a kid again.

Starting my life from scratch with my friend Jackson.

SIENNA

I was right in the middle of reading C.J. McShane's new MC novel, *My Brother's Keeper*, and the sound of motorcycles followed by my doorbell ringing sent chills down my spine. I ran from the kitchen to the living room window and pulled the blinds to the side. One motorcycle sat in the center of the drive, facing the street, with a man sitting on it. The other, which was clearly Vince's bike, sat in the drive facing the street, but he wasn't on it.

I quickly moved to the other side of the blinds and peered toward the porch. Vince stood with his hands in his pockets rocking back and forth on the balls of his feet.

Holy shit.

I ran to the bathroom, checked my hair, and made every effort to calm my nerves. I had no idea why he had come to my house, but I hoped it was at least to talk with me like an adult. I couldn't help but wonder who he brought with him and why. After staring into the mirror blankly for what seemed like an eternity, I ran to the door and opened it slowly.

"Hi," I said.

It sounded foolish, but I had no idea what else to say. It had been four months since we'd seen each other, and as with any other shitty time in my life, the time passed at an extremely slow rate, making the days seem like months. In many respects, I felt I had been away from Vince for a decade.

His face wasn't cleanly shaven, but it was close. He looked like he had a few days growth of beard, seemed slightly thinner than normal, but not unhealthy. The expression on his face seemed to be one of worry. He raked his hair away from his eyes and did his best to smile.

"Hi," he said.

I guess I'll say something.

"So…"

He raised his hand, cleared his throat, and shook his head from side to side. "Hold up a minute."

I stood in the doorway and wondered just what was going on. As I began to run through scenarios in my head, I wondered if something happened to his mother. Before I had a chance to ask, he cleared his throat again and began to speak.

"Look, I made a mistake. I blamed you for things and you didn't deserve it. You did nothing wrong. And me?" he paused, shrugged his shoulders, and chuckled. "I'm far from perfect, and I did everything wrong. I'm selfish, self-righteous, and I apologize for being so blind and stubborn to not even be able to see how imperfect I really am."

I inhaled a breath and considered speaking. He immediately raised his hand again to stop me.

"I'm sorry for what I did to you, and I hope you can find a way to forgive me," he said.

I couldn't believe what I was hearing. All at once, my throat constricted, I felt flush, and I was afraid I was going to faint. But surprisingly, I didn't say a word.

"I'm just going to cut to it. Sienna, I love you and I can't possibly live without you. Will you take me back?" he asked.

I had rehearsed what I wanted to say over and over in my head if this day came. After reading for four months on a daily basis, thinking in my down time, and planting a hundred flowers, I decided if I took him back, I was going to be demanding of some things and do the best that a 125 pound girl could to make him feel like shit.

I widened my eyes and cocked my head to the side. "Take you back? Really?"

He nodded his head. "Will you?"

As much as I wanted to just say *yes* and immediately pick up where we left off, I wanted to make sure he understood how I felt.

"So?" he asked, standing with is shoulders perma-shrugged.

"If I do, there are gonna be some conditions. Gimme a minute, I'm thinking," I said.

I shifted my eyes from Vince to the man in the driveway. I wondered who he was and what he was doing with Vince at this particular moment in time. Obviously a Selected Sinner, and more than likely doing some job with Vince or acting as his muscle on trying to intimidate someone, it seemed odd Vince would bring him to my home.

"So, who's he?" I asked as I tossed my head toward the driveway.

"A friend," he responded.

I widened my eyes comically and nodded my head in my best sarcastic manner. "Oh, so you've got friends now?"

He nodded his head. "One."

Vince didn't have male friends, and he didn't run with any of the Sinners that I knew of. My guess was that this guy somehow convinced Vince to come talk to me after a long night or a drunken confession on Vince's part.

"Tell him to come here," I said.

"Jackson, come here for a minute," Vince hollered over his shoulder.

Jackson?

"What's his name?" I asked.

"Jackson," he said.

I narrowed my eyes and stared. "Jackson?"

He nodded his head once. "Yeah, Jackson."

Vince had no idea his mother had told me of his childhood friend, Jackson. Hearing the man's name made goosebumps rise along my arms and caused my heart to race. I gazed over Vince's shoulder and focused on Jackson, and all of a sudden my perception of him changed. He looked like he actually cared.

I grinned.

"Jackson Shephard," the man said as he stepped onto the porch and extended his hand.

I shook his hand and smiled. "Sienna Boyco."

As he leaned back and crossed his arms, his mouth curled into a smirk. "What can I do for you?"

He looked like a fighter. He was big, muscular, tattooed, and had a permanent smirk on his face like he knew something I didn't. I gazed back at him knowing ninety percent of the population on earth would run from this guy, but all in all I felt extremely comfortable with him and I didn't really know why.

"Just stand over there," I said as I pointed to the edge of the porch. "I want a witness."

"You've got it, Boyco," he said as he stepped to the side.

I shifted my eyes from Jackson to Vince and gave him my best angry glare.

"Okay. Here's my response. Yes, I will take you back under these conditions. One, we start up right where we left off. Two, you never, and I mean *never* do what you did to me again. If we ever have an issue that is worthy of creating waves in our relationship, we talk first, react later. And three, you're going to go to your mothers and tell her you're sorry, and I mean like *now*. And Sunday dinner starts again tomorrow," I paused and crossed my arms in front of my chest in standard Vince fashion. "Take it or leave it."

He didn't make me wait long.

He nodded his head and smiled. "I'll take it."

I shifted my eyes toward Jackson. "You witnessed it."

Still smiling his shitty little smirk, he nodded his head once and pointed at me. "Sure did."

Vince cocked his head to the side. "Go for a ride?"

"Sure, let me get my glasses," I said.

"Looks like we're headed to mom's place next, huh?" Jackson asked as he coughed out a laugh.

Vince shrugged his shoulders. "Guess so."

"Good," he said. "We can stop and get Em."

"Okay, let me get my glasses," I said as I turned toward the house.

I hurried into the kitchen and as soon as I was behind the cover of the wall I pumped my fist at my side and smiled.

Yes!

I walked out onto the porch, kissed Vince, and followed him to the bike. After I got on, they both started their bikes, and we sat for a few seconds.

I had to know.

"Excuse me, Jackson?" I asked over the sound of the exhaust.

"Yeah," he said with a nod of his head.

"Are you the one who talked him into coming here?" I asked.

He shrugged his shoulders and looked at Vince as if seeking authorization to answer.

"Yeah, he is," Vince said over his shoulder.

I fucking knew it.

Thanks Mom and Dad.

VINCE

I had to be honest with myself before I could be honest with anyone else. Once I realized I was mistaken in my beliefs and opinions of myself, I quickly admitted my faults to God and my mother, and I had one more step to go before I could feel that I was the man I had always portrayed myself as being.

"Brought your bike. Tell you what, that thing'll never die. It's a beast, Pop," I said.

I glanced around the cemetery. Rows upon rows of headstones did nothing to minimize the loss of my father, but I did feel like I had thousands of eyes and ears making sure what I said was exactly what I needed to say.

"So, I came here for a reason. I guess, when you get right down to it, I came here for your respect…"

I paused and shook my head. It was far more difficult than I ever imagined it would be. After a moment, I lowered myself to the ground, sat cross legged, and gazed at the headstone.

"I've spent a lot of time thinking about this, and I want to admit some things to you. I hope I didn't disappoint you too much, and if I did, I'll apologize in advance."

I shifted my eyes up to the trees, and eventually to the blue sky well beyond the cemetery. After scanning the horizon for clouds and finding none, my eyes fell to the gravestone.

"Pop, I lied to you. I told you I quit smoking, and I did. But I started again, quite a few times, and I never came back and told you. So I lied. I know you'd see it that way, and I sure see it that way. I lied to Ma, and hell everyone for that matter."

"You know I told you I quit because you wanted me to, and I'm going to try again. I'm going to do my best, but no promises. We'll just see how it goes."

I uncrossed my legs, stood, and rested my hand on the top of the headstone. "So I've got the girl back, and I'm not going to let her go this time. I know how you and mom tried to have kids after me and always hoped for a girl…"

"Well, I guess in some ways Ma's got one now. She sure likes her, Pop. We're over there for Sunday dinners every week. Brought one of the fellas and his girl a couple of times, and Ma sure enjoyed it. Hell, before you know it we might have that dinner table full of the fellas and their girls. I know it'd make Ma happy to have that house filled with people even if it was just once."

"I'm real sorry if I let you down, Pop. There's one more thing that's been bothering me. It's not a lie in my eyes, but it's the only other thing I could think of that I needed to admit."

I lifted my hand from the gravestone, crossed my arms in front of my chest, and studied the name on the stone.
Vincent Stephen Ames
"Vince"

"When I was a kid, I used to peel the wrapping paper off the packages, to see what I was getting, and wrap 'em back up."

I slapped my hand against the top of the headstone and grinned.

"I'll keep you up to speed on the girl, Pop. And I'm sorry, I really am. I guess all I can say is this…"

"From this day forward I'll do my best to make you proud."

And that's a promise.

SIENNA

Where we left off. That's what I demanded, and it was without a doubt what I received. From the moment we pulled out of the driveway, things were right back to the way they were. I didn't need to forgive Vince, my mind didn't see things the way other people did. What happened wasn't his fault, it was him acting in a manner that was in accordance with his beliefs and the moral code he lived by. He wasn't right, nor was he wrong. He simply made a decision.

Would I have made it?

No.

Did I agree that it was appropriate?

No.

But it wasn't my place to second guess the man I fell in love with. I fell in love with who Vince was, and who he was played a great part in his decision making. For me to condemn him for being himself would be to admit I wasn't actually in love with *him*, only parts of him.

And that wasn't the case.

Not at all.

"This back yard is amazing," I said as I shifted my eyes around the yard.

The back yard at Vince's mother's house was huge and had been landscaped professionally. The home being built on three lots left a yard three times wider than the other yards on the block, but it had the same depth.

There was a large waterfall in the center decorated with limestone rocks that trickled down into a small pond, and the pond was filled with fish. A path from the pond in each direction led to the back side of the yard, each path taking a different route, but meeting at a large gazebo which was placed on a concrete patio.

The distance between the back of the home and the gazebo was slightly sheltered by the waterfall, but able to be openly viewed to each side by anyone in the corners of the yard, or the neighbors.

The perimeter of the yard was decorated by a flower garden and various small trees, which I suspected were Japanese Maples. I knew very little about flowers or landscaping until Vince and I broke up, and only then did I use gardening as an outlet. Seeing the magnificent yard was breathtaking, but it left me sad for Vince's mother, who I was quite sure had the work done with the hope of filling it with her children.

Children she was never blessed with.

"I like what you did with your yard. It looks nice," he said.

"It's okay," I said, shrugging my shoulders as I continued to look around.

"Come here," he said as he walked toward the gazebo.

He was dressed in jeans, a white tee shirt, and his boots. I lagged behind him intentionally as he walked away, just so I could watch him walk. Something about a man in jeans and a perfectly clean white tee shirt had always made me weak in the knees. As he stepped onto the platform of the gazebo, he turned to face me and grinned.

"What?" I asked.

"I like that dress," he said.

I typically didn't wear dresses, but Vince had bought me the dress to wear for our dinner. It was the anniversary of his father's death, and it just so happened the day fell on a Sunday. Instead of mourning, he and his mother had a ritual of celebrating, which I thought was pretty ingenious.

Vince, Emily, Jackson, Axton, Avery, and I had all come for dinner, and as they were all inside talking to Anita, Vince and I were taking a quick tour of the yard. It was nice to see Vince opening up to the other Sinners, and I especially liked Axton. He was pretty mean looking, but he was like a father to Vince, and even though he was extremely intense and seemed to be harsh at times, he always had Vince's best interest at heart.

"Well, you bought it," I said.

He glanced over each of my shoulders, toward the back of the house. After seeing what I expected he wanted to, he pointed to the wooden table in the center of the gazebo.

"Bend over and pull it up," he said as he motioned toward the table.

I turned toward the house. I couldn't see the back door, but I could see everything beside it, including the windows I knew were in the dining room.

"Are you kidding me?" I asked as I turned to face Vince.

He shook his head, folded his arms in front of his chest, and glared. "Do I look like it?"

"We're in the *yard*. And we've got to get in there to eat in a minute," I said.

The *thought* of doing it was a huge turn-on, but actually doing it was another story. As he stood and continued to glare at me, I felt myself getting wetter with each passing second. After what seemed like forever, but was realistically a few seconds, I couldn't take it any longer.

"Are you serious?" I asked.

With his arms still folded in front of his chest, he nodded his head once. "I want to finger your little pussy."

With my back facing the house, and the waterfall directly behind me, I was protected from the view of anyone at the back door, but the remaining ten windows in the house had a clear shot at what we were doing. If there was anyone in the great room, dining room, upstairs bedrooms, or bathrooms, they would see everything.

All in all, it was perfect.

I walked to the table, bent over slightly, and flipped the dress over my hips.

"No panties," he said as he ran his hand along my inner thigh.

"Nope," I responded, my legs twitching in response to his touch.

I felt his finger penetrate me. After sliding it in and out of my dripping wet pussy a few times, he obviously added another finger. I bit my lower lip and began to moan at the pressure of both fingers being forced deep inside me. As I pressed my chest onto the top of the wooden table, I lifted myself onto my tip-toes.

Either from intending to do so or by accident, and I didn't really care which it was, the tips of his fingers were rubbing my g-spot each time he pushed them deep inside of me. I closed my eyes and turned my head to the side, resting it flat on the table, and allowed myself to relax onto the heels of my feet.

"Holy shit that feels good," I said softly.

And it did. My love for Vince and his desire to please me made me perpetually wet for him, but being in the back yard while everyone prepared for dinner was book boyfriend dream land for me.

Within what seemed like seconds, but was more than likely minutes, I began to tingle from head to toe.

"Come on, Sienna," he breathed into my ear.

Just shut up and keep going.

"Come on, babe," he breathed.

Shut up. Just…hit…that…spot…again…

"Come on, do it," he said.

Please, be quiet.

His fingers continued to massage my g-spot, and I did my best to filter out his requests to have me come. I was almost there.

"Dinner's almost ready," I heard his mother shout.

I opened my eyes, fully expecting to see her. Still sheltered by the waterfall, and out of view of the door, I was safe. I closed my eyes, and realized my heart was beating ten-fold of what was normal.

A few more strokes of his fingers, and my breathing was louder than anything else in the yard. I raised myself onto my toes, lowered myself, raised up again, and relaxed.

"Oh holy fuuuuuuuck…"

I collapsed onto the table and gasped for my next breath.

The faint sound of what I thought was his zipper was followed by his hand pressing on my back. Him fingering me in the yard was one thing, but him fucking me was another. If he thought for one minute that I was going to let…

I inhaled a slow breath as I felt the pressure of his massive cock slide inside of me. As it reached bottom, I exhaled and grabbed the edges of the table in my hands. As I held the table firm in my hands, I turned and looked his direction over my shoulder.

His jeans were around his thighs, and his perfectly pressed white tee shirt was all bunched up around his mid-section. I felt like I should protest, and really didn't think fucking in his mother's back yard in the evening sun was the best idea I had ever heard, but it wasn't necessarily the worst, either.

Without speaking, I sighed, turned around, and held the table tight.

It must have been all the confirmation he needed.

He began to fuck me. Not the type of fucking he had given me in the past when he really wanted to prove a point or show me who was boss. Not like the day he drove the couch into the wall, or the evening he fucked me across the living room carpet until he had scabs on his knees and my ass was covered in carpet burns.

Not like that.

But a good, solid, steady, deep, predictable stroke.

The kind of stroke a girl can get lost in feeling. The kind of stroke only the right man can give; a man with a big, thick, long cock.

The slow stroke that allows a girl to feel every inch of the shaft as it slides in, and every inch of it as it slides out, almost counting the inches with each stroke, anticipating feeling the rim as it passes the lips each time. The stroke that is so predictable she can bite her lower lip just before the head bottoms out, because it's impossible for every inch of that big thick cock to penetrate her fully.

Yeah, that stroke.

"Fuck yes," I grunted as he fucked me. "Right there, that's it."

His hands gripped my waist, and pulled me back ever so slightly as he pushed himself into me. As he pulled his hips back, he pushed me with his hands, making sure his cock slid right to the point of tickling my pussy lips.

He continued to fuck me in the same manner until my head was spinning and I was close to reaching my second back yard orgasm.

"You two coming in?"

I opened my eyes, recognizing the voice as Axton's. Vince didn't change his pace or slow his stroke, but kept fucking me as if nothing was going on. Although I really couldn't hear our breathing, our skin touching, or his grunting, everything seemed to be amplified now, and I could hear everything.

"Where the fuck are you?"

Shit, he's getting closer.

Vince's cock continued to slide inside of me, slide out, and slide back in. The same pace, the same intensity, and the same great fucking feeling.

Fuck it.

I closed my eyes and bit my bottom lip. The thought of Axton walking around looking for us was weird, but with my eyes closed, it really didn't matter. Strangely, I felt comfort in *not* knowing where he was or what he was seeing, but while Vince was fucking me, I imagined Axton standing behind the waterfall watching Vince fuck me.

And I liked it.

I clenched my eyes tight and focused on the feeling of his thick cock.

"Food's ready."

Yeah, so am I.

A few more strokes and I was done. My pussy began to clench around his cock and I felt him begin to swell inside of me. His rhythmic thrusting continued as his hands gripped my hips a little tighter, and I felt my muscles begin to tighten.

I lifted myself onto my tip-toes and held it for a second…

And relaxed.

The intensity of my orgasm was beyond anything I had ever experienced with Vince or alone. I felt as if my head exploded as he held his cock deep inside of me. For a few seconds of heightened hypersensitivity, I could feel his cock throbbing inside of me.

Eventually, my climax lessened and I opened my eyes.

"Holy shit," I whispered as I turned and glanced over my shoulder.

Vince slowly pulled his cock from inside of me and started to stroke it rapidly.

"What are you…"

He raised his left hand to his lips. "Shhh. Watch."

With his jeans around his thighs and his wrinkled shirt dangling at the base of his cock, he jacked it like his life depended on it. Watching him stroke his cock was something I always wanted to see, and seeing it was quickly exceeding my expectations.

Within a few seconds his breathing increased and he leaned back onto his heels.

"Oh fuck," he sighed.

And he began to erupt.

Cum spurted out of the tip of his cock, landing six feet away onto the concrete deck Another spurt, this time landing a few feet away, followed by a third, landing at his feet.

Holy fuck that's hot.

He opened his eyes and grinned.

"You didn't…" I whispered as I nodded my head toward his waist.

He shook his head. "I wanted you to see what you do to me."

I tugged at the bottom of my dress, attempting to minimize the wrinkles and the soon to be asked questions.

"That was fucking hot," I said.

He pulled up his jeans, buckled his belt, and did his best to make his shirt look neat.

"Come on before we get in trouble," he said as he walked past me.

I glanced down at the puddles of cum on the concrete. "Uhhm, what about all that? Someone will slip and fall."

He shrugged his shoulders.

I shrugged mine and followed him into the house.

Everyone was standing around the table talking.

"Glad you could make it," Axton said.

"We were just taking a tour," Vince said.

I grinned at Avery and immediately felt guilty, so I shifted my eyes to the table.

"Been talking to Otis?" Axton asked.

I glanced up. Axton's eyes were fixed on Vince's.

"Who's Otis?" I asked.

Axton shifted his eyes toward me. "He's one of the fellas. His Ol' Lady's got a flower garden and gazebo just like what's out there. They sure like it."

I nodded my head and grinned. Axton shifted his eyes back to Vince and smiled. "They use it a lot. I was just wondering if ol' Vince here had been talking to Otis about it. Maybe getting a few pointers."

Axton chuckled and turned to face me.

"So how you doing, Kid?" he asked.

"Good," I said.

"I bet you are," he said with a nod. "I bet you are."

VINCE

If I ever felt like something was important enough to be *important*, it was pretty damned important.

"I told you once, I don't think I should just have to keep repeating myself," I said.

"Well, that is a sketch made on a note pad. A sketch. It's not a precision drawing, and..."

I was done listening to this asshole, and was about ready to either beat the living shit out of him or go elsewhere.

"What you think because I'm a fucking biker I'm some dumb fuck?" I asked.

He shook his head. "That's not an accurate statement."

I pointed toward the drawing and tossed my hands in the air. "I didn't draw that fucker with a crayon; I drew it with an architect's pencil. That, that right fucking there, *that's* what I want."

"Very well. Identical to what is depicted?" he asked.

I nodded my head. "Exactly."

He glanced at the drawing, shook his head from side to side, and sighed heavily. "But, the dimensions, it's not drawn to scale, and it's..."

"Who says it's not drawn to scale?" I asked.

"Well, I assume based on the disproportionate nature, and the sheer size of the..."

"Just. Like. The. Fucking. Drawing," I said flatly.

He picked up the paper, nodded his head, and shifted his eyes toward the parking lot where I had parked my bike.

"And, the manner in which you'll resolve payment?" he asked.

I reached inside my cut, pulled out a banded stack of hundred dollar bills, and flopped it onto the edge of the counter.

"Cash. That ought to get you started," I said.

He picked up the bills, flipped through them, and grinned. "It certainly will."

"Your name?" he asked as he picked up a clipboard.

I pointed to the drawing, shifted my finger toward the money he held, and nodded my head.

"Name's Vince, that's it. No phone number, no address. I'll be back in a week," I said.

"The pleasure's mine, Mr. Vince," he said.

"Exactly like the drawing," I said.

He glanced down at the drawing, nodded his head once, and grinned. "It will be."

And as far as I was concerned, that was all that mattered.

SIENNA

There should come a time in every girl's life when she feels she can safely exhale. At least that's what I had always believed. I doubted each and every girl on the earth reached that point, and the thought saddened me that some didn't, but I did.

And I was grateful when the day finally came.

"I had no idea there were carriage rides in Old Town," I said.

The man driving the carriage was actually wearing a top hat, which was pretty cool in my opinion. The carriage was white and rather ornate, with carvings along the sides and on the armrests. The seats were red velvet and quite comfortable for a wooden carriage. As the man whipped the reigns up and down the Clydesdale horses picked up the pace slightly.

We'd been in the carriage for thirty minutes, taking a tour of Old Town in downtown Wichita. Vince had spent the entire time checking his watch, so I realized he must have had other plans, but I had no idea what they were.

The evening was perfect, and for Kansas in the fall, rather enjoyable. It was just under sixty degrees, the dark sky overhead was filled with stars, and there wasn't a cloud in sight. As we sipped our hot apple cider, the carriage came around the corner.

"The Keen Kutter building," the man said as he motioned toward the brick building on our right side.

Vince checked his watch.

"Built in 1906 by Wurster Construction, the building was used by Keen Kutter until the early 1920's when Winchester Arms merged with Keen Kutter to utilize…"

Vince checked his watch again.

The carriage slowed down slightly, and the sound of the horse's hooves slapping against the brick street became almost musical. I took a sip of cider and gazed off to the left at the renovated one hundred year old buildings that had been developed into housing, eateries, and bars.

Vince checked his watch.

I shook my head and turned to the side and watched as two people walked by hand in hand, probably on their way to the wine bar half way down the block. It was almost midnight and the bars were all that was really left open. I shifted my eyes toward the front of the carriage, only to see that Vince had moved to the seat in front of me.

The carriage seated six people, and Vince had rented the entire carriage to give us privacy. Although he had been seated at my side all night, he obviously got bored and moved.

"What are you doing?" I asked.

He shoved his hands deep into the pockets of his coat and leaned forward.

"Sienna, I can say this without hesitation," he said. "You are the only woman I have ever loved. I know that now, I *know* it."

"Awwe, thank you," I said as I leaned forward and kissed him.

"I want this to last forever," he said.

"The ride?" I asked with a grin.

He shook his head. "This. You and me."

"Me too," I said.

"So," he said as he raised himself from the seat.

He removed his right hand from his jacket, lowered himself onto one knee, and raised his hand in front of me. I glanced at his hand.

Oh God...

Vince.

"Sienna, I would be the proudest man on earth if you would agree to marry me," he said.

I bit into my lip and nodded my head, incapable of speaking. I mouthed the words "I will" as tears began to well in my eyes.

I reached for the ring and nodded my head again. I had read about this moment in thousands of books, but nothing could have prepared me for what was happening. He shook his head, reached for my hand, and slipped the ring onto my finger.

I glanced down at the ring. It was a ridiculously huge round diamond, and the sides of the ring were covered in smaller diamonds, fading into small slivers at the bottom.

It was breathtaking.

"I love you," I said as I felt the tears rolling down my cheeks.

Vince turned toward the man driving and nodded his head. The man raised his hand to his mouth, pulled the reigns downward, and stopped the carriage. As the carriage came to a halt, the man whistled a shrill whistle loud enough for the entire city to hear.

"And off to the left, you can see the not so historic Warren Theatre parking garage," he said with a slight laugh as he pointed toward the structure on the left.

Vince turned to the left and stared, pulling me in his arms as he did so. Under the streetlights and illuminated enough for me to see I wasn't the only one crying, he looked peaceful and content.

I was in heaven.

A huge boom, followed by another, and yet another caused me to jump in my seat. The top of the parking garage illuminated underneath the fireworks display over our heads. It was just like the Fourth of July, the sky glowing with pinks, reds, blues, and yellows, one burst after the other.

I smiled as I stared out at the display, only to see the someone's head clearing the top of the roof and peering down below.

The unmistakable "Whoop" of Biscuit making a cat-call made me giggle, and I waved at him from the carriage.

"Congrats, Motherfuckers!" I heard Jackson scream.

"All of this," I said as I waved toward the fireworks. "You're amazing."

"No, you're amazing," he said.

"I'm just surprised…" I paused and shook my head.

The next day was November 9th, the anniversary of our first kiss. I found it odd he didn't wait until the next day to propose.

"What?" he asked.

I shrugged my shoulders and admired my ring. "Nothing."

"Surprised I didn't wait 'till the 9th?" he asked.

I nodded my head. He pointed to his watch. "It's the 9th. It's been the 9th for some time now."

I realized it was past midnight, and the 9th of November.

A true romantic, the love of my life had just proposed to me on the anniversary of our first kiss. Directly above us the fireworks continued to explode, illuminating the sky entirely. I pointed up at the sky, down at my ring, and shook my head.

"What?" he asked.

"This," I said.

"What about it?" he asked.

"*This* is the money shot," I said.

He grinned and pulled me in for a kiss. "It sure is."

And it was. The perfect night. The perfect man. The perfect romantic moment. If our lives were ever written into a book, it would be the perfect...

Money shot.

EPILOGUE

AXTON BISHOP

The fellas in my club weren't simply friends, brothers, or people who I expected to have my back when times were tough. Each and every one of them was a part of a machine. In the absence of one man, the machine would be incomplete. In the absence of some men, the machine would break down.

It took time, but Vince had become a critical component in the machine. Without him there was no doubt in my mind, the machine would cease to exist.

I held my head high and walked as straight as possible. It was something I had never imagined I would have to do, but I agreed to do so as a matter of respect. Well, that and I couldn't imagine anyone else doing it with such devotion.

The slight tug on my right arm reminded me of my commitment. I blinked my eyes, lowered my chin, and waited.

He shifted his eyes upward and gazed at me blankly. "Who gives this woman to be married to this man on this beautiful day?"

"I do. Axton Bishop," I responded with a proud nod.

"And, Mr. Bishop, do I have your blessing to move forward with this ceremony of marriage?" he asked.

I lowered my chin and smiled. "Yes, Sir. You do."

Sienna pinched my arm.

You little shit.

The pastor motioned for her to come forward. I stepped aside, turned and walked to the open seat beside Avery and sat down.

It seemed strange for me to be dressed in a tuxedo for a biker wedding, but I should have known Vince wouldn't do anything traditional to the one percenter. He was a romantic at heart, and I admired him for it.

The pastor shifted his eyes throughout the crowd. The entire yard was decorated and filled with chairs, a stage, band, and rented dance floor. Vince's mother's home was perfect for the wedding, and she sure seemed excited to plan the event entirely; no expense had been spared.

"Marriage is a solemn institution to be held in honor by all, it is the cornerstone of the family and of the community. It requires of those who undertake it a complete and unreserved giving of one's self. It is not to be entered into lightly, as marriage is a sincere and mutual commitment to love one another," he said.

He turned and exchanged glances at Vince and Sienna. "This commitment symbolizes the intimate sharing of two lives and still enhances the individuality of each of you."

"Will rings be exchanged as a symbol of this union in marriage?"

Vince nodded his head and motioned toward the ring bearer. Biscuit grinned, raised the silk pillow, and waited as Vince removed the rings and handed them to the pastor.

"A ring is a circle with no beginning and no end. Love without end is what we hope to achieve in marriage. As this ring is placed upon your fingers remember that it is your love for one another that has brought you here, and it is that love that will guide you down the pathways of your lives."

The pastor turned toward Vince and nodded his head.

Vince gazed into Sienna's eyes and held the ring in his hand. "I promise to you to have all the patience required to comfort you through the life we share and as we grow and learn to love one another. I promise to be quick to listen, slow to speak, and understanding of all you may need, desire, or require of me. Above all, I promise to love you today and every day following no less than the previous, and to never anger beyond what words cannot repair."

The pastor nodded his head.

Vince slipped the ring on Sienna's finger.

The pastor turned to face Sienna.

She grinned, reached for the ring, and held it between her fingers. "I promise to be understanding of your needs, accepting of your shortcomings, and open to your requests of me. I promise to be loving of you now, tomorrow, and for every day we share, and to place my love for you above all other needs. Above all, I promise when you do anger, to be patient, and allow time to pass and wounds to heal, for man is imperfect, and the world knows this to be fact."

The pastor nodded his head.

Sienna placed the ring on Vince's finger.

"Repeat after me," he said. "With this ring I make this vow to you before God, before witness, and before my brothers."

They each repeated the vow.

"Stephen Vincent Ames, do you take this woman to be your wedded wife? Do you promise to love her, comfort her, honor and keep her in sickness and in health, remaining faithful to her as long as you both shall live?"

"Yes, Sir. I do," Vince said.

"Sienna Ghee Boyco, do you take this man to be your wedded husband? Do you promise to love him, comfort him, honor and keep him in sickness and in health, remaining faithful to him as long as you both shall live?"

"I certainly do," Sienna responded.

The pastor glanced at each of them and bowed his head slightly. "Then by the power vested in me, I now pronounce you husband and wife. You may kiss the bride."

They kissed a kiss I damned sure wouldn't have kissed at my wedding. After a few *get a room* remarks were shouted by various Sinners, they separated and turned to face the crowd.

I couldn't have been more proud of one of my boys and his new wife. I turned toward Avery, smiled, and kissed her.

"I love you," I said.

"I love you," she responded.

Avery looked remarkable in her dress. She made me proud in what she had done with Jackson, work, life, and finally making amends with her parents. One day I would make her my wife, I was sure of it. When the day came, I would stand proud before my brothers and take the vow with honor and respect.

As the evening turned into night, and the alcohol became part of the occasion, the DJ tapped his finger on the microphone and got everyone's attention.

"I'd like to make an announcement," he said. "It's time for the father-daughter dance. The song chosen was by the daughter, and I want to make sure everyone in attendance is ready. Axton?"

He motioned toward me with his free hand.

Oh shit, that's my cue.

It was the least I could do for a member of my family whose father was deceased. Participating in the dance was a matter of respect.

I turned to the side and reached for Sienna's hand, fully expecting a slow dance. She raised her hand in the air and pulled it away from me as she shook her head. When she kicked her shoes to the side, I realized I might be in trouble.

I wrinkled my brow and stared.

Her mouth curled into a smirk as she turned her head and shouted over her shoulder at the DJ.

"Hit it," she said with a nod.

The music started and the floor began to shake. It wasn't what I expected, but I had given my word I'd do the dance with her. Without hesitation, I grabbed the lapels of my jacket, pulled it off, and tossed it to Anita. I couldn't wear a jacket and dance to the song she'd chosen, there was no way.

I glanced around the dance floor. Every person in attendance had their eyes on me.

And as *"Christmas in Hollis,"* by Run DMC played, I came to realize although we were all Selected Sinners, we were all different.

But for that moment, Sienna and I were exactly the same.

And I danced like it was the last time I would ever have a chance.